DEATH AT LA FENICE

DEATH AT LA FENICE

Donna Leon

Thorndike Press
Waterville, Maine USA

This Large Print edition is published by Thorndike Press, USA.

Published in 2003 in the U.S. by arrangement with HarperCollins Publishers, Inc.

U.S. Softcover   ISBN 0–7862–5107–7 (General Series Edition)

The text of this Large Print edition is unabridged.
Other aspects of the book may vary from the original edition.

Set in 16 pt. New Times Roman.

Printed in Great Britain on acid-free paper.

Library of Congress Cataloging-in-Publication Data

Leon, Donna.
    Death at La Fenice / Donna Leon.
      p.   cm.
    ISBN 0–7862–5107–7 (lg. print : sc : alk. paper)
    1. Brunetti, Guido (Fictitious character)—Fiction. 2. Police—Italy—Venice—Fiction. 3. Venice (Italy)—Fiction 4. Opera—Fiction 5. Large type books. I. Title.
    PR3562.E534 D4 2003
    813'.54—dc21   2002043099

For my mother

Ah, signor, son rea di morte
E la morte io sol vi chiedo;
Il mio fallo tardi vedo;
Con quel ferro un sen ferite
Che non merita pietà.

Ah, sir, I'm guilty to death
And all I ask is death;
Too late I see my sin.
With your sword pierce this breast,
Which merits no pity.

—Così Fan Tutte

CHAPTER ONE

The third gong, announcing that the opera was about to continue, sounded discreetly through the lobbies and bars of Teatro La Fenice. In response, the audience stabbed out cigarettes, finished drinks and conversations, and started to filter back into the theater. The hall, brightly lit between acts, hummed with the talk of those returning to their seats. Here a jewel flashed, there a mink cape was adjusted over a naked shoulder or an infinitesimal speck of dust was flicked from a satin lapel. The upper galleries filled up first, followed by the orchestra seats and then the three rows of boxes.

The lights dimmed, the hall grew dark, and the tension created by an ongoing performance mounted as the audience waited for the conductor to reappear on the podium. Slowly the hum of voices faded, the members of the orchestra stopped fidgeting in their seats, and the universal silence announced everyone's readiness for the third and final act.

The silence lengthened, grew heavy. From the first gallery, there came a burst of coughing; someone dropped a book, perhaps a purse; but the door to the corridor behind the orchestra pit remained closed.

The first to talk were the players in the

orchestra. A second violinist leaned over to the woman next to him and asked if she had made her vacation plans. In the second row, a bassoonist told an oboist that the Benetton sales were starting next day. The people in the first tiers of boxes, who could best see the musicians, soon imitated their soft chatter. The galleries joined in, and then those in the orchestra seats, as though the wealthy would be the last to give in to this sort of behavior.

The hum grew to a murmur. Minutes passed. Suddenly the folds of the dense green velvet curtain were pulled back and Aamdeo Fasini, the theater's artistic director, stepped awkwardly through the narrow opening. The technician in the light box above the second gallery, with no idea of what was going on, decided to center a hot white spot on the man at center stage. Blinded, Fasini shot up his arm to shield his eyes. Still holding his arm raised in front of him, as if to protect himself from a blow, he began to speak: 'Ladies and gentlemen,' and then he stopped, gesturing wildly with his left hand to the technician, who, realizing his error, switched off the light. Released from his temporary blindness, the man on the stage started again. 'Ladies and gentlemen, I regret to inform you that Maestro Wellauer is unable to continue the performance.' Whispers, questions, rose from the audience, silk rustled as heads turned, but he continued to speak above the noise. 'His

2

place will be taken by Maestro Longhi.' Before the hum could rise to drown him out, he asked, voice insistently calm, 'Is there a doctor in the audience?'

His question met a long pause, then people began to look around them: who would be the one to present himself? Almost a full minute passed. Finally, a hand rose slowly in one of the first rows of the orchestra, and a woman got out of her seat. Fasini waved a hand to one of the uniformed ushers at the back of the house, and the young man hurried to the end of the row where the woman now stood. 'If you would, Dottoressa,' Fasini said, sounding as if he were in pain and needed the doctor for himself. 'Please go backstage with the usher.'

He glanced up into the horseshoe of the still-darkened hall, tried to smile, failed, and abandoned the attempt. 'Excuse, ladies and gentlemen, the difficulty. The opera will now continue.'

Turning, the artistic director fumbled at the curtain, unable for a moment to find the opening through which he had come. Disembodied hands parted the curtain from behind, and he slipped through, finding himself in the bare garret where Violetta was soon to die. From out in front, he heard the tentative applause that greeted the substitute conductor as he took his place on the podium.

Singers, chorus members, stagehands appeared from all around him, as curious as

3

the audience had been but far more vocal. Though the power of his position usually protected him from contact with members of the company as low in standing as these, the director could not now avoid them, their questions, their whispers. 'It's nothing, nothing,' he said to no one in particular, then he waved at them all, trying to clear them, with that gesture, from the stage upon which they flocked. The music of the prelude was drawing to a close; soon the curtain would open on the evening's Violetta, who now sat nervously on the edge of the cot at the center of the stage. Fasini redoubled the intensity of his gestures, and singers and stagehands began to move off to the wings, where they continued to whisper among themselves. He snarled a furious *'Silenzio'* and waited for it to take effect. When he saw the curtains inching apart to reveal the stage, he hurried to join the stage manager, who stood off to stage right, beside the doctor. A short, dark woman, she stood directly under a No Smoking sign, with an unlighted cigarette in her hand.

'Good evening, Doctor,' Fasini said, forcing himself to smile. She dropped the cigarette into the pocket of her jacket and shook his hand. 'What is it?' she finally asked as, from behind them, Violetta began to read the letter from Germont père.

Fasini rubbed his hands together briskly, as if the gesture would help him decide what to

4

say. 'Maestro Wellauer has been . . .' he began, but he found no satisfactory way to finish the sentence.

'Is he sick?' asked the doctor impatiently.

'No, no, he's not sick,' Fasini said, and then words left him. He returned to rubbing his hands together.

'Perhaps I had better see him,' she said, making it a question. 'Is he here in the theater?'

When Fasini continued incapable of speech, she asked, 'Has he been taken somewhere else?'

This prodded the director. 'No, no. He's in the dressing room.'

'Then hadn't we better go there?'

'Yes, of course, Doctor,' he agreed, glad of the suggestion. He led her off to the right, past a grand piano and a harp draped with a dull green dust cover, down a narrow corridor. He stopped at the end, before a closed door. A tall man stood in front of it.

'Matteo,' Fasini began, turning back toward the doctor. 'This is Doctor—'

'Zorzi,' she supplied curtly. This hardly seemed a time for formal introductions.

At the arrival of his superior and someone he was told was a doctor, Matteo, the assistant stage manager, was all too eager to step away from the door. Fasini moved past him, pulled the door half open, looked back over his shoulder, then allowed the doctor to precede him into the small room.

Death had distorted the features of the man who was slumped across the easy chair at the center of the room. His eyes stared out at nothingness; his lips were pulled back in a fierce grimace. His body canted heavily to one side, head thrust against the chair back. A trail of dark liquid stained the starched and gleaming front of his shirt. For a moment, the doctor thought it was blood. She took a step closer and smelled, rather than saw, that it was coffee. The scent that mingled with the coffee was equally distinctive, the cutting, sour almond smell she had only read about.

She had seen so much of death that it was unnecessary for her to try to find his pulse, but she did place the fingers of her right hand under his upraised chin. Nothing, but she noticed that the skin was still warm. She stepped back from the body and looked around. On the floor in front of him were a small saucer and the cup that had held the coffee that trailed down the front of his shirt. She knelt and placed the back of her fingers against the side of the cup, but it was cold to the touch.

Rising, she spoke to the two men who stood near the door, content to leave her to the business of death. 'Have you called the police?' she asked.

'Yes, yes,' Fasini muttered, not really hearing her question.

6

'Signore,' she said, speaking clearly and raising her voice so that there could be no question of his hearing her. 'There's nothing I can do here. This is a matter for the police. Have you called them?'

'Yes,' he repeated, but he still gave no sign that he had heard or understood what she said. He stood staring down at the dead man, trying to grasp the horror, and the scandal, of what he saw.

Abruptly the doctor pushed her way past him and out into the corridor. The assistant stage manager followed her. 'Call the police,' she commanded him. When he nodded and moved off to do as she had ordered, she reached into her pocket for the cigarette she had dropped there, fingered it back into shape, and lit it. She pulled in a deep breath of smoke and glanced down at her watch. Mickey's left hand stood between the ten and the eleven, and his right was just on seven. She leaned back against the wall and waited for the police to arrive.

CHAPTER TWO

Because this was Venice, the police came by boat, blue light flashing on the forward cabin. They pulled up at the side of the small canal behind the theater, and four men got out,

7

three in blue uniform and one in civilian clothes. Quickly they walked up the *calle*, or narrow street, alongside the theater and continued through the stage entrance, where the *portiere*, who had been warned of their arrival, pushed the button that released the turnstile and allowed them to walk freely into the backstage area. He pointed silently to a staircase.

At the top of the first flight of steps, they were met by the still-stunned director. He started to extend his hand to the civilian, who seemed to be in charge, but forgot about the gesture and wheeled around, saying over his shoulder, 'This way.' Advancing down a short corridor, he stopped at the door to the conductor's dressing room. There he stopped and, reduced to gestures, pointed inside.

Guido Brunetti, a commissario of police for the city, was the first through the door. When he saw the body in the chair, he held up his hand and signaled the uniformed officers not to come any farther into the room. The man was clearly dead, body twisted backward, face horribly distorted, so there was no need to search for a sign of life; there would be none.

The dead man was as familiar to Brunetti as he was to most people in the Western world, if not because they had actually seen him on the podium, then because they had, for more than four decades, seen his face, with its chiseled Germanic jaw, its too-long hair that had

8

remained raven black well into his sixties, on the covers of magazines and the front pages of newspapers. Brunetti had seen him conduct twice, years before, and he had, during the performance, found himself watching the conductor, not the orchestra. As if in the grip of a demon, or a deity, Wellauer's body had swept back and forth above the podium, left hand clutched half open, as if he wanted to rip the sound from the violins. In his right hand, the baton was a weapon, flashing now here, now there, a thunderbolt that summoned up waves of sound. But now, in death, all sign of the deity had fled, and there remained only the leering demon's mask.

Brunetti turned his eyes away and glanced around the room. He saw the cup lying on the floor, the saucer not far from it. That explained the dark stains on the shirt and, Brunetti was sure, the horribly twisted features.

Still only a short distance into the room, Brunetti remained still and let his eyes roam, taking note of what he saw, uncertain about what any of it might come to mean, curious. He was a surprisingly neat man: tie carefully knotted, hair shorter than was the fashion; even his ears lay close to his head, as if reluctant to call attention to themselves. His clothing marked him as Italian. The cadence of his speech announced that he was Venetian. His eyes were all policeman.

9

He reached forward and touched the back of the dead man's wrist, but the body was cold, the skin dry to the touch. He took one last look around and turned to one of the men who stood behind him. He told him to call the medical examiner and the photographer. He told the second officer to go downstairs and speak to the *portiere*. Who was backstage that night? Have the *portiere* make a list. To the third, he said he wanted the names of anyone who had spoken to the Maestro that evening, either before the performance or during the intermissions.

He stepped to the left and opened the door to a small bathroom. The single window was closed, as the one in the dressing room had been. In the closet hung a dark overcoat and three starched white shirts.

He went back into the dressing room and across to the body. With the back of his fingers, he pushed aside the lapels of the dead man's jacket and pulled open the inner pocket. He found a handkerchief, and holding it by a corner, he pulled it out slowly. There was nothing else in the pocket. He repeated the same process with the side pockets, finding the usual things: a few thousand lire in small bills; a key with a plastic tag attached to it, probably the key to this room; a comb; another handkerchief. He didn't want to disturb the body until it had been photographed, so he left the pockets of the trousers until later.

The three policemen, satisfied that there was a certifiable victim, had gone off to follow Brunetti's orders. The director of the theater had disappeared. Brunetti stepped out into the corridor, hoping to find him and get some idea of how long ago the body had been discovered. Instead he found a small, dark woman, leaning against the wall, smoking. From behind them came deep waves of music.

'What's that?' Brunetti asked.

'*La Traviata,*' the woman replied simply.

'I know,' he said. 'Does that mean they went on with the performance?'

' "Even if the whole world falls," ' she said, giving it that heavy weight and emphasis usually reserved for quotations.

'Is that something from *Traviata*?' he asked.

'No; *Turandot,*' she responded, voice calm.

'Yes, but still,' he protested. 'Out of respect for the man.'

She shrugged, tossed her cigarette to the cement floor, ground it out with her foot.

'And you are?' he finally asked.

'Barbara Zorzi,' she answered, then amended it, though he hadn't asked. 'Dr. Barbara Zorzi. I was in the audience when they asked for a doctor, so I came back here and found him, at exactly ten thirty-five. His body was still warm, so I'd estimate he had been dead for less than half an hour. The coffee cup on the floor was cold.'

'You touched it?'

'Only with the back of my fingers. I thought it might be important to know if it was still warm. It wasn't.' She took another cigarette from her bag, offered him one, didn't seem surprised when he refused, and lit it for herself.

'Anything else, Doctor?'

'It smells like cyanide,' she answered. 'I've read about it, and we worked with it once, in pharmacology. The professor wouldn't let us smell it; he said even the fumes were dangerous.'

'Is it really that toxic?' he asked.

'Yes. I forget how little is necessary to kill a person; far less than a gram. And it's instantaneous. Everything simply stops—heart, lungs. He would have been dead, or at least unconscious, before the cup hit the floor.'

'Did you know him?' Brunetti asked.

She shook her head. 'No more than anyone who likes opera knew him. Or anyone who reads *Gente*,' she added, naming a gossip magazine he found it difficult to believe she would read.

She looked up at him and asked, 'Is that all?'

'Yes, Doctor, I think so. Would you leave your name with one of my men so that we can contact you if we have to?'

'Zorzi, Barbara,' she said, not at all impressed by his official voice and manner. 'I'm the only one in the phone book.'

12

She dropped the cigarette and stepped on it, then extended her hand to him. 'Goodbye, then. I hope this doesn't become too ugly.' He didn't know if she meant for the Maestro, the theater, the city, or for him, so he merely nodded his thanks and shook her hand. As she left, it struck Brunetti how strangely similar his work was to that of a doctor. They met over the dead, both asking 'Why?' But after they found the answer to that question, their paths parted, the doctor going backward in time to find the physical cause, and he going forward to find the person responsible.

Fifteen minutes later, the medical examiner arrived, bringing with him a photographer and two white-jacketed attendants whose job it would be to take the body to the Civil Hospital. Brunetti greeted Dr. Rizzardi warmly and explained as much as he had learned about the probable time of death. Together, they went back to the dressing room. Rizzardi, a fastidiously dressed man, pulled on latex gloves, checked his watch automatically, and knelt beside the body. Brunetti watched him as he examined the victim, oddly touched to see that he treated the corpse with the same respect he would give to a living patient, touching it softly and, when necessary, turning it gently, helping the awkward movement of stiffening flesh with practiced hands.

'Could you take the things from his pockets,

Doctor?' Brunetti asked, since he didn't have gloves and didn't want to add his prints to anything that might be found. The doctor complied, but all he found was a slim wallet, alligator perhaps, which he pulled out by one corner and placed on the table beside him.

He got to his feet and stripped off his gloves. 'Poison. Obviously. I'd say it was cyanide; in fact, I'm sure it was, though I can't tell you that officially until after the autopsy. But from the way his body's bent backward, it can't be anything else.' Brunetti noticed that the doctor had closed the dead man's eyes and attempted to ease the corners of his distorted mouth. 'It's Wellauer, isn't it?' the doctor asked, though the question was hardly necessary.

When Brunetti nodded, the doctor exclaimed, *'Maria Vergine*, the mayor's not going to like this at all.'

'Then let the mayor find out who did it,' Brunetti shot back.

'Yes, stupid of me. Sorry, Guido. We should be thinking of the family.'

As if on cue, one of the three uniformed policemen came to the door and signaled Brunetti. When he emerged from the room, he saw Fasini standing next to a woman he assumed was the Maestro's daughter. She was tall, taller than the director, taller even than Brunetti, and to that she had added a crown of blond hair. Like the Maestro, she had a Slavic

14

tilt to her cheekbones and eyes of a blue so clear as to be almost glacial.

When she saw Brunetti emerge from the dressing room, she took two quick steps away from the director. 'What's wrong?' she asked in heavily accented Italian. 'What's happened?'

'I'm sorry, Signorina,' Brunetti began.

Not hearing him, she cut him short and demanded, 'What's happened to my husband?'

Though surprised, Brunetti had the presence of mind to move to his right, effectively blocking her entrance to the room. 'Signora, I'm sorry, but it would be better if you didn't go in there.' Why was it that they always knew what it was you had to tell them? Was it the tone, or did some sort of animal instinct cause us to hear death in the voice that bore the news?

The woman slumped to one side, as though she had been struck. Her hip slammed against the keyboard of the piano, filling the corridor with discordant sound. She braced her body with a stiff outthrust hand, palm smashing more discord from the keys. She said something in a language Brunetti didn't understand, then put her hand to her mouth in a gesture so melodramatic it had to be natural.

It seemed, in this moment, that he had spent his entire life doing this to people, telling them that someone they loved was dead or, worse, had been killed. His brother, Sergio,

15

was an x-ray technician and had to wear a small metallic card pinned to his lapel that would turn a strange color if it was exposed to dangerous amounts of radiation. Had he worn a similar device, sensitive to grief or pain or death, it would have changed color permanently long ago.

She opened her eyes and looked at him. 'I want to see him.'

'I think it would be better if you didn't,' he answered, knowing that this was true.

'What happened?' She strove for calm, and she achieved it.

'I think it was poison,' he said, though in fact he knew.

'Someone killed him?' she asked with astonishment that appeared to be real. Or practiced.

'I'm sorry, Signora. There are no answers I can give you now. Is there someone here who can take you home?' From behind them, he could hear the sudden crash of applause, then wave upon wave of it. She gave no sign that she had heard it or his question, simply stared at him and moved her mouth silently.

'Is there anyone in the theater who can take you home, Signora?'

She nodded, at last understanding him. 'Yes, yes,' she said, then added in a softer voice, 'I need to sit.' He was prepared for this, the sudden blow of reality that sets in after the first shock. It was this that knocked people

16

down.

He put his arm under hers and led her out into the backstage area. Though tall, she was so slender that her weight was easy to support. The only space he could see was a small cubicle on the left, crowded with light panels and equipment he didn't recognize. He lowered her into the chair in front of the panel and signaled to one of the uniformed officers, who had appeared from the wing, which swarmed now with people in costume, taking bows and crowding into groups as soon as the curtain was closed.

'Go down to the bar and get a glass of brandy and a glass of water,' he ordered the policeman.

Signora Wellauer sat in the straight-backed wooden chair, hands grasping the seat on either side of her, and stared at the floor. She shook her head from side to side in negation or in response to some inner conversation.

'Signora, Signora, are your friends in the theater?'

She ignored him and continued with her silent dialogue.

'Signora,' he repeated, this time placing his hand on her shoulder. 'Your friends, are they here?'

'Welti,' she said, not looking up. 'I told them to meet me back here.'

The officer returned, carrying two glasses. Brunetti took the smaller one and handed it to her. 'Drink this, Signora,' he said. She took it and drank it down absently, then did the same with the water when he handed that to her, as though there were no difference between them.

He took the empty glasses and set them aside.

'When did you see him, Signora?'

'What?'

'When did you see him?'

'Helmut?'

'Yes, Signora. When did you see him?'

'We came in together. Tonight. Then I came back after . . .' Her voice trailed off.

'After what, Signora?' he asked.

She studied his face for a moment before she answered. 'After the second act. But we didn't speak. I was too late. He just said—no, he didn't say anything.' He couldn't tell if her confusion was caused by shock or by difficulty with the language, but he was certain she was past the point where she could be asked questions.

Behind them, another wave of applause crashed out at them, rising and falling as the singers continued to take their curtain calls. Her eyes left him, and she lowered her head, though she seemed to have finished with her inner dialogue.

He told the officer to stay with her, adding that some friends would come to find her. When they did, she was free to go with them.

18

Leaving her, he went back to the dressing room, where the medical examiner and the photographer, who had arrived while Brunetti was speaking to Signora Wellauer, were preparing to leave.

'Is there anything else?' Dr. Rizzardi asked Brunetti when he came in.

'No. The autopsy?'

'Tomorrow.'

'Will you do it?'

Rizzardi thought for a moment before he answered. 'I'm not scheduled, but since I examined the body, the *questore* will probably ask me to do it.'

'What time?'

'About eleven. I should be finished by early afternoon.'

'I'll come out,' Brunetti said.

'It's not necessary, Guido. You don't have to come to San Michele. You can call, or I'll call your office.'

'Thanks, Ettore, but I'd like to come out. It's been too long since I was there. I'd like to visit my father's grave.'

'As you like.' They shook hands, and Rizzardi started for the door. He paused a moment, then added, 'He was the last of the giants, Guido. He shouldn't have died like this. I'm sorry this happened.'

'So am I, Ettore, so am I.' The doctor left, and the photographer followed after him. As soon as they were gone, one of the two ambulance attendants who had been standing by the window, smoking and looking at the people who passed through the small *campo* below, turned and moved toward the body, which now lay on a stretcher on the floor.

'Can we take him out now?' he asked in a disinterested voice.

'No,' Brunetti said. 'Wait until everyone's left the theater.'

The attendant who had remained near the window flipped his cigarette outside and came to stand at the opposite end of the stretcher. 'That'll be a long time, won't it?' he asked, making no attempt to disguise his annoyance. Short and squat, he spoke with a noticeable Neapolitan accent.

'I don't know how long it'll be, but wait until the theater's empty.'

The Neapolitan pushed back the sleeve of his white jacket and made a business of checking his watch. 'Well, we're scheduled to go off shift at midnight, and if we wait much longer, we won't get back to the hospital until after that.'

The first one chimed in now. 'Our union rules say we aren't supposed to be kept working after our shift unless we've been given twenty-four hours' notice. I don't know what we're supposed to do about something like this.' He indicated the stretcher with the point of his shoe, as though it were something they'd found on the street.

For a moment, Brunetti was tempted to reason with them. That passed quickly. 'You two stay here, and you don't open the door to this room until I tell you to.' When they didn't respond, he asked, 'Do you understand? Both of you?' Still no answer. 'Do you understand?' he repeated.

'But the union rules—'

'Damn your union, and damn its rules,' Brunetti exploded. 'You take him out of here before I tell you to, and you'll be in jail the first time you spit on the sidewalk or swear in public. I don't want a circus when you remove him. So you wait until I tell you you can leave.' Without waiting to ask if they now understood him, Brunetti turned and slammed out of the room.

In the open area at the end of the corridor he found chaos. People in and out of costume milled about; he could tell by their eager glances toward the closed door of the dressing room that the news of death had spread. He watched as the news spread even further, watched as two heads came together and then one turned sharply to stare down the length of the corridor at that door, behind which was hidden what they could only guess at. Did they want a sight of the body? Or only something to talk about in the bars tomorrow?

When he got back to Signora Wellauer, a man and a woman, both considerably older than she, were with her, the woman kneeling

21

by her side. She had her arms around the widow, who was now openly sobbing. The uniformed policeman approached Brunetti. 'I told you they can go,' Brunetti told him.

'Do you want me to go with them, sir?'

'Yes. Did they tell you where she lives?'

'By San Molisè, sir.'

'Good; that's close enough,' Brunetti said, then added, 'Don't let them talk to anyone,' thinking of reporters, who were sure to have heard by now. 'Don't take her out the stage entrance. See if there's some way to go through the theater.'

'Yes, sir,' the officer answered, snapping out a salute so crisp Brunetti wished the ambulance attendants could have seen it.

'Sir?' he heard from behind him, and turned to see Corporal Miotti, the youngest of the three officers he had brought with him.

'What is it, Miotti?'

'I've got a list of the people who were here tonight: chorus, orchestra, stage crew, singers.'

'How many?'

'More than a hundred, sir,' he said with a sigh, as if to apologize for the hundreds of hours of work the list represented.

'Well,' Brunetti said, then shrugged it away. 'Go to the *portiere* and find out how you get through those turnstiles down there. What sort of identification do you have to have?' The corporal scribbled away in a notebook as

22

Brunetti continued to speak. 'How else can you get in? Is it possible to get back here from the theater itself? Who did he come in with this evening? What time? Did anyone go into his dressing room during the performance? And the coffee, did it come up from the bar, or was it brought in from outside?' He paused for a moment, thinking. 'And see what you can find out about messages, letters, phone calls.'

'Is that all, sir?' Miotti asked.

'Call the Questura and get someone to call the German police.' Before Miotti could object, he said, 'Tell them to call that German translator—what's her name?'

'Boldacci, sir.'

'Yes. Tell them to call her and have her call the German police. I don't care how late it is. Tell her to request a complete dossier on Wellauer. Tomorrow morning, if possible.'

'Yes, sir.'

Brunetti nodded. The officer saluted and, notebook in hand, went back toward the flight of steps that would take him to the stage entrance.

'And, Corporal,' Brunetti said to his retreating back.

'Yes, sir?' he asked, pausing at the top of the steps.

'Be polite.'

Miotti nodded, wheeled around, and was gone. The fact that he could say this to an officer without offending him made Brunetti

23

newly grateful that he had been transferred back to Venice after five years in Naples.

Though the final curtain calls had been taken more than twenty minutes before, the people backstage gave no sign of leaving. A few who seemed to have more sense of purpose went among the rest, taking things from them: pieces of costume, belts, walking sticks, wigs. One man walked directly in front of Brunetti, carrying what looked like a dead animal. Brunetti looked again and saw that the man's hands were filled with women's wigs. From across the area behind the curtain, Brunetti saw Follin appear, the officer he had sent to call the medical examiner.

He came up to Brunetti and said, 'I thought you might want to talk to the singers, sir, so I asked them to wait upstairs. And the director too. They didn't seem to like it, but I explained what happened, so they agreed. But they still didn't like it.'

Opera singers, Brunetti found himself thinking, then, repeating the thought, opera singers. 'Good work. Where are they?'

'At the top of the stairs, sir,' he said, pointing toward a short flight that continued to the top floors of the theater. He handed Brunetti a copy of that night's program.

Brunetti glanced down the list of names, recognizing one or two, then started up the stairs. 'Who was the most impatient, Follin?' Brunetti asked when they reached the top.

'The soprano, Signora Petrelli,' the officer answered, pointing toward a door that stood at the end of the corridor to the right.

'Good,' said Brunetti, turning left. 'Then we'll leave Signora Petrelli for the last.' Follin's smile made Brunetti wonder what the encounter between the eager policeman and the reluctant prima donna had been like.

'Francesco Dardi—Giorgio Germont,' read the typed cardboard rectangle that was tacked to the door of the first dressing room on his left. He knocked twice and heard an immediate cry of *'Avanti!'*

Seated at the small dressing table and busy wiping off his makeup was a baritone whose name Brunetti had recognized. Francesco Dardi was a short man, whose broad stomach pressed hard against the front of the dressing table as he leaned forward to see what he was doing. 'Excuse me, gentlemen, if I don't stand to greet you,' he said, carefully toweling black makeup from around his left eye.

Brunetti nodded in response but said nothing.

After a moment, Dardi looked away from the mirror and up at the two men. 'Well?' he asked, then returned to his makeup.

'Have you heard about this evening?' Brunetti asked.

'You mean about Wellauer?'

'Yes.'

When his question got him no more than

25

this monosyllabic reply, Dardi set down the towel and turned to look at the two policemen. 'May I be of help, gentlemen?' he asked, directing the question at Brunetti.

Since this was more to his liking, Brunetti smiled and answered pleasantly. 'Yes, perhaps you can.' He glanced down at the piece of paper in his hand, as if he needed to be reminded of the man's name. 'Signor Dardi, as you've heard by now, Maestro Wellauer died this evening.'

The singer acknowledged this news with a slight bow of his head, nothing more.

Brunetti continued. 'I'd like to know as much as you can tell me about tonight, about what went on during the first two acts of the performance.' He paused for a moment, and Dardi nodded again but said nothing.

'Did you speak to the Maestro this evening?'

'I saw him briefly,' Dardi said, swinging around in his chair and going back to the business of removing his makeup. 'When I came in, he was talking to one of the lighting technicians, something about the first act. I said *"Buona sera"* to him, then came up here to begin with my makeup. As you can see,' he said, gesturing at his image in the mirror, 'it takes a long time.'

'What time was it you saw him?' asked Brunetti.

'At about seven, I'd say. Perhaps a bit later,

maybe quarter after, but certainly no later than that.'

'And did you see him at any time after that?'

'Do you mean up here or backstage?'

'Either.'

'The only time I saw him after that was from the stage, when he was on the podium.'

'Was the Maestro with anyone when you saw him this evening?'

'I told you he was with one of the lighting crew.'

'Yes, I remember that. Was he with anyone else?'

'With Franco Santore. In the bar. They had a few words, but just as I was leaving.'

Although he recognized the name, Brunetti asked, 'And this Signor Santore, who is he?'

Dardi didn't seem at all surprised by Brunetti's display of ignorance. After all, why should a policeman recognize the name of one of the most famous theatrical directors in Italy?

'He's the director,' Dardi explained. He finished with the towel and tossed it on the table in front of him. 'This is his production.' The singer took a silk tie from where it lay on the far right side of the table, slipped it under the collar of his shirt, and carefully knotted it. 'Is there anything else you'd like?' he asked, voice neutral.

'No, I think that will be all. Thank you for your help. If we want to speak to you again,

Signor Dardi, where will we find you?'

'The Gritti.' The singer gave Brunetti a quick, puzzled glance, as if he wanted to know if other hotels actually existed in Venice but was somehow afraid to ask.

Brunetti thanked him and went out into the hallway with Follin. 'We'll try the tenor next, shall we?' he asked as he glanced down at the program in his hand.

Nodding, Follin led him along the corridor to a door on the opposite side.

Brunetti knocked, paused a moment, heard nothing. He knocked again and heard a noise from inside, which he chose to interpret as an invitation to enter. When he did, he found a short, thin man, sitting fully dressed, coat over the arm of his chair, poised in an attitude learned in drama class, one that was meant to denote 'annoyed impatience.'

'Ah, Signor Echeveste,' Brunetti gushed, walking quickly to him and extending his hand so that the other didn't have to rise. 'It is a tremendous honor to meet you.' Had Brunetti been enrolled in the same class, he would have been working on the assignment 'awe in the presence of staggering talent.'

Like a frozen stream in early March, Echeveste's anger melted under the warmth of Brunetti's flattery. With some difficulty, the young tenor pushed himself up from the chair and made a small, formal bow to Brunetti.

'And whom have I the honor to meet?' he

asked in slightly accented Italian.

'Commissario Brunetti, sir. I represent the police in this most unfortunate event.'

'Ah, yes,' replied the other, as though he'd once heard of the police, long ago, but had quite forgotten what they did. 'You're here, then, for all of this,' he said, and paused, gesturing limply with his hand, waiting for someone to supply him with the proper word. Bidden, it came: '. . . this unfortunate affair with the Maestro.'

'Yes, I am. Most unfortunate, most regrettable,' Brunetti babbled, all the time keeping his eyes on the tenor's. 'Would it be too much trouble for you to answer a few questions?'

'No, of course not,' answered Echeveste, and he sank gracefully back into his chair, but not before carefully hiking up his trousers at the knee so as to preserve their knife-edged crease. 'I'd like to be of help. His death is a great loss to the world of music.'

In the face of so stunning a platitude, Brunetti could do no more than bow his head reverently for a moment, then raise it to ask, 'At what time did you reach the theater?'

Echeveste thought for a moment before he answered. 'I'd say it was about seven-thirty. I was late. Delayed. You understand?' and somehow, in the question, managed to convey the image of slipping reluctantly away from crumpled sheets and female allure.

29

'And why were you late?' Brunetti asked, knowing he was not supposed to and waiting to see how the question affected the fantasy.

'I was having my hair cut,' the tenor replied.

'And the name of your barber?' Brunetti asked politely.

The tenor named a shop only a few streets from the theater. Brunetti glanced at Follin, who made a note. He would check tomorrow.

'And when you arrived at the theater, did you see the Maestro?'

'No, no. I saw no one.'

'And it was about seven-thirty when you arrived?'

'Yes. As nearly as I can remember.'

'Did you see or speak to anyone when you came in?'

'No, I didn't. No one at all.'

Even before Brunetti could comment on the strangeness of that, Echeveste explained. 'I didn't come in, you see, through the stage entrance. I came in through the orchestra.'

'I didn't realize that was possible,' Brunetti said, interested that there was access to the backstage area that way.

'Well,' Echeveste said, looking down at his hands. 'It usually isn't, but I have a friend who is an usher, and he let me in, so I didn't have to use the stage entrance.'

'Could you tell me why you did this, Signor Echeveste?'

The tenor raised a dismissive hand and

allowed it to float languidly in front of them for a moment, as if hoping it would erase or answer the question. It did neither. He put the hand on top of the other and said, simply, 'I was afraid.'

'Afraid?'

'Of the Maestro. I'd been late for two rehearsals, and he'd been very angry about it, shouting. He could be very unpleasant when he was angry. And I didn't want to have to go through it again.' Brunetti suspected that it was only respect for the dead that kept any word stronger than 'unpleasant' from being used.

'So you came in that way to avoid seeing him?'

'Yes.'

'Did you see or speak to him at any time? Other than from the stage?'

'No, I didn't.'

Brunetti got to his feet and repeated his very theatrical smile. 'Thank you very much for your time, Signor Echeveste.'

'My pleasure,' the other replied, rising from his seat. He looked at Follin, then back to Brunetti, and asked, 'Am I free to go now?'

'Of course. If you'd just tell me where you're staying?'

'The Gritti,' he answered, with the same puzzled glance Dardi had given. It was enough to make a man wonder if there *were* other hotels in the city.

31

CHAPTER THREE

When Brunetti emerged from the dressing room, he found Miotti waiting for him. The young officer explained that Franco Santore, the director, had refused to wait, saying that anyone who wanted to speak to him could find him at the Hotel Fenice, along the side of the theater. Brunetti nodded, almost pleased to be assured of the presence of other hotels in the city.

'That leaves us the soprano,' said Brunetti, heading down the corridor. The usual cardboard tag was stuck to the door. 'Flavia Petrelli—Violetta Valéry.' Below this, there was a line of what appeared to be Chinese characters sketched with a fine black pen.

He knocked at the door and signaled with a nod that the other two could remain outside.

'*Avanti!*' he heard, and opened the door.

Two women were waiting for him in the room, and it surprised him that he couldn't tell which of them was the soprano. Like everyone in Italy, he knew of 'La Petrelli.' Brunetti had seen her sing only once, some years ago, and had a vague memory of seeing pictures of her in the newspapers.

The darker of the two women stood with her back to the dressing table, while the other sat in a straight wooden chair against the far

32

wall. Neither of them spoke when he came in, and Brunetti used the silence to study them.

He guessed the woman who was standing to be in her late twenties or early thirties. She wore a purple sweater and a long black skirt that brushed against a pair of black leather boots. The boots were low-heeled and of glove-quality leather, and Brunetti vaguely recalled walking past the window of Fratelli Rossetti with his wife and hearing her exclaim at the madness of spending half a million lire for a pair of boots. These boots, he felt sure. She had shoulder-length black hair with a natural curl that would allow it to be cut with a spoon and still look perfect. Her eyes were out of place with her olive coloring, a clear green that made him think of glass but then, remembering those boots, of emeralds.

The seated woman appeared to be a few years older and wore her hair, in which there were a few specks of gray, cropped close to her head, like one of the Roman emperors of the centuries of decline. The severity of the cut emphasized the fineness of bone and nose.

He took a few steps toward the seated woman and made a motion that could have been taken for a bow. 'Signora Petrelli?' he asked. She nodded but said nothing. 'I'm honored to meet you and regret only that it has to be in these unfortunate circumstances.' Since she was one of the leading opera singers of the day, he found irresistible the temptation to speak to her in the excessive language of opera, as if he were playing a part.

She nodded again, doing nothing to remove the burden of speech from him.

'I'd like to speak to you about the death of Maestro Wellauer.' He glanced across the room to the other woman and added, 'And speak to you too,' leaving it to one of them to supply the second woman's name.

'Brett Lynch,' the singer supplied. 'My friend and secretary.'

'Is that an American name?' he asked the woman whose name it was.

'Yes, it is,' Signora Petrelli answered for her.

'Then would it be better if we were to speak in English?' he asked, not a little bit proud of the ease with which he could switch from one language to the other.

'It would be easier if we spoke in Italian,' the American said, speaking for the first time and using an Italian that displayed not the least accent. His reaction was entirely involuntary and was noticed by both women. 'Unless you'd like to speak in Veneziano,' she added, slipping casually into the local dialect, which she spoke perfectly. 'But then Flavia might have trouble following what we say.' It was entirely deadpan, but Brunetti realized it would be a long time before he'd flaunt his English again.

'Italian, then,' he said, turning back to Signora Petrelli. 'Will you answer a few

34

questions?'

'Certainly,' she answered. 'Would you like a chair, Signor . . .'

'Brunetti,' he supplied. 'Commissario of police.'

The title appeared not to impress her in the least. 'Would you like a chair, Dottor Brunetti?'

'No, thank you.' He pulled his notebook from his pocket, took the pen that was stuck between the pages, and prepared to give the appearance of taking notes, something he seldom did, preferring to let his eyes and mind roam freely during the first questioning.

Signora Petrelli waited until he had uncapped his pen, then asked, 'What is it you would like to know?'

'Did you see or speak to the Maestro tonight?' Then, before she could offer it, he continued, 'Aside from while you were on the stage, of course.'

'No more than to say "*Buona sera*" when I came in and to wish one another "*In boca al lupo.*" Nothing more than that.'

'And that was the only time you spoke to the Maestro?'

Before she answered, she glanced across toward the other woman. He kept his eyes on the soprano, so he had no idea of the other's expression. The pause lengthened, but before he could repeat the question, the soprano finally answered. "No, I didn't see him again. I

35

saw him from the stage, of course, as you pointed out, but we didn't speak again.'

'Not at all?'

'No, not at all,' came her instant reply.

'And during the intervals? Where were you?'

'Here. With Signorina Lynch.'

'And you, Signorina Lynch?' he asked, pronouncing her name with complete lack of accent, though he had to concentrate to do it. 'Where were you during the performance?'

'Here in the dressing room for most of the first act. I went downstairs for *"Sempre libera,"* but then I came back up here. And I was here for the rest of the performance,' she replied calmly.

He looked around the bare room, searching for something that could possibly have occupied her for that length of time. She caught his glance and pulled a slim volume from the pocket of her skirt. On it he saw Chinese characters such as those on the name card on the door.

'I was reading,' she explained, holding the book toward him. She gave him an entirely friendly smile, as though she were now ready to talk about the book, if he so desired.

'And did you speak to Maestro Wellauer during the evening?'

'As Signora Petrelli told you, we spoke to him when we came in, but after that I didn't see him again.' Brunetti, quelling the impulse to say that, no, Signora Petrelli had not mentioned that they had come in together, let her continue. 'I couldn't see him from where I was standing backstage, and I was here in the dressing room during both of the intervals.'

'Here with Signora Petrelli?'

This time it was the American who glanced toward the other woman before she answered. 'Yes, with Signora Petrelli, just as she told you.'

Brunetti closed his notebook, in which he had done no more than scribble the American's last name, as if to capture the full horror of a word composed of five consonants. 'In case there should be other questions, could you tell me where I might find you, Signora Petrelli?'

'Cannaregio 6134,' she said, surprising him by naming an entirely residential part of the city.

'Is that your apartment, Signora?'

'No, it's mine,' interrupted the other woman. 'I'll be there, too.'

He reopened his notebook and wrote down the address. Without missing a beat, he asked, 'And the phone number?'

She gave him that as well, telling him that it was not listed, then added that the address was near the basilica of SS. Giovanni e Paolo.

Putting on his formal self, he bowed slightly and said, 'Thank you both, Signore, and I'm sorry for your difficulty at this time.'

If either one of them found the words

strange, neither gave any sign of it. After more polite exchanges, he left the dressing room and led the two officers who had been waiting for him outside down the narrow flight of stairs that led to the backstage area.

The third officer waited at the bottom of the steps.

'Well?' Brunetti asked him.

He smiled, pleased to have something to report 'Both Santore, the director, and La Petrelli spoke to him in his dressing room. Santore went in before the performance, and she went in after the first act.'

'Who told you?'

'One of the stagehands. He said that Santore seemed to be angry when he left, but this was just an impression the man had. He didn't hear any shouting or anything.'

'And Signora Petrelli?'

'Well, the man said he wasn't sure it was La Petrelli but that she was wearing a blue costume.'

Miotti interrupted here. 'She wears a blue dress in the first act.'

Brunetti gave him a quizzical look.

Was it possible that Miotti lowered his head before he spoke? 'I saw a rehearsal last week, sir. And she wears a blue dress in the first act.'

'Thank you, Miotti,' Brunetti said, voice level.

'It's my girlfriend, sir. Her cousin's in the chorus and he gets us tickets.'

Brunetti nodded, smiling, but he realized he would have liked it more if he hadn't said that.

The officer who had been making his report shot back his cuff and looked at his watch. 'Go on,' Brunetti told him.

'He said he saw her come out toward the end of the interval, and he said she was angry, very angry.'

'At the end of the first interval?'

'Yes, sir. He was sure of that.'

Taking a cue from the policeman, Brunetti said, 'It's late, and I'm not sure we can do much more here tonight.' The others glanced around at the now empty theater. 'Tomorrow, see if you can find anyone else who might have seen her. Or seen anyone else go in.' Their mood seemed to lighten when he spoke of tomorrow. 'That will be all for tonight. You can go.' When they started to move away, he called, 'Miotti, have they taken his body to the hospital yet?'

'I don't know, sir,' he said, almost guiltily, as though afraid this would cancel out the approval he had received a moment before.

'Wait here while I find out,' Brunetti told him.

He walked back to the dressing room and opened the door without bothering to knock. The two attendants sat in easy chairs, feet on the table that stood between them. On the floor beside them, covered by a sheet, entirely ignored, lay one of the greatest musicians of

39

the century.

They looked up when Brunetti came in but gave no acknowledgment. 'You can take him to the hospital now,' he said, then turned and left the room, careful to close the door behind him.

Miotti was where he had left him, glancing through a notebook that was very similar to the one Brunetti carried. 'Let's go and have a drink,' Brunetti said. 'The hotel is probably the only place open at this hour.' He sighed, tired now. 'And I could use a drink.' He started off to his left, but he found himself walking back toward the stage. The staircase seemed to have disappeared. He had been inside the theater for so long, up and down stairs, along corridors and back down them, that he was completely disoriented and had no idea how to get out.

Miotti touched him lightly on the arm and said, 'This way, sir,' leading him to the left and down the flight of steps they had first come up more than two hours before.

At the bottom, the *portiere*, seeing Miotti's uniform, reached under the counter at which he sat and pushed the button that released the turnstile blocking the exit of the theater. He gestured that all they had to do was push. Knowing that Miotti would already have questioned the man about who had come in and out of the theater that night, Brunetti didn't bother to ask him any questions but

40

passed directly out of the theater and into the empty *campo* beyond the door.

Before they started up the narrow street that led to the hotel, Miotti asked, 'Are you going to need me for this, sir?'

'You don't have to worry about having a drink while you're still in uniform,' Brunetti assured him.

'No, its not that, sir.' Perhaps the boy was simply tired.

'What is it, then?'

'Well, sir, the *portiere* is a friend of my father's, so I thought that if I went back now, and maybe I asked him to come and have a drink, maybe he'd tell me something more than he did before.' When Brunetti didn't respond, he said quickly, 'It was just an idea, sir. I don't mean to . . .'

'No, it's a good idea. Very good. Go back and talk to him. I'll see you tomorrow morning. No need to get there before nine, I think.'

'Thank you, sir,' Miotti said with an eager smile. He snapped out a salute that Brunetti answered with a cursory wave of his hand, and the young man turned back toward the theater and the business of being a policeman.

CHAPTER FOUR

Brunetti walked up toward the hotel, still lighted, even at this hour when the rest of the city was darkened and sleeping. Once the capital of the dissipations of a continent, Venice had become a sleepy provincial town that virtually ceased to exist after nine or ten at night. During the summer months, she could remember her courtesan past and sparkle, as long as the tourists paid and the good weather held, but in the winter, she became a tired old crone, eager to crawl early to bed, leaving her deserted streets to cats and memories of the past.

But these were the hours when, for Brunetti, the city became most beautiful, just as they were the same hours when he, Venetian to the bone, could sense some of her past glory. The darkness of the night hid the moss that crept up the steps of the *palazzi* lining the Grand Canal, obscured the cracks in the walls of churches, and covered the patches of plaster missing from the facades of public buildings. Like many women of a certain age, the city needed the help of deceptive light to recapture her vanished beauty. A boat that, during the day, was making a delivery of soap powder or cabbages, at night became a numinous form, floating toward some mysterious destination. The fogs that were common in these winter days could transform people and objects, even turn long-haired teenagers, hanging around a street corner and sharing a cigarette, into mysterious phantoms from the past.

He glanced up at the stars, seen clearly above the darkness of the unlighted street, and noticed their beauty. Holding their image in mind, he continued toward the hotel.

The lobby was empty and had the abandoned look common to public places at night. Behind the reception desk, the night potter sat, chair tilted back against the wall, that day's pink sporting newspaper open before him. An old man in a green-and-black-striped apron was busy spreading sawdust on the marble floor of the lobby and sweeping it clean. When Brunetti saw that he had trailed his way through the fine wooden chips and couldn't traverse the lobby without tracking a path across the already swept floor, he looked at the old man and said, '*Scusi.*'

'It's nothing,' the old man said, and trailed after him with his broom. The man behind the newspaper didn't even bother to look up.

Brunetti continued on into the lobby of the hotel. Six or seven clusters of large stuffed chairs were pulled up around low tables. Brunetti threaded his way through them and went to join the only person in the room. If the press was to be believed, the man sitting there was the best stage director currently working in Italy. Two years before, Brunetti had seen his production of a Pirandello play at the Goldoni Theater and had been impressed with it, far more with the direction than with the acting, which had been mediocre. Santore was known to be homosexual, but in the theatrical world where a mixed marriage was one between a man and a woman, his personal life had never served as an impediment to his success. And now he was said to have been seen angrily leaving the dressing room of a man who had died violently not too long afterward.

Santore rose to his feet as Brunetti approached. They shook hands and exchanged names. Santore was a man of average height and build, but he had the face of a boxer at the end of an unlucky career. His nose was squat, its skin large-pored. His mouth was broad, his lips thick and moist. He asked Brunetti if he would like a drink, and from that mouth came words spoken in the purest of Florentine accents, pronounced with the clarity and grace of an actor. Brunetti thought Dante must have sounded like this.

When Brunetti accepted his suggestion that they have brandy, Santore went off for some. Left alone, Brunetti looked down at the book the other man had left open on the table in front of him, then pulled it toward him.

Santore came back, carrying two snifters,

44

each generously filled with brandy.

'Thanks,' Brunetti said, accepting the glass and taking a large swallow. He pointed at the book and decided to begin with that, rather than with the usual obvious questions about where he had been, what he had done. 'Aeschylus?'

Santore smiled at the question, hiding any surprise he might have felt that a policeman could read the title in Greek.

'Are you reading it for pleasure, or for work?'

'I suppose you could call it work,' Santore answered, and sipped at his brandy. 'I'm supposed to begin work on a new production of the *Agamemnon* in Rome in three weeks.'

'In Greek?' Brunetti asked, but it was clear that he didn't mean it.

'No, in translation.' Santore was silent for a moment, but then he allowed his curiosity to get the better of him. 'How is it that a policeman reads Greek?'

Brunetti swirled the liquid around in his glass. 'Four years of it. But a long time ago. I've forgotten almost all I knew.'

'But you can still recognize Aeschylus?'

'I can read the letters. I'm afraid that's all that's left.' He took another swallow of his drink and added, 'I've always liked it about the Greeks that they kept the violence off the stage.'

'Unlike us?' Santore asked, then asked

45

again, 'Unlike this?'

'Yes, unlike this,' Brunetti admitted, not even bothering to wonder how Santore would have learned that the death had been violent. The theater was small, so he had probably learned that even before the police did, probably even before they had been called.

'Did you speak to him this evening?' There was no need to use a name.

'Yes. We had an argument before the first curtain. We met in the bar and went back to his dressing room. That's where it started.' Santore spoke without hesitation. 'I don't remember if we were shouting at each other, but our voices were raised.'

'What were you arguing about?' Brunetti asked, as calmly as if he'd been talking to an old friend and equally certain that he would get the truth in response.

'We had come to a verbal agreement about this production. I kept my part of it. Helmut refused to keep his.'

Instead of asking Santore to clarify the remark, Brunetti finished his brandy and set the glass on the table between them, waiting for him to continue.

Santore cupped his hands around the bottom of his glass and rolled it slowly from side to side. 'I agreed to direct this production because he promised to help a friend of mine to get a job this summer, at the Halle Festival. It isn't a big festival, and the part wasn't an

46

important one, but Helmut agreed to speak to the directors and ask that my friend be given the part. Helmut was going to be conducting just the one opera there.' Santore brought the glass to his lips and took a sip. 'That's what the argument was about.'

'What did you say during the argument?'

'I'm not sure I remember everything I said, or what he said, but I do remember saying that I thought what he'd done, since I'd already done my part, was dishonest and immoral.' He sighed. 'You always ended up talking like him, when you talked to Helmut.'

'What did he say to that?'

'He laughed.'

'Why?'

Before he answered, Santore asked, 'Would you like another drink? I'm going to have one.'

Brunetti nodded, grateful. This time, while Santore was gone, he laid his head against the back of the chair and closed his eyes.

He opened them when he heard Santore's steps approach. He took the glass that the other man handed him and asked, as if there had been no break in the conversation, 'Why did he laugh?'

Santore lowered himself into his chair, this time holding the glass with one hand cupped under it. 'Part of it, I suppose, is that Helmut thought himself above common morality. Or perhaps he thought he'd managed to create his own, different from ours, better.' Brunetti said nothing, so he continued. 'It's almost as if he alone had the right to define what morality meant, almost as if he thought no one else had the right to use the term. He certainly thought I had no right to use it.' He shrugged, sipped.

'Why would he think that?'

'Because of my homosexuality,' the other answered simply, suggesting that he considered the issue equal in importance to, say, a choice of newspaper.

'Is that the reason he refused to help your friend?'

'In the end, yes,' Santore said. 'At first, he said it was because Saverio wasn't good enough, didn't have enough stage experience. But the real reason came later, when he accused me of wanting a favor for my lover.' He leaned forward and put his glass down on the table. 'Helmut has always seen himself as a sort of guardian of public morals,' he said, then corrected his grammar. 'Saw himself.'

'And is he?' Brunetti asked.

'Is who what?' Santore asked, all grammar forgotten in his confusion.

'Is he your lover, this singer?'

'Oh, no. He's not. More's the pity.'

'Is he homosexual?'

'No, not that, either.'

'Then why did Wellauer refuse?'

Santore looked at him directly and asked, 'How much do you know about him?'

'Very little, and that only about his life as a

48

musician, and only what's been in the newspapers and magazines all these years. But about him as a man I know nothing.' And that, Brunetti realized, was beginning to interest him a great deal, for the answer to his death must lie there, as it always did.

Santore said nothing, so Brunetti prompted him. 'Never speak ill of the dead, *vero*? Is that it?'

'And never speak ill of someone you might have to work with again,' Santore added.

Brunetti surprised himself by saying, 'That hardly seems to be the case here. What ill is to be spoken?'

Santore glanced across at the policeman and studied his face, giving it the sort of speculative look that he might give to an actor or a singer he was deciding how to use in a performance. 'It's mostly rumor,' he finally said.

'What sort of rumor?'

'That he was a Nazi. No one knows for sure, or if they ever knew, no one is saying, or whatever they might have said in the past has been forgotten, dropped into that place where memory does not follow. He conducted for them while they were in power. It's even said he conducted for the Führer. But he said he had to do it to save some of the people in his orchestra, who were Jews. And they did survive the war, those who were Jews, and managed to play in the orchestra all through

49

the war years. And so did he, play and survive. And somehow his reputation never suffered because of all those years or because of those intimate concerts for the Führer. After the war,' Santore continued, voice strangely calm, 'he said he had been "morally opposed" and had conducted against his will.' He took a small sip of his drink. 'I've no idea what's true, whether he was a member of the party or not, what his involvement was. And I suppose I don't care.'

'Then why do you mention it?' Brunetti asked.

Santore laughed out loud, his voice filling the empty room. 'I suppose because I believe it's true.'

Brunetti smiled. 'That could be the case.'

'And probably because I do care?'

'That as well,' Brunetti agreed.

They allowed the silence to expand between them until Brunetti asked, 'How much *do* you know?'

'I know that he gave those concerts all during the war. And I know that, in one case, the daughter of one of his musicians went to him in private and begged him to help her father. And I know that the musician survived the war.'

'And the daughter?'

'She survived the war.'

'Well, then?' Brunetti asked.

'Then nothing, I suppose.' Santore

shrugged. 'Besides, it's always been easy to forget the man's past and think only of his genius. There was no one like him, and I'm afraid there's no conductor like him left.'

'Is that why you agreed to direct this production for him—because it was convenient to forget his past?' It was a question, not an insult, and Santore clearly took it as such.

'Yes,' he answered softly. 'I chose to direct it so that my friend would get the chance to sing with him. So it was convenient for me to forget all that I knew or suspected, or at least to ignore it. I'm not sure it matters all that much, not anymore.'

Brunetti watched an idea appear in Santore's face. 'But now he won't get to sing with Helmut, ever,' and he added, to let Brunetti know that the purpose of the conversation had never been far beneath its surface, 'which would seem to argue that I had no reason to kill him.'

'Yes, that would seem to follow,' Brunetti agreed, with no apparent interest, then asked, 'Did you ever work with him before?'

'Yes. Six years ago. In Berlin.'

'Your homosexuality didn't present difficulties then?'

'No. It never presented real difficulties, once I was famous enough for him to want to work with me. Helmut's stand, as a sort of guardian angel of Western morality or biblical standards, was pretty well known, but you can't survive very long in this world if you refuse to work with homosexuals. Helmut just made his own sort of moral truce with us.'

'And you did the same with him?'

'Certainly. As a musician, he was as close to perfection as a man could come. It was worth putting up with the man to be able to work with the musician.'

'Was there anything else about the man you found objectionable?'

Santore thought a long time before he answered this. 'No, there's nothing else I knew about him that would make me dislike him. I don't find the Germans sympathetic, and he was very Germanic. But its not dislike or liking that I'm talking about. It was this sense of moral superiority he seemed to carry about with him, as if it was—he was—a lantern in dark times.' Santore grimaced at the last phrase. 'No, that's not right. It must be the hour or the brandy. Besides, he was an old man, and now he's dead.'

Going back to an earlier question, Brunetti asked, 'What did you say to him during the argument?'

'The usual things one says in an argument,' Santore said wearily. 'I called him a liar, and he called me a faggot. Then I said some unpleasant things about the production, about the music and his conducting, and he said the same things about the stage direction. The usual things.' He stopped speaking and slumped in his chair.

'Did you threaten him?'

Santore's eyes shot to Brunetti's face. He couldn't disguise his shock at the question. 'He was an old man.'

'Are you sorry he's dead?'

This was another question the director wasn't prepared to hear. He thought for a time before he answered it. 'No, not for the death of the man. For his wife, yes. This will be . . .' he began, but then didn't finish the sentence. 'For the death of the musician, yes, I'm very sorry about that. He was old, and he was at the end of his career. I think he knew that.'

'What do you mean?'

'The conducting, it didn't have its old glory somehow, didn't have that old fire. I'm not a musician, so I can't be clear about just what it was. But something was missing.' He paused and shook his head. 'No, maybe it's just my anger.'

'Did you talk to anyone about this?'

'No; one doesn't complain about God.' He paused for a moment, then said, 'Yes, I did. I mentioned it to Flavia.'

'La Signora Petrelli?'

'Yes.'

'And what did she say?'

'She'd worked with him before; often, I think. She was bothered by the difference in him, spoke to me about it once.'

'What did she say?'

'Nothing specific; just that it was like working with one of the younger conductors, someone with little experience.'

'Did anyone else mention it?'

'No, no one; at least not to me.'

'Was your friend Saverio in the theater tonight?'

'Saverio's in Naples,' Santore responded coldly.

'I see.' It had been the wrong question. The mood of easy intimacy was gone. 'How much longer will you be in Venice, Signor Santore?'

'I usually leave after the *prima* has been successfully performed. But Helmut's death will change things. I'll probably be here for another few days, until the new conductor is fully at home with the production.' When Brunetti made no response to this, he asked, 'Will I be allowed to go back to Florence?'

'When?'

'Three days. Four. I have to stay for at least one performance with the new conductor. But then I'd like to go home.'

'There's no reason you can't go,' Brunetti said, and stood. 'All we'll need is an address where we can reach you, but you can certainly give that to one of my men at the theater tomorrow.' He extended his hand. Santore got to his feet and took it. 'Thank you for the brandy. And good luck with the *Agamemnon*.' Santore smiled his thanks, and saying nothing else, Brunetti left.

CHAPTER FIVE

Brunetti decided to walk home, to take advantage of the star-studded sky and the deserted streets. He paused in front of the hotel, measuring distances. The map of the city that lay imprinted in the minds of all Venetians showed him that the shortest way was across the Rialto Bridge. He cut across Campo San Fantin and into the labyrinth of narrow streets that wound back toward the bridge. No one passed him as he walked, and he had the strange sensation of having the sleeping city entirely to himself. At San Luca, he passed the pharmacy, one of the few places that were open all night, except for the train station, where slept the homeless and the mad.

And then he was at the water's edge, the bridge to his right. How typically Venetian it was, looking, from a distance, lofty and ethereal but revealing itself, upon closer reflection, to be firmly grounded in the mud of the city.

Across the bridge, he walked through the now abandoned market. It was usually a cross to bear, shoving and pushing through the crowded street, through herds of tourists jammed together between vegetable stalls on

55

one side and shops filled with the worst sort of tourist junk on the other, but tonight he had it to himself and could stride freely. Ahead of him, in the middle of the street, a pair of lovers stood, glued hip to hip, blind to the beauty about them but perhaps, after all, somehow inspired by it.

At the clock, he turned left, glad to be almost home. Five minutes brought him to his favorite shop, Biancat, the florist, whose windows offered the city a daily explosion of beauty. Tonight, through the clinging humidity of the glass, tubs of yellow roses preened themselves, while behind them lurked a cloud of pale jasmine. He walked quickly past the second window, crowded with lurid orchids, which always looked faintly cannibalistic to him.

He let himself into the *palazzo* in which he lived, bracing himself, as he always had to do when he was tired, for the task of climbing the ninety-four steps to their fourth-floor apartment. The previous owner had built the apartment illegally more than thirty years before, simply added another floor to the existing building without bothering with official permission of any sort. This situation had somehow been obscured when Brunetti bought the apartment ten years ago, and ever since, he had lived in recurrent fear of being confronted with a summons to legalize the obvious. He trembled at the prospect of the

Herculean task of getting the permits that would authenticate both that the apartment existed and that he had a right to live there. The mere fact that the walls were there and he lived within them would hardly be thought relevant. The bribes would be ruinous.

He opened the door, glad of the warmth and smell he associated with the apartment: lavender, wax, the scent of something cooking in the kitchen at the back; it was a mixture that represented to him, in a way he couldn't explain, the existence of sanity in the daily madness that was his work.

'Is that you, Guido?' Paola called from the living room. He wondered who else she might be expecting at two in the morning, but he didn't ask.

'Yes,' he called back, kicking off his shoes and removing his coat, just now beginning to accept how tired he was.

'Would you like some tea?' She came into the hall and kissed him lightly on the cheek.

He nodded, making no attempt to hide his exhaustion from her. Trailing her down the hall toward the kitchen, he took a chair while she filled the kettle and put it on the stove to boil. She pulled down a bag of dried leaves from a cupboard above her head, opened it, sniffed, and asked, 'Verbena?'

'Fine, fine,' he answered, too tired to care.

She tossed a handful of dried leaves into the terra-cotta teapot that had been his grandmother's and came over to stand behind him. She kissed the back of his head, right on the spot where his hair was beginning to thin. 'What is it?'

'At La Fenice. Someone poisoned the conductor.'

'Wellauer?'

'Yes.'

She placed her hands on his shoulders and gave them a gentle squeeze that he found encouraging. No comment was necessary; it was obvious to both of them that the press would make a sensation of the death and become screamingly insistent that the culprit be found as quickly as possible. Either he or Paola could have written the editorials that would appear in the morning, were probably being written even now.

The kettle shot out a burst of steam, and Paola went to pour the water into the chipped pot. As always, he found her mere physical presence comforting, found solace in observing the easy efficiency with which she moved and did things. Like many Venetian women, Paola was fair-skinned and had the red-gold hair so often seen in portraits of the women of the seventeenth century. Not beautiful by any ordinary canon, she had a nose that was a bit too long and a chin that was more than a bit too determined. He liked both.

'Any ideas?' she asked, bringing the pot and two mugs to the table. She sat opposite him,

58

poured out the aromatic tea, then went back to the cupboard and returned with an immense jar of honey.

'Its too early,' he said, spooning honey into his mug. He swirled it around, clicking his spoon against the side of the mug, then spoke in rhythm with the clicking of the spoon. 'There's a young wife, a soprano who lied about not seeing him before he died, and a gay director who had an argument with him before he was killed.'

'Maybe you ought to try to sell the story. It sounds like something we'd see on TV.'

'And a dead genius,' he added.

'Yes, that would help.' Paola sipped at her tea, then blew on it to cool it. 'How much younger is the wife?'

'Easily young enough to be his daughter. Thirty years, I'd say.'

'OK,' she said, using one of the Americanisms toward which her vocabulary was prone. 'I say it was the wife.'

Though he had repeatedly asked her not to do this, she insisted on choosing a suspect at the beginning of any investigation he worked on, and she was generally wrong, for she always opted for the most obvious choice. Once, exasperated beyond bearing, he'd asked her why she insisted on doing it, and she'd explained that since she had written her dissertation on Henry James, she considered herself entitled to the release of finding the obvious in real life, since she'd never found it in his novels. Nothing Brunetti had ever done could stop her from making her choice, and nothing could ever induce her to inject any subtlety into her selection.

'Which means,' he said, still swirling his spoon, 'that it will turn out to be someone in the chorus.'

'Or the butler.'

'Hmm,' he agreed, and drank his tea. They sat in companionable silence until the tea was gone. He took both mugs and placed them in the sink, and set the teapot on the counter beside it, safe from harm.

CHAPTER SIX

The morning after the conductor's body was found, Brunetti arrived at his office a bit before nine, to discover that an event almost as marvelous as that of the night before had transpired: his immediate superior, Vice-Questore Giuseppe Patta, was already in his office and had been calling for Brunetti for almost half an hour. This fact was revealed to him first by the porter who stood just inside the entrance to the building, then by an officer he met on the stairs, then by the secretary who worked for him and the two other commissarios of the city. Making no attempt to hurry, Brunetti checked his mail, phoned the switchboard to see if there had been any calls, and at last went down the flight of stairs that led to his superior's office.

Cavaliere Giuseppe Patta had been sent to Venice three years before in an attempt to introduce new blood into the criminal justice system. In this case, the blood had been Sicilian and had proved to be incompatible with that of Venice. Patta used an onyx cigarette holder and had been known, upon occasion, to carry a silver-headed walking stick. Though the first had made Brunetti stare and the second laugh, he tried to reserve judgment until he had worked long enough with the man to decide if he had a right to these affectations. It had taken Brunetti less than a month to decide that though the affectations did suit the man, he had little right to them. The vice-questore's work schedule included a long coffee each summer morning on the terrace of the Gritti, and, in the winter, at Florian's. Lunch was usually taken at the Cipriani pool or Harry's Bar, and he usually decided at about four to 'call it a day.' Few others would so name it. Brunetti had quickly learned, as well, that Patta was to be addressed, at all times, as 'Vice-Questore' or the even grander 'Cavaliere,' the provenance of which title remained obscure. Not only did he insist that his title be used, but he had to be addressed formally as *lei*, leaving it to the

61

rabble to call one another by the familiar, *tu*.

Patta preferred not to be disturbed by any of the more distressing details of crime or other such messiness. One of the few things that could drive him to run his fingers through the graceful curls at his temples was a suggestion in the press that the police were in any way lax in their duties. It did not matter what the press chose to comment on: that a child had managed to slip through a police cordon to give a flower to a visiting dignitary or that notice had been taken of the open sale of drugs by African street vendors. Any suggestion that so little as hinted at anything less than a police stranglehold on the inhabitants of the city sent Patta into paroxysms of accusation, most of which fell upon his three commissarios. His ire was usually expressed in long memos to them, in which the crimes of omission by the police were made to sound infinitely more heinous than those of commission by the criminal population.

Patta had been known, as the result of a suggestion in the press, to declare various 'crime alerts,' in which he singled out a particular crime, much in the way he would select an especially rich dessert from the cloth-draped sweet table in a restaurant, and announced in the press that, this week, the crime in question would be wiped out or, at least, minimized. Brunetti could not, when he read of the most recent 'crime alert'—for this was information that was generally revealed to him only by the press—help but think of the scene in *Casablanca* in which the order was given to 'round up the usual suspects.' That was done, a few teenagers were sentenced to jail for a month or so, and things went back to normal until the press's attentions once again provoked an 'alert.'

Brunetti often mused that the crime rate in Venice was low—one of the lowest in Europe and certainly the lowest in Italy—because the criminals, and they were almost always thieves, simply didn't know how to get away. Only a resident could navigate the spiderweb of narrow *calles*, could know in advance that this one was a dead end or that one ended in a canal. And the Venetians, the native population, tended to be law-abiding, if only because their tradition and history had given them an excessive respect for the rights of private property and the imperative need to see to its safekeeping. So there was very little crime, and when there was an act of violence or, much more rarely, a murder, the criminal was quickly and easily found: the husband, the neighbor, the business partner. Usually all they had to do was round up the usual suspects.

But Wellauer's death, Brunetti knew, was different. He was a famous man, no doubt the most famous conductor of the age, and he had been killed in Venice's little jewel of an opera house. Because it was Brunetti's case, the vice-questore would find him directly responsible for any bad publicity that might attach to the police.

He knocked on the door and waited to be told to enter. When the shout came, Brunetti pushed open the door and saw Patta where he knew he would be seated, poised as he knew he would find him, sitting behind his enormous desk, bent over a paper that was made important by the scrutiny he gave it. Even in a country of handsome men, Patta was shockingly handsome, with a chiseled Roman profile, wide-spaced and piercing eyes, and the body of an athlete, though he was well into his fifties. He preferred, when photographed for the papers, to be taken in left profile.

'So you've finally come,' Patta said, suggesting that Brunetti was hours late rather than on time. 'I thought I'd have to wait all morning for you,' he added, which Brunetti thought was overplaying the role. When Brunetti made no response to either remark, Patta demanded, 'What have you got?'

Brunetti pulled that morning's *Gazzettino* from his pocket and answered, 'The paper, sir. Its right here on page one.' Then, before Patta could stop him, he read out, ' "Famous Maestro Found Dead. Murder Suspected." ' He offered the paper to his superior.

Patta kept his voice level but dismissed the paper with a wave. 'I've already read that. I meant what have you found out?'

Brunetti reached into the pocket of his jacket and pulled out his notebook. There was nothing written in it except for the name, address, and phone number of the American woman, but so long as he was kept standing in front of the seated Patta, there was no way the other man could see that the pages were virtually empty. Pointedly, he wet the finger of one hand and leafed slowly through the pages. 'The room was unlocked, and there was no key in the door. That means that anyone could have gone in or out at any time during the performance.'

'Where was the poison?'

'In the coffee, I think. But I won't know until after the autopsy and the lab report.'

'When's the autopsy?'

'This morning, I think. At eleven.'

'Good. What else?'

Brunetti turned a page, exposing fresh emptiness. 'I spoke to the singers at the theater. The baritone saw him, but only to say hello. The tenor says he didn't see him, and the soprano says she saw him only when she came into the theater.' He glanced down at Patta, who waited. 'The tenor's telling the truth. The soprano's lying.'

'Why do you say that?' Patta snapped.

'Because I think it's true, sir.'

With exaggerated patience, as if he were speaking to an especially slow child, Patta asked, 'And why, Commissario, do you think it's true?'

'Because she was seen going into his dressing room after the first act.' Brunetti didn't bother to clarify that this was only a suggestion from a witness, not yet confirmed. His interview had suggested she wasn't telling the truth, perhaps about that, perhaps about something else.

'I also spoke to the director,' Brunetti continued. 'He had an argument with the conductor before the performance began. But he didn't see him again during the performance. I think he's telling the truth.' Patta didn't bother to ask him why he thought this.

'Anything else?'

'I sent a message to the police in Berlin last night.' He made a business of leafing through his notebook. 'The message went out at—'

'Never mind.' Patta cut him off. 'What did they say?'

'They'll fax down a full report today, any information they have on Wellauer or his wife.'

'What about the wife? Did you speak to her?'

'Not more than a few words. She was very upset. I don't think anyone could have talked to her.'

'Where was she?'

'When I spoke to her?'

'No, during the performance.'

66

'She was sitting in the audience, in the orchestra. She said she went back to see him after the second act but got there too late to speak to him, that they never spoke.'

'You mean she was backstage when he died?' Patta asked with an eagerness so strong Brunetti almost believed the man would need little more to arrest her for the crime.

'Yes, but I don't know whether she saw him, whether she went into the dressing room.'

'Well, make it your business to find out.' Even Patta realized that his tone had been too harsh. He added, 'Sit down, Brunetti.'

'Thank you, sir,' he said, closing his notebook and slipping it into his pocket before taking a seat opposite his superior. Patta's chair, he knew, was a few centimeters higher than this one, something the vice-questore undoubtedly regarded as a delicate psychological advantage.

'How long was she back there?'

'I don't know, sir. She was very upset when I spoke to her, so her story wasn't very clear.'

'Could she have gone into the dressing room?' Patta asked.

'She might have. I don't know.'

'It sounds like you're making excuses for her,' said Patta, then added, 'Is she pretty?' Brunetti realized Patta must have found out about the difference in age between the dead man and his widow.

'If you like tall blonds,' Brunetti said.

'Don't you?'

'My wife doesn't permit me to, sir.'

Patta thrust around for a way to pull the conversation back together. 'Did anyone else go into the dressing room during the performance? Where did the coffee come from?'

'There's a bar on the ground floor of the theater. Probably from there.'

'Find out.'

'Yes, sir.'

'Now pay attention, Brunetti.' Brunetti nodded. 'I want the name of anyone who was in the dressing room, or near it, last night. And I want to find out more about the wife. How long they've been married, where she comes from, that sort of thing.' Brunetti nodded.

'Brunetti?' Patta suddenly asked.

'Yes, sir?'

'Why aren't you taking notes?'

Brunetti permitted himself the smallest of smiles. 'Oh, I never forget anything you say, sir.'

Patta chose, for reasons of his own, to give this a literal reading. 'I don't believe what she told you about not seeing him. People don't start to do things and then change their minds. I'm sure there's something here. It probably has something to do with the difference in their ages.' It was rumored that Patta had spent two years studying psychology at the University of Palermo before changing to the law. But it was unblemished fact that, after an undistinguished career as a student, he had taken his degree and, soon thereafter, as a direct result of his father's very distinguished career in the Christian Democratic party, had been appointed a vice-commissario of police. And now, after more than twenty years, he was vice-questore of the police of Venice.

Patta having apparently finished with his orders, Brunetti prepared himself for what was coming, the speech about the honor of the city. As night the day, the thought gave birth to Patta's words. 'You might not understand this, Commissario, but this is one of the most famous artists of our era. And he was killed here in our city, Venice'—which name never failed to sound faintly ridiculous coming from Patta, with his Sicilian accent. 'We have to do everything in our power to see that this crime is solved; we cannot allow this crime to blot the reputation, the very honor, of our city.' There were times when Brunetti was tempted to take notes of what the man said.

As Patta continued in this vein, Brunetti decided that if something was said about the glorious musical history of the city, he'd take Paola flowers that afternoon. 'This is the city of Vivaldi. Mozart was here. We have a debt to pay to the world of music.' Irises, he thought; she liked them best of all. And she'd put them in the tall blue Murano vase.

'I want you to stop whatever you're working

on and devote yourself entirely to this. I've looked at the duty rosters,' Patta continued, surprising Brunetti that he even knew they existed, 'and I've assigned you two men to help you with this.' Please let it not be Alvise and Riverre, and I'll take her two dozen. 'Alvise and Riverre. They're good, solid men.' Roughly translated, that meant they were loyal to Patta.

'And I want to see progress in this. Do you understand?'

'Yes, sir,' Brunetti replied blandly.

'Right, then. That's all. I've got work to do, and I'm sure you've got a lot to get busy with.'

'Yes, sir,' Brunetti repeated, rising and going toward the door. He wondered what the parting shot would be. Hadn't Patta taken his last vacation in London?

'And good hunting, Brunetti.'

Yes, London. 'Thank you, sir,' he said quietly, and let himself out of the office.

CHAPTER SEVEN

For the next hour, Brunetti busied himself reading through the reports of the crime in the four major papers. *Il Gazzettino*, as was to be expected, put it all over the front page and saw it as a crime that somehow compromised the city and put it at risk. It editorialized that the

70

police must quickly find the person responsible, not so much to bring that person to justice as to remove the blot from the honor of Venice. Reading it, Brunetti reflected on Patta's having read this article instead of waiting for his usual *L'Osservatore Romano*, which wasn't on the newsstands until ten.

La Repubblica viewed the event in light of recent political developments, suggesting a relationship so subtle that only the journalist, or a psychiatrist, could grasp it. *Corriere della Sera* behaved as though the man had died in his bed and devoted a full page to an objective analysis of his contribution to the world of music, drawing special attention to his having championed the cause of certain modern composers.

He saved *L'Unità* for last. Predictably, it screamed the first thing that came into its head—in this case, vengeance, which, predictably, it had got confused with justice. An editorial hinted broadly at the same old secrets in high places and dragged out, not surprisingly, poor old Sindona, dead in his jail cell, and asked the patently rhetorical question of whether there wasn't some dark connection between these two 'frighteningly similar' deaths. Aside from the fact that they were both old men who died of cyanide poisoning, there was little similarity, frightening or not, that Brunetti could see.

Not for the first time in his career, Brunetti

71

reflected upon the possible advantage of censorship of the press. In the past, the German people had got along very well with a government that demanded it, and the American government seemed to fare similarly well with a population that wanted it.

He turned back to the long story in the *Corriere*, and tossed the three other papers into the wastebasket. He read through the article a second time, occasionally taking notes. If not the most famous conductor in the world, Wellauer was certainly ranked high among them. He had first conducted before the last war, the prodigy of the Berlin Conservatory. Not much was written about the war years, save that he had continued to conduct in his native Germany. It was in the fifties that his career had taken off and he had joined the international glitter set, flying from one continent to another to conduct a single concert, then going off to a third to conduct an opera.

In the midst of the tinsel and the fame, he had remained the consummate musician, exacting both precision and delicacy from any orchestra he directed, insisting upon absolute fidelity to the score as written. Even the reputation he had acquired of being imperious or difficult paled before the universal praise that greeted his absolute devotion to his art.

The article paid little attention to his personal life, save to mention that his current

72

wife was his third and that the second had taken her life, twenty years before. His residences were given as Berlin, Gstaad, New York, and Venice.

The picture that appeared on the front page was not a recent one. In it, Wellauer appeared in profile, talking with Maria Callas, who was in costume and was obviously the prime subject of the photograph. It seemed strange to him that the paper would print a photo that was at least thirty years old.

He reached down into the wastebasket and grabbed back the *Gazzettino*. It, as usual, had a photo of the place where the death had occurred, the dull, balanced facade of Teatro La Fenice. Next to it was a smaller photo of the stage entrance, out of which something was being carried by two uniformed men. The picture below was a recent full-face publicity still of the Maestro: white tie, shock of silver hair swept back from his angular face. There was the faint Slavic tilt to the eyes, which appeared curiously light under the dark brows that overshadowed them. The nose was entirely too long for the face, but the effect of those eyes was so strong that the slight defect hardly seemed worth notice. The mouth was broad, the lips full and fleshy, a strangely sensual contrast with the austerity of the eyes. Brunetti tried to remember the face as he had seen it the night before, tightened and distorted by death, but the power of this photo was enough to supplant that image. He stared at those pale eyes and tried to imagine a hatred so strong that it would lead someone to destroy this man.

His speculations were interrupted by the arrival of one of the secretaries, with the report that had come down from the police in Berlin, already translated into Italian.

Before he began to read it, Brunetti reminded himself that Wellauer was a sort of living monument and the Germans were always on the lookout for heroes, so what he read was very likely to reflect both of those things. This meant that some truths would be there only by suggestion, others by omission. Hadn't many musicians and artists belonged to the Nazi Party? But who remembered that now, after all these years?

He opened the report and began to read the Italian text, the German useless to him. Wellauer had no criminal record whatsoever, not even a driving violation. His apartment in Gstaad had been robbed twice; both times, nothing had been recovered, no one apprehended, and the insurance had made good, though the totals had been enormous.

Brunetti waded through two more paragraphs of Germanic exactitude until he came to the suicide of the second wife. She had hanged herself in the basement of their Munich apartment on 30 April 1968, after what the report referred to as 'a long period of depression.' No suicide note had been found. She had left three children, twin boys and a girl, then aged seven and twelve. Wellauer had himself discovered the body and, after the funeral, had gone into a period of complete seclusion that lasted six months.

The police had paid no attention to him until his marriage, two years ago, to Elizabeth Balintffy, a Hungarian by birth, a doctor by training and profession, and a German by her first marriage, which had ended in divorce three years before her marriage to Wellauer. She had no criminal record, either in Germany or in Hungary. She had one child by the first marriage, a daughter, Alexandra, aged thirteen.

Brunetti looked, and looked in vain, for some reference to what Wellauer had done during the war years. There was mention of his first marriage, in 1936, to the daughter of a German industrialist, and his divorce after the war. Between those dates, the man seemed not to have existed, which, to Brunetti, spoke very eloquently of what he had been doing or, at any rate, supporting. This, however, was a suspicion about which he was likely to get very little confirmation, especially not in an official report from the German police.

Wellauer was, in short, as clean as a man could possibly wish to be. But still, someone had put cyanide in his coffee. Experience had taught Brunetti that people killed one another primarily for two reasons: money and sex. The order wasn't important, and the second was very often called love, but he had, in fifteen years spent among the murderous, encountered few exceptions to that rule.

Well before eleven, he had finished with the German police report. He called down to the laboratory, only to learn that nothing had been done, no fingerprints taken from the cup or from the other surfaces in the dressing room, which remained sealed, a fact that, he was told, had already prompted three phone calls from the theater. He yelled a bit at that, but he knew it was useless. He spoke briefly with Miotti, who said he'd learned nothing further from the *portiere* the night before, save that the conductor was a 'cold one,' the wife very pleasant and friendly, and La Petrelli not at all to his liking. The *portiere* gave no reason for this, falling back, instead, on the explanation that she was *antipatica*. For him, that was enough.

There was no sense in sending either Alvise or Riverre to take prints, not until the lab could determine if prints other than those of the conductor were on the cup. No need for haste here.

Disgruntled that he would miss lunch, Brunetti left his office a little after noon and walked to the bar on the corner, where he had a sandwich and a glass of wine, not at all pleased with either. Though everyone in the bar knew who he was, no one asked him about the death, though one old man did rustle his newspaper suggestively. Brunetti walked down to the San Zaccaria stop and caught the number 5 boat, which would take him to the cemetery island of San Michele, cutting through the Arsenale and along the back side of the island. He seldom visited the cemetery, somehow not having acquired the cult of the dead so common among Italians.

He had come here in the past; in fact, one of his first memories was of being taken here as a child to help tend the grave of his grandmother, killed in Treviso during the Allied bombing of that city during the war. He remembered how colorful the graves were, blanketed with flowers, and how neat, each precise rectangle separated from the others by razor-edged patches of green. And, in the midst of this, how grim the people, almost all women, who came carrying those armloads of flowers. How drab and shabby they were, as if all their love for color and neatness was exhausted by the need to care for those spirits in the ground, leaving none left over for themselves.

And now, some thirty-five years later, the graves were just as neat, the flowers still explosive with color, but the people who passed among the graves looked as if they belonged to the world of the living, were no longer those wraiths of the postwar years. His father's grave was easily found, not too far from Stravinsky. The Russian was safe; he would remain there, untouched, for as long as the cemetery remained or people remembered his music. His father's tenancy was far more precarious, for the time was arriving when his grave would be opened and his bones taken to be put in an ossuary in one of the long, crowded walls of the cemetery.

The plot, however, was neatly tended; his brother was more conscientious than he. The carnations that stood in the glass vase set in the earth of the grave were new; the frost of three nights earlier would have killed any that had been placed here before. He bent down and brushed aside a few leaves that the wind had blown up against the vase. He straightened up, then stooped to pick up a cigarette butt that lay beside the headstone. He stood again and looked at the picture displayed upon the front of the stone. He saw his own eyes, his own jaw, and the too-big ears that had skipped over him and his brother and gone, instead, to their sons.

'Ciao, Papà,' he said, but then he couldn't think of anything else to say. He walked down to the end of the row of graves and dropped the cigarette butt into a large metal can set in the earth.

At the office of the cemetery, he announced his name and his rank and was shown into a small waiting room by a man who told him to wait, the doctor would be with him soon. There was nothing to read in the room, so he contented himself with looking out the only window, which gave onto the enclosed cloister about which the buildings of the cemetery had been built.

At the beginning of his career, Brunetti had asked to attend the autopsy of the victim of the first murder he had investigated, a prostitute killed by her pimp. He had watched intently as the body was rolled into the operating theater, stared fascinated as the white sheet was pulled back from her nearly perfect body. And as the doctor raised the scalpel above the flesh, ready to begin the long butterfly incision, Brunetti had pitched forward and fainted amid the medical students with whom he sat. They had calmly carried him out into the hall and left him, groggy, on a chair before hurrying back to watch. Since then, he had seen the victims of many murders, seen the human body rent by knives, guns, even bombs, but he had never learned to look on them calmly, and he could never again bring himself to watch the calculated violation of an autopsy.

The door to the small waiting room opened, and Rizzardi, dressed as impeccably as he had been the night before, entered. He smelled of expensive soap, not of the carbolic that Brunetti couldn't help associating with his work.

'Good afternoon, Guido,' he said, and

extended a hand. 'I'm sorry you bothered to come all the way out here. I could easily have phoned you with what little I learned.'

'That's all right, Ettore; I wanted to come out anyway. And there won't be anything until those fools in the lab give me a report. And it's certainly too soon to speak to the widow.'

'Then let me give you what I have,' the doctor said, closing his eyes and beginning to recite from memory. Brunetti removed the notebook from his pocket and took down what he heard. 'The man was in excellent health. If I didn't know his age, seventy-four, I would have guessed him to be at least ten years younger, early sixties, perhaps even late fifties. Muscles in excellent tone, probably through exercise added to a generally healthy body. No sign of disease in the internal organs. He can't have been a drinker; liver was perfect. Strange to see in a man his age. Didn't smoke, though I think he might have, years ago, and stopped. I'd say he was good for another ten or twenty years.' Finished, he opened his eyes and looked at Brunetti.

'And the cause of death?' Brunetti asked.

'Potassium cyanide. In the coffee. I'd estimate he ingested about thirty milligrams, more than enough to kill him.' He paused for a moment, then added, 'I'd never actually seen it before. Remarkable effect.' His voice trailed off, and he lapsed into a reverie that Brunetti found unsettling.

After a moment, Brunetti asked, 'Is it as quick as I've read it is?'

'Yes, I think it is,' the doctor answered. 'As I said, I've never seen a case before, not a real one. I'd just read about it.'

'Instantaneous?'

Rizzardi thought for a moment before he answered. 'Yes, I suppose it is, or so close as to make it the same thing. He might have had a moment to realize what was happening, but he would have thought it was a stroke or a heart attack. In any case, well before he could have realized what it was, he would have been dead.'

'What's the actual cause of death?'

'Everything stops. Everything simply stops working: heart, lungs, brain.'

'In seconds?'

'Yes. Five. Ten at the most.'

'No wonder they use it,' Brunetti said.

'Who?'

'Spies, in spy novels. With capsules hidden in hollow teeth.'

'Um,' Rizzardi muttered. If he found Brunetti's comparison at all strange, he gave no indication of it. 'Yes, there's no question that it's fast, but there are others that are much more deadly.' In response to Brunetti's raised eyebrows, he explained, 'Botulism. The same amount that killed him could probably kill half of Italy.'

There seemed little to be gained from this

subject, regardless of the doctor's evident enthusiasm for it, so Brunetti asked, 'Is there anything else?'

'It looks like he's been under treatment for the last few weeks. Do you know if he had a cold or flu or something like that.'

'No,' Brunetti said, shaking his head. 'We don't know anything yet. Why?'

'There were signs of injections. There was no indication of drug abuse, so I imagine it was antibiotics, perhaps a vitamin, some normal procedure. In fact, the traces were so faint that it might not even have been injections; they could have been simple bruises.'

'But not drugs?'

'No, not likely,' the doctor said. 'He could easily have given himself an injection in the right hip—he was right-handed—but a right-handed person can't give himself an injection in the right arm or left buttock, at least not where I found the mark. And as I said, he was in excellent health. I would have seen signs of drug use, if there had been any.' He paused a moment and then added, 'Besides, I'm not even sure that's what they are. In my report, I'll simply enter them as subcutaneous bleeding.' Brunetti could tell from his voice that he considered the marks a triviality and already regretted mentioning them.

'Anything else?'

'No, nothing. Whoever did this robbed him of at least another ten years of life.'

As was usual with him, Rizzardi displayed, and probably felt, no curiosity whatsoever about who might have committed the crime. In the years he'd known him, Brunetti had never heard the doctor ask about the criminal. At times, he had become interested in, even fascinated by, a particularly inventive means of death, but he seemed never to care about who had done it or if the person had been found.

'Thanks, Ettore,' Brunetti said, and shook the doctor's hand. 'I wish they would work this fast in the lab.'

'I doubt that their curiosity is as compelling as mine,' Rizzardi said, again confirming Brunetti in the belief that he would never understand the man.

CHAPTER EIGHT

On the boat back to the city, he decided to stop in unannounced and see if Flavia Petrelli had perhaps remembered that she had spoken to the Maestro the night before. Buoyed by the sense of having something to do, he got off the boat at Fondamente Nuove and walked toward the hospital, which shared a common wall with the basilica of SS. Giovanni e Paolo. Like all street addresses in Venice, the one the American had given him was virtually meaningless in a city with only six different names for street addresses and a numbering system without plan or reason. The only way to find it was to get to the church and ask someone who lived in the neighborhood. She ought to be easy to find. Foreigners tended to live in more fashionable parts of Venice, not this solidly middle-class area, and very few foreigners managed to sound as if they had grown up here, as Brett Lynch did.

In front of the church, he inquired first for the number, then for the American, but the woman he had approached had no idea of where to find either. She told him to go and ask Maria, saying the name as if she expected him to know exactly which Maria she meant. Maria, it turned out, ran the news-stand in front of the grammar school, and if Maria didn't know where she lived, then the American didn't live in the neighborhood.

At the bottom of the bridge in front of the basilica, he found Maria, a white-haired woman of indeterminate age who sat inside her kiosk, dispensing newspapers as though they were fortunes and she the Sibyl. He gave her the number he was looking for, and she replied, 'Ah, Signorina Lynch,' saying it with a smile and giving the name the two syllables demanded by Italian. Straight down Calle della Testa, first right, fourth bell, and would he mind taking her newspapers along with him?

Brunetti found the door with no trouble.

The name was carved into a brass plate, scratched and tarnished with age, that stood next to the bell. He rang once and, after a moment, a voice through the intercom asked who he was. He resisted the desire to announce that he had come to deliver the papers, and, instead, simply gave his name and title. Whoever it was he had spoken to said nothing, but the door snapped open in front of him, allowing him to enter the building. A single flight of stairs lay off to the right, and he began to climb, noting with pleasure the slight concavity that hundreds of years of use had hollowed out of each step. He liked the way the declivity forced him to walk up the center of the staircase. He went up a double flight, then another. At the fourth turn, the stairway suddenly broadened out, and the original, worn marble steps were replaced by slabs of clean-cut Istrian marble. This part of the building had been extensively restored, and very recently.

The stairs ended at a black metal door. As he approached it, he sensed that he was being examined through the minuscule spyhole that was cut above the top lock. Before he could raise his hand to knock, the door was pulled open by Brett Lynch, who stepped aside and asked him to come in.

He muttered the ritual 'Permesso' without which an Italian could never enter another person's house. She smiled but didn't offer her hand and turned to lead him down the hallway into the main room of the apartment.

He was surprised to find himself in a vast open space, easily ten meters by fifteen. The wooden floor was made of the thick oak beams used to support the oldest roofs in the city. The walls had been stripped of paint and plaster and taken down to the original brick. The most remarkable thing in the room was the tremendous brightness that glared from the uncovered skylights, six of them, set in triple pairs on either side of the peaked ceiling. Whoever had received permission to alter the external structure of a building this old, Brunetti reflected, either had powerful friends or had blackmailed both the mayor and the city planner. And it had all been done recently; the smell of fresh wood told him that.

He turned his attention from the house to its owner. The previous night, he had failed to notice how tall she was, tall in that angular way Americans seemed to find attractive. But her body, he noticed, had none of the frailty that often came with tallness. She looked healthy, fit, a quality that was heightened by her clear skin and eyes. He found that he was staring at her, struck by the intelligence in her eyes, struck as well by the fact that he was seeking to find cunning in them. He was curious about his own refusal to accept her for what she seemed to be, an attractive, intelligent woman.

Flavia Petrelli sat, rather artistically, he

thought, just to the left of one of the long windows that filled the left side of the room and through which, at a distance, he could see the bell tower of San Marco. She made no acknowledgment of his presence other than a faint nod, which he returned before saying to the other, 'I brought you your papers.'

He was careful to hand them to her with the front page exposed, turned so that she would see the pictures and read the shouting headlines. She glanced down at them, quickly folded them shut, and said, 'Thank you,' before turning to toss them on a low table.

'I compliment you on your home, Miss Lynch.'

'Thank you,' was her minimal reply.

'It's unusual to see so much light, so many skylights in a building of this age,' he said, prying.

'Yes, it is, isn't it?' she said blandly.

'Come, Commissario,' interrupted Flavia Petrelli, 'certainly you didn't come here to discuss interior design.'

As if to offset the brusqueness of her friend's remark, Brett Lynch said, 'Please have a seat, Dottor Brunetti,' and motioned him to a low divan that stood in front of a long glass table at the center of the room. 'Would you like some coffee?' she asked, the bright hostess, this a purely social call.

Though he had little desire for coffee, he said he'd like some, so as to see how the singer would respond to his declaration that he was there for a while and had no sense of haste. She turned her attention back to a musical score that lay on her lap and ignored him while her friend disappeared to make the coffee.

While she was busy with the coffee and while Petrelli was busy ignoring him, he took a careful look around the apartment. The wall he faced was filled with books from floor to ceiling. He easily recognized the Italian ones by the way their titles ran from bottom to top, the English by their titles running top to bottom. More than half of the books were printed in characters he assumed to be Chinese. All of them looked as if they had been read more than once. Interspersed among the books were pieces of ceramic— bowls and small human figures—that appeared no more than faintly Oriental to him. One shelf was taken up with boxed sets of compact discs, suggesting that they were complete operas. To their left stood very complicated-looking stereo equipment, and in the far corners two large speakers stood on wooden pedestals. The only pictures on the walls were bright modern splashes that didn't appeal to him.

After a short time, Lynch returned from the kitchen, carrying a silver tray on which stood two small espresso cups, spoons, and a silver sugar bowl. Today, he noticed, she was wearing jeans that had never heard of America and another pair of those boots, this pair a dark reddish brown. A color for each day of the week? What was it in this woman that irritated him so? The fact that she was a foreigner who spoke his language as well as he did and lived in a house he could never hope to afford?

She set the cup down in front of him and he thanked her, waiting for her to take a seat opposite him. He offered to spoon sugar into the second cup, but she shook her head in refusal. He spooned two sugars into his own cup and sat back on the sofa. 'I've just come from San Michele,' he said by way of introduction. 'The cause of death was cyanide.' She raised her cup to her lips, sipped. 'It was in the coffee.'

She replaced her cup in the saucer and placed both on the table.

Flavia Petrelli glanced up from the score, but it was the other who spoke. 'Then at least it was quick. How thoughtful of whoever did it.' She turned to her friend. 'Did you want coffee, Flavia?'

Brunetti thought it all a bit too theatrical, but he ignored this and asked the question she had clearly meant to prepare by her remark. 'Am I to take it that you didn't like the Maestro, Miss Lynch?'

'No,' she answered, looking at him directly. 'I didn't like him, and he didn't like me.'

'Was there any particular reason?'

She moved a hand dismissively. 'We disagreed about many things.' That, he supposed, was meant to be sufficient reason.

He turned to Petrelli. 'Was your rapport with the Maestro different from your friend's?'

She closed the score and set it carefully at her feet before she answered. 'Yes, it was. Helmut and I always worked well together. We had a great deal of professional respect for one another.'

'And personal?'

'That too, of course,' she answered quickly. 'But our relationship was primarily professional.'

'What, if I might ask, were your personal feelings toward him?' If she was prepared for the question, she nevertheless seemed not to like it. She shifted in her seat, and he was struck by how obvious she was making her discomfort at the question. He had read about her for years and knew her to be a better actress than this. If she had something to hide in her relationship with Wellauer, she knew how to hide it; she would not sit there like a schoolgirl squirming around when asked about her first boyfriend.

He allowed the silence to grow, intentionally not repeating his question.

Finally, she said, with some reluctance, 'I didn't like him.'

When she added nothing to this, Brunetti said, 'If I might repeat my question to Miss

90

Lynch, was there a particular reason for that?' How polite we're being, he thought. The old man is lying, cold and eviscerated, across the *laguna*, and we sit here engaged in grammatical niceties—a subjunctive here, a conditional there: Would you be so kind as to tell me? Could you please tell me? For a moment, he wished himself back in Naples, where he'd spent those awful years dealing with people who ignored the subtlety of words and responded to kicks and blows.

Signora Petrelli cut in on his reverie by saying, 'There was no real reason. He was simply *antipatico*.' Ah, thought Brunetti, hearing that word again, how much better than any exercise in grammar. Just haul out this explanation of any human discord, that someone was *antipatico*, that some nameless transport of cordiality hadn't been struck between people, and everything was supposed to be miraculously clear. It was vague, and it was insufficient, but it appeared to be all that he was going to get.

'Was it mutual?' he asked, unperturbed. 'Did the Maestro find something in you to dislike?'

She glanced across at Brett Lynch, who was again sipping at her coffee. If something passed between them, Brunetti didn't see it.

Finally, as though displeased with the character she was playing, Petrelli raised one hand in an open-fingered gesture, one he recognized from the publicity still of her as Norma that had appeared in the papers that morning. Dramatically, she thrust the hand away from her and said, '*Basta*. Enough of all of this.' Brunetti was fascinated by the change in her, for the gesture had carried away years with it. She got abruptly to her feet, and the rigidity disappeared from her features.

She turned to face him. 'You're bound to hear all of this sooner or later, so it's better that I tell you.' He heard the slight tap of porcelain as the other woman set her saucer down on the table, but he kept his eyes on the singer. 'He accused me of being a lesbian, and he accused Brett of being my lover.' She paused, waiting to see what his response would be. When he made none, she continued. 'It started the third day of rehearsal. Nothing direct or clear; just the way he spoke to me, the way he referred to Brett.' Again she paused, waiting for his response, and again there was none. 'By the end of the first week, I said something to him, and that developed into an argument, and at the end of that he said he wanted to write to my husband.' She paused to correct herself. 'My ex-husband.' She waited for the impact of that to register on Brunetti.

Curious, he asked, 'Why would he do that?'

'My husband is Spanish. But my divorce is Italian. So is the decree that gives me custody of our children. If my husband were to bring an accusation like that against me in this country . . .' She allowed her voice to trail off, making it clear what she thought the chances would be of her keeping her children.

'And the children?' he asked.

She shook her head in confusion, not understanding the question.

'The children. Where are they?'

'In school, where they should be. We live in Milan, and they go to school there. I don't think it's right to drag them along to wherever I happen to be singing.' She came closer to him, then sat at the end of the sofa. When he glanced at her friend, he saw that she sat with her face turned away, looking off at the bell tower, almost as if this conversation in no way involved her.

For a long time, no one said anything. Brunetti considered what he had just been told and wondered whether it was the cause of his instinctive backing away from the American. He and Paola had enough friends of variegated sexuality for him to believe that, even if the accusation was true, this would not be the reason.

'Well?' the singer finally said.

'Well what?' he asked.

'Aren't you going to ask if it's true?'

He dismissed the question with a shake of his head. 'Whether it's true or not is irrelevant. All that's important is whether he would have gone through with his threat to tell your husband.' Brett Lynch had turned back to face him with speculative eyes.

When she spoke, her voice was level. 'He would have done it. Anyone who knew him well would have known that. And Flavia's husband would move mountains to get custody of the children.' When she said her friend's name, she glanced over at her, and their eyes locked for a moment. She moved down in her seat, shoved her hands into her pockets, and stretched her feet out in front of her.

Brunetti studied her. Was it those gleaming boots, the careless display of wealth in this apartment, that caused him to feel such resentment toward her? He tried to clear his mind, to see her for the first time, a woman in her early thirties who had offered him her hospitality and, now, appeared to be offering him her trust. Unlike her employer—if that's what Petrelli was—she didn't bother with dramatic gestures or try in any way to highlight the sharp Anglo-Saxon beauty of her face.

He noticed that the strands of her beautifully cut hair were damp at the neck, as though she had not long ago stepped from either a bath or a shower. Turning his attention to Flavia Petrelli, he thought that she had about her, too, the fresh smell of a woman who had just finished bathing. He suddenly found himself embroiled in an erotic fantasy of the two women entwined, naked, in the shower, breasts pushed up against breasts, and he was amazed at the power of the fantasy to

94

stir him. Oh, God, how much easier it had been in Naples, with a kick and a shove.

The American released him from his reverie by asking, 'Does this mean you think Flavia could have done it? Or that I could have?'

'It's far too early to speak like that,' he said, though this was hardly true. 'It's far too early to speak of suspects.'

'But it's not too early to speak of motive,' the singer said.

'No, it's not,' he agreed. He hardly needed to point out that she now appeared to have one.

'I suppose that means I've got one as well,' added her friend, as strange a declaration of love as Brunetti had ever heard. Or friendship? Or loyalty to an employer? And people said Italians were complicated.

He decided to temporize. 'As I said, it's too early to talk of suspects.' He decided to change the topic. 'How long will you be in the city, Signora?'

'Until the end of the performances,' she said. 'That's another two weeks. Until the end of the month. Though I'd like to go back to Milan for the weekends.' It was phrased as a statement, but it was clear that she was asking for permission. He nodded, the gesture conveying both understanding and police permission to leave the city.

She continued. 'After that, I don't know. I

95

haven't any other engagements until—' she paused, looking across at her friend, who supplied immediately, 'Covent Garden, on the fifth of January.'

'And you'll be in Italy until then?' he asked.

'Certainly. Either here or in Milan.'

'And you, Miss Lynch?' he asked, turning to her.

Her glance was cool, as cool as her answer. 'I'll be in Milan, as well.' Though it was hardly necessary, she added, 'With Flavia.'

He took his notebook from his pocket then and asked if he could have the address in Milan where they would be. Flavia Petrelli gave it to him and, unasked, supplied the phone number. He wrote down both, put the notebook back in his pocket, and stood.

'Thank you both for your time,' he said formally.

'Will you want to speak to me again?' the singer asked.

'That depends on what I'm told by other people,' Brunetti said, regretting the menace in it but not the honesty. Understanding only the first, she picked up the score and opened it, posing it on her lap. He no longer interested her.

He took a step toward the door and, as he did, stepped into one of the beams of light that washed across the floor. Looking up toward its source, he turned to the American and asked, finally, 'How did you manage to get those

96

skylights?'

She crossed in front of him and went into the hallway, stopped before the door, and asked him, 'Do you mean how did I get the skylights themselves or the permits to build them?'

'The permits.'

Smiling, she answered, 'I bribed the city planner.'

'How much?' he asked automatically, calculating the total area of the windows. Six of them, each about a meter square.

She had obviously lived in Venice long enough not to be offended by the indelicacy of the question. She smiled more broadly and answered, 'Twelve million lire,' as though she were giving the outside temperature.

That made it, Brunetti calculated, about half a month's salary a window.

'But that was two years ago,' she added by way of explanation. 'I'm told prices have risen since then.'

He nodded. In Venice, even graft was subject to inflation.

They shook hands at the door, and he was surprised at the warmth of the smile she gave him, as though their talk of bribery had somehow made them fellow conspirators. She thanked him for having come, though there was no need for that. He responded with equal politeness and found real warmth in his voice. Had it taken so little to win him over? Had her display of corruptibility rendered her more human? He said goodbye and mused on this last question as he walked down the stairs, glad again to feel their sea-like unevenness under his feet.

CHAPTER NINE

Back at the Questura, he learned that officers Alvise and Riverre had gone to the Maestro's apartment and looked through his personal effects, coming away with documents and papers, which were now being translated into Italian. He called down to the lab, but they still had no results on fingerprints, though they had confirmed the self-evident, that the poison was in the coffee. Miotti was nowhere to be found; presumably he was still at the theater. At a loss for what to do, knowing that he would have to speak to her soon, Brunetti called the Maestro's widow and asked if it would be possible for her to receive him that afternoon. After an initial and entirely understandable reluctance, she asked him to come at four. He rooted around in the top drawer of his desk and found half a package of *bussolai*, the salty Venetian pretzels he loved so much. He ate them while he looked through the notes he had taken on the German police report.

A half hour before his appointment with

Signora Wellauer, he left his office and walked slowly up toward Piazza San Marco. Along the way, he paused to look into shop windows, shocked, as he always was when in the center of the city, by how quickly their composition was changing. It seemed to him that all the shops that served the native population—pharmacies, shoemakers, groceries—were slowly and inexorably disappearing, replaced by slick boutiques and souvenir shops that catered to the tourists, filled with luminescent plastic gondolas from Taiwan and papier-mâché masks from Hong Kong. It was the desires of the transients, not the needs of the residents, that the city's merchants answered. He wondered how long it would take before the entire city became a sort of living museum, a place fit only for visiting and not for inhabiting.

As if to exacerbate his reflections, a group of off-season tourists wandered by, led by a raised umbrella. Water on his left, he passed through the piazza, amazed by the people who seemed to find the pigeons more interesting than the basilica.

He crossed the bridge after Campo San Moisè, turned right, then right again, and into a narrow *calle* that ended in a huge wooden door.

He rang and heard a disembodied, mechanical voice ask who he was. He gave his name and, seconds later, heard the snap that released the lock on the door. He stepped into a newly restored hall, its ceiling beams stripped to their original wood and varnished to a high gloss. The floor, he noticed with a Venetian eye, was made of inlaid marble tiles set in a geometric pattern of waves and swirls. From the gentle undulance of it, he guessed that it was original to the building, perhaps early fifteenth century.

He began to climb the broad, space-wasting steps. At each landing there was a single metal door; the singleness spoke of wealth and the metal of the desire to protect it. Engraved nameplates told him to keep ascending. The steps ended, five flights up, at another metal door. He rang the bell and a few moments later was greeted by the woman he had spoken to in the theater the night before, the Maestro's widow.

He took her extended hand, muttered, 'Permesso,' and crossed into the apartment.

If she had slept the night before, there was no sign of it in her face. She wore no makeup, so the intense pallor of her face was accented, as were the dark smudges beneath her eyes. But even under the fatigue, the structure of great beauty was visible. The bones of her cheeks would carry her into great age safely, and the line of her nose would always create a profile that people would turn to see again.

'I'm Commissario Brunetti. We spoke last night.'

'Yes, I remember,' she replied. 'Please come this way.' She led him down a corridor to a large study. In one corner, there was a fireplace with a small open fire. Two chairs separated by a table stood in front of the fire. She waved him to one of the chairs and sat in the other. On the table, a burning cigarette rested in a full ashtray. Behind her was a large window, through which he could see the ocher rooftops of the city. On the walls hung what his children insisted on calling 'real' paintings.

'Would you like a drink, Dottor Brunetti? Or perhaps tea?' She repeated the Italian phrases as though she had learned them by rote from a grammar book, but he found it interesting that she would know his proper title.

'Please don't go to any trouble, Signora,' he said, responding in kind.

'Two of your policemen were here this morning. They took some things away with them.' It was evident that her Italian wasn't adequate to name the things that had been removed.

'Would it help if we spoke English?' he asked in that language.

'Oh, yes,' she said, smiling for the first time and giving him a hint of what her full beauty would be. 'That would be much easier for me.' Her face softened, and some of the signs of stress disappeared. Even her body seemed to relax as the language difficulty was removed.

'I've just been here a few times, to Venice, and I'm embarrassed by how badly I speak Italian.'

In other circumstances, the situation would have demanded that he deny this and praise her ability with the language. Instead he said, 'I realize, Signora, how difficult this is for you, and I want to express my condolences to you and your family.' Why was it that the words with which we confronted death always sounded so inadequate, so blatantly false? 'He was a great musician, and the loss to the world of music is enormous. But I'm sure yours must be far worse.' Stilted and artificial, it was the best he could do.

He noticed a number of telegrams sitting next to the ashtray, some open, some not. She must have been hearing much the same thing all day long, but she gave no indication of that and, instead, said simply, 'Thank you.' She reached into the pocket of her sweater and pulled out a package of cigarettes. She took one of them from the pack and raised it to her lips, but then she saw the cigarette still smoking in the ashtray. She tossed fresh cigarette and package on the table and pulled the lighted cigarette from the ashtray. She took a deep breath of smoke, held it for a long time, then expelled with obvious reluctance.

'Yes, he will be missed by the world of music,' she said. Before he could reflect on the strangeness of this, she added, 'And here as well.' Though there was only a millimeter of ash on the end of it, she flicked her cigarette at the ashtray, then bent forward and scraped the sides, as though it were a pencil she wanted to sharpen.

He reached into his pocket and took out his notebook, opened it to a page on which he kept a scribbled list of new books he wanted to read. He had noticed the night before that she was almost beautiful, would become unquestionably so from certain angles and in certain lights. Under the weariness that veiled her face today, that beauty was still evident. She had wide-spaced blue eyes and naturally blond hair, which today she wore pulled back and knotted simply at her neck.

'Do you know what killed him?' she asked.

'I spoke to the pathologist this morning. It was potassium cyanide. It was in the coffee he drank.'

'So it was fast. There is at least that.'

'Yes,' he agreed. 'It would have been almost instantaneous.' He jotted something in his notebook, then asked, 'Are you familiar with the poison?'

She shot him a quick glance before she answered, 'No more than any other doctor would be.'

He flipped a page. 'The pathologist suggested that it's not easily come by, cyanide,' he lied.

She said nothing, so he asked, 'How did your husband seem to you last night, Signora?

Was there anything strange or in any way peculiar about his behavior?'

Continuing to wipe her cigarette against the edge of the ashtray, she answered, 'No; I thought he was quite the same as always.'

'And how was that, if I might ask?'

'A bit tense, withdrawn. He didn't like to speak to anyone before a performance, or during intermissions. He didn't like to be distracted by anything.'

That seemed normal enough to him. 'Did he appear any more nervous than usual last night?'

She considered this for a moment. 'No, I can't say that he was. We walked to the theater at about seven. It's very close.' He nodded. 'I went to my seat, even though it was early. The ushers were used to seeing me at rehearsals, so they let me in. Helmut went backstage to change and take a look at the score.'

'Excuse me, Signora, but I think I read in one of the papers that your husband was famous for conducting without a score.'

She smiled at this. 'Oh, he did, he did. But he always kept one in the dressing room, and he'd look over it before the performance and during the intervals.'

'Is that why he didn't want to be interrupted during the intervals?'

'Yes.'

'You said you went backstage to speak to him last night.' She said nothing, so he asked,

104

'Was that normal?'

'No; as I told you, he didn't like anyone to talk to him during a performance. He said it destroyed his concentration. But last night, he asked me to go back after the second act.'

'Was anyone with you when he asked you?'

Her voice took on a sharp edge. 'Do you mean, do I have a witness that he asked me?' Brunetti nodded. 'No, Dottor Brunetti, I don't have a witness. But I was surprised.'

'Why?'

'Because Helmut seldom did things that were . . . I'm not sure of the words to use . . . out of the ordinary. He seldom did things that were not part of his routine. So it surprised me that he asked me to go and see him during a performance.'

'But you went?'

'Yes, I went.'

'Why did he want to see you?'

'I don't know. I met friends in the foyer, and I stopped to talk to them for a few minutes. I'd forgotten that during a performance, you can't get backstage from the orchestra, that you have to go upstairs to the boxes. So by the time I finally got backstage and to his dressing room, the second bell was already ringing for the end of the interval.'

'Did you speak to him?'

She hesitated a long time before she answered. 'Yes, but not more than to say hello and ask him what he wanted to tell me. But then we heard—' She paused here and stabbed out her cigarette. She took a long time doing this, moving the dead stump around and around in the ashtray. Finally, she dropped it and continued, though something had changed in her voice. 'We heard the second bell. There was no time to speak. I said I'd see him after the performance, and I went back to my seat. I got there just as the lights were going down. I waited for the curtain to go up, for the performance to continue, but you know . . . you know what happened.'

'Was that the first time you thought that anything was wrong?'

She reached for the package and pulled another cigarette from it. Brunetti took the lighter from the table and lit it for her. 'Thank you,' she said, blowing the smoke away from him.

'And was that the first time you realized that something was wrong?' he repeated.

'Yes.'

'In the last few weeks, had your husband's behavior been different in any way?' When she didn't answer, he prompted: 'Nervous, irritable in any way?'

'I understood the question,' she said shortly, then looked at him nervously and said, 'I'm sorry.'

He decided it was better to remain silent than to acknowledge her apology.

She paused for a moment and then

answered. 'No, he seemed much the same as ever. He always loved *Traviata*, and he loved this city.'

'And the rehearsals went well? Peacefully?'

'I'm not sure I understand that question.'

'Did your husband have any difficulty with the other people engaged in the production?'

'No, not that I know of,' she answered after a short pause.

Brunetti decided it was time to bring his questions to a more personal level. He flipped a few pages in his notebook, glanced down at it, and asked, 'Who is it that lives here, Signora?'

If she was surprised by the sudden change of subject, she gave no sign of it. 'My husband and I and a maid who sleeps in.'

'How long has she worked for you, this maid?'

'She has worked for Helmut for about twenty years, I think. I met her only when we came to Venice for the first time.'

'And when was that?'

'Two years ago.'

'Yes?' he prodded.

'She lives here in the apartment year round, while we're away.' Immediately she corrected herself: 'While we were away.'

'Her name?'

'Hilda Breddes.'

'She's not Italian?'

'No; Belgian.'

He made a note of this. 'How long were you and the Maestro married?'

'Two years. We met in Berlin, where I was working.'

'Under what circumstances?'

'He was conducting *Tristan*. I went backstage with friends of mine who were also friends of his. We all went to dinner after the performance.'

'How long did you know each other before you were married?'

'About six months.' She busied herself with sharpening her cigarette.

'You said that you were working in Berlin, yet you are Hungarian.' When she didn't comment, he asked, 'Isn't this true?'

'Yes; by birth I am. But I am now a German citizen. My first husband, as I'm sure you've been informed, was German, and I took his nationality when we moved to Germany after our marriage.'

She stubbed out her cigarette and looked at Brunetti, as if declaring that she would now devote all her attention to his questions. He wondered that it was these factual issues on which she had decided to focus, for all of them were matters of public record. All her answers about her marriages had been true; he knew because Paola, hopelessly addicted to the gutter press, had filled him in on the details that morning.

'Isn't that unusual?' he asked.

108

'Isn't what unusual?'

'Your being permitted to move to Germany and take German citizenship.'

She smiled at that, but not, he thought, in amusement. 'Not so unusual as you here in the West seem to think.' Was it scorn? 'I was a married woman, married to a German. His work in Hungary was finished, and he went back to his own country. I applied for permission to go with my husband, and it was granted. Even under the old government, we were not savages. The family is very important to Hungarians.' From the way she said it, Brunetti suspected she believed it to be of only minimal importance to Italians.

'Is he the father of your child?'

The question clearly startled her. 'Who?'

'Your first husband.'

'Yes, he is.' She reached for another cigarette.

'Does he still live in Germany?' Brunetti asked as he lit her cigarette, though he knew that the man taught at the University of Heidelberg.

'Yes, he does.'

'Is it true that, before marrying the Maestro, you were a doctor?'

'Commissario,' she began, voice tight with an anger she did little to contain or disguise, 'I am still a doctor, and I shall always be a doctor. At the moment, I don't have a practice, but believe me, I am still a doctor.'

'I apologize, Doctor,' he said, meaning it and regretting his stupidity. He quickly changed the subject. 'Your daughter, does she live here with you?'

He saw the impulsive motion toward the cigarette package, watched as she glided her hand toward the burning cigarette and picked that up instead. 'No, she lives with her grandparents in Munich. It would be too difficult for her to go to a foreign-language school while we were here, so we decided it would be best for her to go to study in Munich.'

'With your former husband's parents?'

'Yes.'

'How old is she, your daughter?'

'Thirteen.'

His own daughter, Chiara, was the same age, and he realized how unkind it would be to force her to attend school in a foreign country. 'Will you resume your medical practice now?'

She thought awhile before she answered this. 'I don't know. Perhaps. I would like to heal people. But it's too early to think about that.' Brunetti bowed his head in silent agreement.

'If you will permit me, Signora, and perhaps forgive me in advance for the question, could you tell me if you have any idea of the sort of financial arrangements your husband made?'

'You mean what happens to the money?' Remarkably direct.

'Yes.'

She answered quickly. 'I know only what Helmut told me. We didn't have a formal agreement, nothing written, the way people do today when they marry.' Her tone dismissed such thinking. 'It is my understanding that five people will inherit his estate.'

'And they are?'

'His children by his previous marriages. He had one by the first and three by the second. And myself.'

'And your daughter?'

'No,' she said immediately. 'Only his natural children.'

It seemed normal enough to Brunetti that a man would want to leave his money to children of his own blood. 'Have you any idea of the amount involved?' Widows usually did and just as usually said they did not.

'I think it is a great deal of money. But his agent or his lawyer would be able to tell you more about that than I can.' Strangely enough, it sounded to him as if she really didn't know. Stranger still, it sounded as if she didn't care.

The signs of fatigue he had seen in her when he entered had grown more pronounced during their conversation. The line of her shoulders was less straight; twin lines ran down from her nose to the corners of her mouth. 'I have only a few more questions,' he said.

'Would you like something to drink?' It was clear that she was being no more than formally polite.

'Thank you, but no. I'll ask these questions and then leave you.' She nodded tiredly, almost as if she knew that these were the questions he had come to ask.

'Signora, I would like to know something about your relationship with your husband.' He watched her grow visibly more distant and self-protective. He prodded. 'The difference in age between you was considerable.'

'Yes, it was.'

He remained silent, waiting. She finally said, stating, not admitting, and he liked her for that, 'Helmut was thirty-seven years older than I.' That would make her a few years older than he had judged her to be, just Paola's age. Wellauer was just eight years younger than Brunetti's grandfather. As strange as he found that thought, Brunetti tried to give no sign of it. What was it like for this woman, with a husband almost two generations older than she? He saw that she was shifting uncomfortably under the intensity of his gaze, and he glanced away for a moment, as if thinking about how to phrase his next question.

'Did the difference to your ages create any difficulties in your marriage?' How transparent was the cloud of euphemism that always surrounded such a union. Though polite, the question was still a voyeur's leer, and he was embarrassed by it.

Her silence stretched out for so long that he didn't know if it spoke of her disgust with his curiosity or her annoyance at the artificiality with which he expressed it. Suddenly sounding very tired, she said, 'Because of the difference in our ages, in our generations, we saw the world differently, but I married him because I was in love with him.' Brunetti's instinct told him that he had just heard the truth, but the same instinct also told him that he had heard only the singular. His humanity prevented him from asking about the omission.

As a sign that he was finished, he closed the notebook and slipped it back into his pocket. 'Thank you, Signora. It was very kind of you to see me at this time.' He trailed off, unwilling to lapse again into euphemism or platitude. 'Have you made arrangements for the funeral?'

'Tomorrow. At ten. At San Moisè. Helmut loved the city and always hoped that he would have the privilege of being buried here.'

The little that Brunetti had heard and read about the conductor made him doubt that the dead man would have viewed privilege as anything other than what he could bestow, but perhaps Venice had sufficient grandeur to be an exception. 'I hope you have no objection if I attend.'

'No, of course not.'

'I have one more question, also a painful one. Do you know of anyone who might have wanted to harm your husband? Is there anyone with whom he recently argued, anyone he might have had reason to fear?'

Her smile was small, but it was a smile. 'Does that mean,' she asked, 'can I think of anyone who might have wanted to kill him?'

Brunetti nodded.

'His career was very long, and I'm sure he offended many people during it. Some people disliked him, surely. But I can't think of anyone who would do this.' Absently, she ran her finger along the arm of her chair. 'And no one who loved music could do this.'

He rose to his feet and extended his hand. 'Thank you, Signora, for your time and your patience.' She stood and took his hand. 'Please don't bother,' he said, meaning that he would see himself out of the apartment. She dismissed his suggestion with a shake of her head and led him down the hall. At the door, they shook hands again, neither speaking. He left the apartment troubled by the interview, not quite sure if the reason was only the platitudes and excessive courtesies on his part or something he had been too dull to catch.

CHAPTER TEN

While he was inside, it had grown dark, the suddenly descending early-winter obscurity that added to the desolation that brooded over the city until the release of spring. He decided not to go back to his office, not willing to risk his anger if there was still no report from the lab and not interested in reading the German report again. As he walked, he reflected on how very little he had learned about the dead man. No, he had a great deal of information, but it was all strangely out of focus, too formal and impersonal. A genius, a homophobe, adored by the world of music, a man whom a woman half his age would love, but still a man whose substance was elusive. Brunetti knew some of the facts, but he had no idea of the reality.

He walked on and considered the means by which he had acquired his information. He had the resources of Interpol at his command, he had the full cooperation of the German police, and he had sufficient rank to call upon the entire police system of Italy. Obviously, then, the most reliable way to get accurate information about the man was to address himself to the unfailing source of all information—gossip.

It would be an exaggeration to say that

Brunetti disliked Paola's parents, the Count and Countess Falier, but it would be an equal exaggeration to say that he liked them. They puzzled him in much the same way that a pair of whooping cranes would puzzle someone accustomed to tossing peanuts to the pigeons in the park. They belonged to a rare and elegant species, and Brunetti, after knowing them for almost two decades, had to admit that he had mixed feelings about the inevitability of their extinction.

Count Falier, who numbered two doges on his mother's side, could, and did, trace his family back to the tenth century. There were crusaders perched on the limbs of his family tree, a cardinal or two, a composer of secondary importance, and the former Italian ambassador to the court of King Zog of Albania. Paola's mother was Florentine by birth, though her family had transferred itself to the northern city shortly after that event. They claimed descent from the Medici, and in a kind of genealogical chess that had a strange fascination for people of their circle, she matched her husband's doges with a pope and a textile millionaire, the cardinal with a cousin of Petrarch, the composer with a famous castrato (from whom, sadly, no issue), and the ambassador with Garibaldi's banker.

They lived in a *palazzo* that had belonged to the Falieri for at least three centuries, a vast rambling vault on the Grand Canal that was virtually impossible to heat in the winter and that was kept from imminent collapse only by the constant ministrations of an ever-present horde of masons, builders, plumbers, and electricians, all of whom joined Count Falier willingly in the perpetual Venetian battle against the inexorable forces of time, tide, and industrial pollution.

Brunetti had never counted the rooms in the *palazzo* and had always been embarrassed to ask how many there were. Its four floors were surrounded on three sides by canals, its back propped up by a deconsecrated church. He entered it only on formal occasions: the vigil of Christmas, when they went to eat fish and exchange gifts; the name day of Count Orazio, when, for some reason, they ate pheasant and again gave gifts; and the Feast of the Redeemer, when they went to eat *pasta fagioli* and watch the fireworks soaring above Piazza San Marco. His children loved to visit their grandparents on these occasions, and he knew they went, either by themselves or with Paola, to visit during the year. He chose to believe that it was because of the *palazzo* and the possibilities of exploration it offered, but he had the niggling suspicion that they loved their grandparents and enjoyed their company, twin phenomena that baffled Brunetti utterly.

The count was 'in finance.' Throughout the seventeen years Brunetti had been married to Paola, this was the only description he had ever heard of her father's profession. He was not described as being 'a financier,' no doubt because that might have suggested something manual, like counting money or going to the office. No, the count was 'in finance,' in much the same way that the de Beers were 'in mines,' or von Thyssen 'in steel.'

The countess, for her part, was 'in society,' which meant that she attended the opening nights of Italy's four major opera houses, arranged benefit concerts for the Italian Red Cross, and gave a masked ball for four hundred people each year during Carnevale.

Brunetti, for his part, earned slightly more than three million lire a month as a commissario of police, a sum he calculated to be only a bit more than what his father-in-law paid each month for the right to dock his boat in front of the *palazzo*. A decade ago, the count had attempted to persuade Brunetti to leave the police and join him in a career in banking. He continually pointed out that Brunetti ought not to spend his life in the company of tax evaders, wife beaters, pimps, thieves, and perverts. The offers had come to a sudden halt one Christmas when, goaded beyond patience, Brunetti had pointed out that although he and the count seemed to work among the same people, he at least had the consolation of being able to arrest them, whereas the count was constrained to invite them to dinner.

118

So it was with some trepidation that night that Brunetti asked Paola if it would be possible for them to attend the party her parents were giving the following evening to celebrate the opening of a new exhibition of French impressionist paintings at the Doge's Palace.

'But how did you know about the party?' Paola asked, astonished.

'I read about it in the paper.'

'My parents, and you read about it in the paper?' This seemed to offend Paola's atavistic concept of the family.

'Yes; but will you ask them?'

'Guido, I usually have to threaten you just to get you to go and have Christmas dinner with them, and now you suddenly want to go to one of their parties. Why?'

'Because I want to talk to the sort of people who go to that sort of thing.'

Paola, who had been reading and grading student papers when he came in, carefully set her pen down and graced him with the look she usually reserved for brutal infelicities of language. Though they were not infrequent in the papers that rested under her pen, she was not accustomed to hearing them from her husband. She looked at him a long time, formulating one of the replies he often relished as much as he dreaded. 'I doubt that they could refuse, given the elegance of your request,' she said, then picked up the pen and bent back over the papers.

It was late, and he knew that she was tired, so he busied himself at the counter, making coffee. 'You know you won't sleep if you drink coffee this late,' she said, recognizing what he was doing from the sounds he made.

He passed her on the way to the stove, ruffled her hair, and said, 'I'll think of something to occupy myself.'

She grunted, struck a line through a phrase, and asked, 'Why do you want to meet them?'

'To find out as much as I can about Wellauer. I've been reading about what a genius he was, about his career, about his wives, but I don't have any real idea of what sort of man he was.'

'And you think the sort of people,' she said with heavy emphasis, 'who go to my parents' parties would know about him?'

'I want to know about his private life, and those are the people who would know the sort of thing I want to know.'

'That's the sort of thing you can read about in *STOP*.' It never failed to amaze him that a person who taught English literature at the university could be so intimate with the gutter press.

'Paola,' he said. 'I want to find out things that are true about him. *STOP*'s the sort of place where you read about Mother Teresa's abortion.'

She grunted and turned a page, leaving a

trail of angry blue marks behind her.

He opened the refrigerator and pulled out a liter of milk, splashed some into a pan, and set it on the flame to heat. From long experience, he knew that she would refuse to drink a cup of coffee, no matter how much milk he added to it, insisting that it would keep her awake. But once he had his own, she would sip at it, end up drinking most of it, then sleep like a rock. From the cabinet he pulled down a bag of sweet biscuits they bought for the children and peered into it to see how many were left.

When the coffee was finished boiling up into the top of the double pot, he poured it into a mug, added the steaming milk, spooned in less sugar than he liked, and went to sit across from Paola. Absently, still intent on the paper in front of her, she reached out and took a sip of coffee even before he had a chance to do so. When she put it back on the table, he wrapped his fingers around it but didn't pick it up. She turned a page, reached out for the mug, and looked up at him when he refused to release it.

'Eh?' she asked.

'Not until you agree to call your mother.'

She tried to push his hand away. When he refused to move it, she wrote a rude word on it with her pen. 'You'll have to wear a suit.'

'I always wear a suit when I go to see your parents.'

'Well, you never look like you're happy to

be wearing a suit.'

'All right,' he said, smiling. 'I promise to wear a suit and to look happy that I'm wearing it. So will you call your mother?'

'All right,' she conceded. 'But I meant it about the suit.'

'Yes, my treasure,' he fawned. He let go of the cup and pushed it toward her. When she had taken another sip, he extracted a biscuit from the bag and dipped it into the coffee.

'You are disgusting,' she said, then smiled.

'Simple peasant,' he agreed, shoving the biscuit into his mouth.

Paola never talked much about what it had been like to be raised in the *palazzo*, with an English nanny and a flock of servants, but if he knew anything about all those years, he knew that she had never been permitted to dunk. He saw it as a great lapse in her upbringing and insisted that their children be allowed to do it. She had agreed, but with great reluctance. Neither child, he never failed to point out to her, showed grave signs of moral or physical decline as a result.

From the way she scribbled a hasty comment across the bottom of a page, he knew she was about to come to the end of her patience for that night.

'I'm so tired of their blunt minds, Guido,' she said, capping the pen and tossing it down on the table. 'I'd almost rather deal with murderers. At least they can be punished.'

122

The coffee was finished, or he would have pushed it toward her. Instead he got up and took a bottle of grappa from the cabinet. It was the only comfort he could think of at the moment.

'Wonderful,' she said. 'First coffee, and now grappa. We'll never get to sleep.'

'Shall we try keeping each other awake?' he asked. She glowed.

CHAPTER ELEVEN

The following morning, he arrived at the Questura at eight, carrying with him the day's newspapers, which he read through quickly. There was little new information; most of it had been said the day before. The summaries of Wellauer's career were longer, the cries that the killer be brought to justice more strident, but there was nothing that Brunetti didn't already know.

The lab report was on his desk. The only fingerprints on the cup, in which traces of potassium cyanide were found, were Wellauer's. In the dressing room, there were scores of other prints, far too many to be checked. He decided against having prints taken. Since the only ones on the cup were Wellauer's, there seemed little sense in identifying all those found in the room.

Along with the fingerprint report was a list of articles found in the dressing room. He remembered having seen most of them: the score of *Traviata*, each page crowded with notations in the angular Gothic script of the conductor; a comb, a wallet, change; the clothes he had been wearing and those in the closet; a handkerchief and a package of mints. There had also been a Rolex Oyster, a pen, and a small address book.

The officers who had gone to take a look at the conductor's home—one could hardly call it a search—had written a report, but since they had no idea of what they were supposed to be looking for, Brunetti had little hope that their report would reveal anything of interest or importance. Nevertheless, he picked it up and read through it carefully.

The Maestro had had a remarkably complete wardrobe for a man who spent only a few weeks in the city each year. He marveled at the precision of the notes made about the clothing: 'Black double-vent cashmere jacket (Duca D'Aosta); cobalt and muted-umber sweater, size 52 (Missoni).' For a moment, he wondered if he had lost his bearings and found himself in the Valentino boutique rather than in police headquarters. He flipped to the end and found, as he had feared, the signatures of Alvise and Riverre, the two officers who had written, a year ago, about a body that had been pulled out of the sea at the Lido: 'Appears to have died of suffocation.'

He turned back to the report. The signora, it appeared, did not share her late husband's interest in clothing. Nor, from what he read, did it seem that Alvise and Riverre thought highly of her taste. 'Varese boots, only one pair. Black woolen coat, no label.' They had, however, apparently been impressed by the library, which they described as 'extensive, in three languages and what appears to be Hungarian.'

He turned another page. There were two guest rooms in the apartment, each with a separate bath. Fresh towels, empty closets, Christian Dior soap.

There was no evidence of Signora Wellauer's daughter; nothing in the report suggested the presence in the house of the third member of the family. Neither of the two extra rooms held a teenager's clothes or books or possessions of any kind. Knowing how he was forever finding proof of his own daughter's existence under foot, Brunetti found this strange. Her mother had explained that she was going to school in Munich. But it was a remarkable child who managed to take all of her clutter along with her.

There was a description of the Belgian maid's room, which the two officers appeared to have found too simply furnished, and of the maid, whom they had found subdued but helpful. The last room described was the

Maestro's office, where they had found 'documents.' Some, it seems, had been brought back and looked over by the German translator, who explained, in a page added to the report, that the bulk of them pertained to business and contracts. A datebook had been inspected and judged unimportant.

Brunetti decided to seek out the two authors of this document and thus spare himself the irritation of having to wait for them to respond to his request that they come up to his office. Since it was almost nine, he knew that he would find them down the street at the bar on the other side of the Ponte dei Greci. It was not the precise hour but the fact that it was before noon that made this conclusion inescapable.

Though Brunetti dreaded the assignment of the two men to any case he was working on, he couldn't help liking them. Alvise was a squat man in his late forties, almost a caricature of the dark-skinned Sicilian, save that he came from Tarvisio, on the border with Austria. He was accepted as the resident expert on popular music, this because he had once, fifteen years ago, actually had a program autographed by Mina, the mythic queen of Italian popular singing. Over the years, this event had swelled and expanded—as had Mina—by repeated retelling, until Alvise now suggested, eyes bright with the glitter of satisfied desire, that far more had gone on between them. The retelling seemed not at all affected by the fact that the singer was a head taller than Alvise and was now almost twice his girth.

Riverre, his partner, was a red-haired Palermitano, whose only interests in life appeared to be soccer and women, in that order. The high point in his life to date was having survived the riot in the Brussels soccer stadium. He augmented his account of what he had done there, before the Belgian police arrived, with tales of his triumphs with women, usually foreigners, who, he claimed, fell like wheat before the sickle of his charms.

Brunetti found them, as he had expected, standing at the counter in the bar. Riverre was reading the sports newspaper, and Alvise was talking with Arianna, the woman who owned the bar. Neither noticed Brunetti's arrival until he came up to the bar and ordered a coffee. At that, Alvise smiled in greeting and Riverre pulled his attention away from the paper long enough to greet his superior.

'Two more coffees, Arianna,' Alvise said, 'all three on my bill.'

Brunetti recognized the maneuver, aimed at putting him in the other's debt. By the time the three coffees arrived, Riverre stood with them, and the newspaper had somehow been transformed into a blue-covered case file, which now lay open on the counter.

Brunetti spooned in two sugars and swirled his spoon around. 'Is it you two who went to the Maestro's house?'

'Yes, sir,' brightly, from Alvise.

'And what a house it is!' chimed in Riverre.

'I've just been looking at your report.'

'Arianna, bring us some brioches.'

'I read it with great interest.'

'Thank you, sir.'

'Particularly your comments about his wardrobe. I take it you didn't like those English suits.'

'No, sir,' replied Riverre, as usual not getting it. 'I think they're cut too loose in the leg.'

Alvise, reaching along the counter to open the file, accidentally nudged his partner in the arm, perhaps a bit harder than was necessary. 'Anything else, sir?' he asked.

'Yes. While you were there, did you notice any sign of the signora's daughter?'

'Is there a daughter, sir?' This, predictably, from Riverre.

'Thats why I'm asking you. Was there any sign of a child? Books? Clothes?'

Both showed signs of deep thought. Riverre stared off into space, which he seemed to find closer than most people did, and Alvise looked down at the floor, hands thrust into his uniform pockets. The requisite minute passed before they both answered, 'No, sir,' at the same time, almost as if they had practiced it.

'Nothing at all?'

Again their separate displays, then the

128

simultaneous response: 'No, sir.'

'Did you speak to the maid, the Belgian?'

Riverre rolled his eyes at the memory of the maid, suggesting that any time spent with such a stick of a woman was time wasted, even if she was a foreigner. Alvise contented himself with 'Yes, sir.'

'And did she tell you anything that might be important?'

Riverre drew in a breath, preparing himself to answer, but before he could begin, his partner said, 'Nothing she actually said, sir. But I got the impression she didn't like the signora.'

Riverre couldn't let this pass and asked, with a lurid smile, 'What's not to like there?' putting heavy emphasis on the last word.

Brunetti gave him a cool glance and asked his partner, 'Why?'

'It was nothing I could put my finger on,' he began. Riverre snorted. So much for the effectiveness of his cool glance.

'As I was saying, sir, it was nothing definite, but she seemed much more formal when the signora was there. Be hard for her to be more formal than she was with us, but it just seemed that way. She seemed to, I don't know, get cooler when the signora was there, especially when she had to speak to her.'

'And when was that?'

'When we first went in. We asked her if it would be all right if we had a look around the apartment, at his things. From the way she answered us, I mean the signora, sir, it looked like she didn't like the idea very much. But she told us to go ahead, and then she called the maid and told her to show us where his things were. It was then, when they were talking to each other, that the maid seemed, well, cold. Later, when she was talking to us, she seemed better. Didn't warm up or anything—after all, she is Belgian—but she was better with us, more friendly, than she was with the other one.'

'Did you speak to the signora again?'

'Just before we were leaving, sir. We had the papers with us. She didn't like it that we were taking them with us. It was just a look, but it's the way she made us feel. We asked her if we could take the papers. We had to; it's the regulation.'

'Yes, I know,' Brunetti answered. 'Anything else?'

'Yes,' chirped in Riverre.

'What?'

'She didn't mind it when we looked through his clothing and closets. She sent the maid with us, didn't even bother to come herself. But when we went into the other room, where the papers were, then she came along and told the maid to wait outside. She didn't like us looking at that stuff, sir, papers and things.'

'And what were they?'

'They looked official, sir. It was all in

German, and we brought it back here to be translated.'

'Yes, I've seen the report. What happened to the papers, after they were translated?'

'I don't know, sir,' answered Alvise. 'Either they're still down with the translator or they were sent back to her.'

'Riverre, could you go and find out for me?'

'Now, sir?'

'Yes, now.'

'Yes, sir.' He sketched out something that resembled a salute and moved away from the bar with deliberate slowness.

'And, Riverre,' he called out after him. Riverre turned, hoping to be called back and spared the walk to the Questura and the two flights of stairs. 'If the papers are there, have them sent up to my office.'

Brunetti picked up one of the brioches that lay on a plate in front of them and took a bite. He signaled to Arianna to make him another coffee. 'While you were there,' he asked Alvise, 'did you notice anything else?'

'What kind of things, sir?' As though they were meant to see only those things they were sent to look for.

'Anything. You mentioned the tension between the two women. Did either of them seem to act strangely?'

Alvise thought for a moment, took a bite from one of the brioches, and answered, 'No, sir.' Seeing that Brunetti was disappointed

131

with this answer, he added, 'Only when we took the papers.'

'Do you have any idea why that might be?'

'No, sir. Only she was so different from how she was when we looked at his personal things, as if that didn't matter at all. I'd sort of think that people wouldn't like that, poking around in someone's clothing. But papers are just papers.' Seeing that this last remark had clearly garnered Brunetti's interest, he grew more expansive. 'But maybe it's because he was a genius. Of course, I wouldn't know about that sort of music.' Brunetti braced himself for the inevitable. 'The only singer I know personally is Mina, and she never sang with him. But as I was saying, if he was famous, then maybe the papers might be important. There might be things in them about, you know, music.'

At that moment, Riverre came back. 'Sorry, sir, but the papers have been sent back.'

'How? Mailed?'

'No, sir; the translator took them himself. He said that the widow would probably need some of them.'

Brunetti stepped back from the bar and reached for his wallet. He put ten thousand lire on the counter before either of the two uniformed men could object.

'Thank you, sir,' they both said.

'It's nothing.'

When he turned to leave, neither of them

made a move to accompany him, though both did salute.

The porter at the Questura's door told him that Vice-Questore Patta wanted to see him immediately in his office.

'Gesù Bambino,' Brunetti exclaimed under his breath, an expression he had learned from his mother, who, like him, used it only when pressed beyond the limits of human patience.

At the door to his commander's office, he knocked and was careful to wait for the shouted 'Avanti!' before entering. As he had expected, he found Patta posed behind his desk, a stack of files fanned out in front of him. He ignored Brunetti for a moment, continuing to read the paper he had in his hand. Brunetti contented himself with examining the faint traces of a fresco that had once been painted on the ceiling.

Pasta looked up suddenly, feigned surprise at seeing Brunetti, and asked, 'Where are you?'

Brunetti mirrored Patta's apparent confusion, as though he found the question peculiar but didn't want to call attention to it. 'In your office, sir.'

'No, no, where are you on the case?' Waving Brunetti to one of the low ormolu chairs in front of his desk, he picked up his pen and began to tap it on the desk top.

'I've interviewed the widow and two of the people who were in the dressing room. I've spoken to the doctor, and I know the cause of death.'

'I know all that,' Patta said, increasing the rhythm of the pen and making no attempt to hide his irritation. 'In other words, you've learned nothing important?'

'Yes, sir, I suppose you could put it that way.'

'You know, Brunetti, I've given a lot of thought to this investigation, and I think it might be wise to take you off the case.' Patta's voice was heavy with menace, as though he'd spent the previous night paging through his copy of Machiavelli.

'Yes, sir.'

'I could, I suppose, give it to someone else to investigate. Perhaps then we'd have some real progress.'

'I don't think Mariani's working on anything at the moment.'

It was only with the exercise of great self-restraint that Patta kept himself from wincing at the mention of the name of the younger of the two other commissarios of police, a man of unimpeachable character and impenetrable stupidity who was known to have gotten his job as part of his wife's dowry, she being the niece of the former mayor. His other colleague, Brunetti knew, was currently involved in the investigation of the drug traffic at the port of Marghera. 'Or perhaps you could take it over yourself,' he suggested, and then added with tantalizing lateness, 'sir.'

'Yes, that's always a possibility,' Patta said, either not registering the rudeness or deciding to ignore it. He took a package of dark-papered Russian cigarettes from his desk and fitted one into his onyx holder. Very nice, Brunetti thought; color coordinated. 'I've called you in because I've had some phone calls from the press and from People in High Places,' he said, carefully emphasizing all the capitals. 'And they're very concerned that you've done nothing.' This time, the enunciation fell very heavily upon the singular. He puffed delicately at the cigarette and stared across at Brunetti. 'Did you hear me? They're not pleased.'

'I can see how that would be, sir. I've got a dead genius and no one to blame for it.'

Was he wrong, or did he see Patta mouth that last one silently to himself, perhaps preparing to toss it off himself at lunch today? 'Yes, exactly,' Patta said. His lips moved again. 'And no one to blame for it.' Patta deepened his voice. 'I want that to change. I want someone to blame for it.' Brunetti had never before heard the man so clearly express his idea of justice. Perhaps Brunetti would toss *that* off at lunch today.

'From now on, Brunetti, I want a written report on my desk each morning by'—he paused, trying to remember when the office opened—'by eight,' he said, getting it right.

135

'Yes, sir. Will that be all?' It made little difference to Brunetti whether the report had to be spoken or written; he would still have nothing to report until he had a clearer idea of the man who had been killed. Genius or not, the answer always lay there.

'No, that's not all. What do you plan to do with yourself today?'

'I'm going to go to the funeral. That's in about twenty minutes. And I want to have a look through his papers myself.'

'Is that all?'

'Yes, sir.'

Patta snorted. 'No wonder we're getting nowhere.'

That seemed to signal the end of the interview, so Brunetti got to his feet and went toward the door, wondering how close he would get before Patta would remind him of the written report. He estimated he was still three steps from the door when he heard: 'Remember, eight o'clock.'

His meeting with Patta kept Brunetti from getting to the church of San Moisè until just a few minutes before ten. The black boat carrying the flower-covered casket was already moored to the side of the canal, and three blue-suited men were busy placing the wooden casket on the wheeled metal platform they would use to take it to the door of the church. In the host of people who crowded around the front of the church, Brunetti recognized a few familiar Venetian faces, the usual reporters and photographers from the papers, but he didn't see the widow; she must already have entered the church.

As the three men reached the doors, a fourth man joined them, and they lifted the coffin, placed it with practiced ease on their shoulders, and ascended the two low steps of the church. Brunetti was among the people who followed them inside. He watched the men carry the casket up the center aisle and place it on a low stand before the main altar.

Brunetti took a seat at the end of a pew at the rear of the crowded church. With difficulty, he could see between the heads of the people in front of him to the first row, where the widow, in black, sat between a man and a woman, both gray-haired, probably the people he had seen with her in the theater. Behind her, alone in a pew, sat another woman in black, whom Brunetti assumed to be the maid. Though he'd had no expectations regarding the mass, Brunetti was surprised by the starkness of the ceremony. The most remarkable thing about it was the complete absence of music, even an organ. The familiar words floated over the heads of the crowd, the ageless sprinklings and blessings were performed. Because of its simplicity, the mass was quickly over.

Brunetti waited at the end of the pew as the casket was carried past, waited until the chief mourners left the church. Outside, cameras flashed and reporters surrounded the widow, who cringed back against the elderly man who accompanied her.

Without thinking, Brunetti pushed his way through the crowd and took her other arm. He recognized a few of the photographers, saw that they knew who he was, and ordered them to move away. The men who had surrounded the widow backed off, leaving a path open toward the boats that stood at the side of the *campo*. Supporting her, he led the widow toward the boat, helped her as she stepped down onto the deck, and then followed her into the passenger cabin.

The couple who had been with her in the theater joined her there; the gray-haired woman put her arm around the shoulder of the younger woman, and the man contented himself with sitting beside her and taking her hand. Brunetti placed himself at the cabin door and watched as the boat carrying the casket cast off and began moving slowly up the narrow canal. When they were safely away from the church and the crowds, he ducked his head and went back into the cabin.

'Thank you,' Signora Wellauer said, making no attempt to hide her tears.

There was nothing he could say.

The boat moved out into the Grand Canal and turned left, toward San Marco, which they would have to pass in order to get to the cemetery. Brunetti went back to the cabin door and looked forward, taking his intrusive gaze away from the grief within. The campanile flowed by them, then the checkered rectangularity of the Ducal Palace, and then those happy, carefree domes. When they were approaching the Arsenale canal, Brunetti went up on deck and asked the boatman if he could stop at the embarcadero of the Palasport. He went back into the cabin and heard the three people there conversing in low voices.

'Dottor Brunetti,' the widow said.

He turned from the cabin door and looked back at her.

'Thank you. That would have been too much, back there.'

He nodded in agreement. The boat began the broad left turn that would take them into the canal of the Arsenale. 'I'd like to speak to you again,' he said, 'whenever it would be convenient for you.'

'Is it necessary?'

'Yes, I believe it is.'

The motor hummed a deeper note as the boat pulled toward the landing platform that stood on the right side of the canal.

'When?'

'Tomorrow?'

If she was surprised or the others were offended, they gave no sign. 'All right,' she said. 'In the afternoon.'

'Thank you,' he said as the boat hovered at

the wooden landing. No one answered him, so he left the cabin, jumped from the boat onto the platform, and stood there as the boat pulled back into line, following the casket out into the deeper waters of the *laguna*.

CHAPTER TWELVE

Like most of the *palazzi* on the Grand Canal, Palazzo Falier was originally meant to be approached by boat, and guests were meant to enter by means of the four shallow steps leading down to the landing on the canal. But this entrance had long since been closed off by a heavy metal grating that was opened only when large objects were delivered by boat. In these fallen times, guests arrived by foot, walking from Cà Rezzonico, the nearest vaporetto stop, or from other parts of the city.

Brunetti and Paola approached the *palazzo* by foot, passing in front of the university, then through Campo San Barnaba, after which they turned left and along a narrow canal that led them to the side entrance of the *palazzo*.

They rang the bell and then were ushered into the courtyard by a young man Paola had never seen before. Probably hired for the night.

'At least he's not wearing knee breeches and a wig,' Brunetti remarked as they climbed the

140

exterior staircase. The young man had not bothered to ask who they were or whether they had been invited. Either he had a guest list committed to memory and could recognize everyone who arrived or more likely, he simply did not care whom he let into the *palazzo*.

At the top of the stairs, they heard music coming from the left, where the three enormous reception rooms were located. Following the sound, they went down a mirror-lined hallway, accompanied by their own dim reflections. The huge oaken doors to the first room stood open. Light, music, and the scent of expensive perfume and flowers spilled from beyond them.

The light that filled the room came from two immense Murano glass chandeliers, covered with playful angels and Cupids, which hung from the frescoed ceiling, and from candle-filled stanchions that lined the walls. The music came from a discreet trio in the corner, who played Vivaldi in one of his more repetitive moods. And the scent emanated from the flock of brightly colored and even more brightly chattering women who decorated the room.

A few minutes after he saw them enter, the count approached, bowed to kiss Paola's cheek, and extended his hand to his son-in-law. He was a tall man in his late sixties who, making no attempt to disguise the fact that his hair was thinning, wore it cut short around a tonsure and looked like a particularly studious monk. Paola had his brown eyes and broad mouth but had been spared the large prow of aristocratic nose that was the central feature of his face. His dinner jacket was so well tailored that even had it been pink, the only thing anyone seeing it would have noticed was the cut.

'Your mother is delighted that you *both* could come.' The subtle emphasis alluded to the fact that this was the first time Brunetti had attended one of their parties. 'I hope you will enjoy yourselves.'

'I'm sure we will,' Brunetti replied for them both. For seventeen years, he had avoided calling his father-in-law anything. He couldn't use the title, nor could he bring himself to call the man Papà. 'Orazio,' his Christian name, was too intimate, a baying at the moon of social equality. So Brunetti struggled on, not calling him anything, not even 'Signore.' They did, however, compromise and use the familiar *tu* form of address with each other, though even that did not fall easily from their lips.

The count saw his wife come across the room and smiled, beckoning her to join them. She maneuvered her way through the crowd with a combination of grace and social skill that Brunetti envied, stopping to kiss a cheek here, lightly touch an arm there. He quite enjoyed the countess, stiff and formal in her chains of pearls and layers of black chiffon. As

142

usual, her feet were encased in dagger-pointed shoes with heels as high as curbstones, which still failed to bring her level with her husband's shoulder.

'Paola, Paola,' she cried, making no attempt to hide her delight at seeing her only child. 'I'm so glad you could finally bring Guido with you.' She broke off for a moment to kiss them both. 'I'm so glad to see you here, not just for Christmas or for those awful fireworks.' Not one to keep a cat in a bag, the countess.

'Come,' said the count. 'Let me get you a drink, Guido.'

'Thank you,' he answered, then, to Paola and her mother, 'May we bring you something?'

'No, no. *Mamma* and I will get something in a little while.'

Count Falier led Brunetti across the room, pausing occasionally to exchange a greeting or a word. At the bar, he asked for champagne for himself and a Scotch for his son-in-law.

As he handed the drink to Brunetti, he asked, 'I assume you're here in the line of duty. Is that correct?'

'Yes, it is,' Brunetti answered, glad of the other man's directness.

'Good. Then my time hasn't been wasted.'

'I beg your pardon,' Brunetti said.

Nodding to an enormous woman who had just enthroned herself in front of the piano, the count said, 'I know from Paola that you've

143

been assigned this Wellauer thing. It's bad for the city, a crime like this.' As he spoke, he could not restrain his look of disapproval at the conductor for having gotten himself killed, especially during the social season. 'In any case, when I heard that Paola called to say you both wanted to come tonight, I made a few phone calls. I assumed that you would want to know about his finances.'

'Yes, that correct.' Was there any information this man couldn't get, just by picking up the phone and dialing the right number? 'May I ask what you learned?'

'He wasn't as wealthy as he was generally thought to be.' Brunetti waited for this to be translated into numbers he could understand. He and the count, surely, would have different ideas of what 'wealthy' meant. 'His total holdings, in stocks and bonds and real estate, probably didn't amount to more than ten million deutsche marks. He's got four million francs in Switzerland, at the Union Bank in Lugano, but I doubt that the German tax people will learn anything about that.' As Brunetti was calculating that it would take him approximately three hundred and fifty years to earn such money, the count added, 'His income from performances and recordings must bring in at least three or four million marks a year.'

'I see,' Brunetti acknowledged. 'And the will?'

'I didn't succeed in getting a copy of it,' the count said apologetically. Since the man had been dead only two days, Brunetti believed this was a lapse he could overlook. 'But it's divided equally among his children and his wife. There is talk, however, that he tried to get in touch with his lawyers a few weeks before he died; no one knows why, and it need not have been about his will.'

'What does that mean, "tried to get in touch with"?'

'He called his lawyers' office in Berlin, but apparently there was something wrong with the connection, and he never called back.'

'Did any of the people you spoke to say anything about his personal life?'

The count's glass stopped just short of his mouth with such a sudden motion that some of the pale liquid splashed onto the lapel of the jacket. He glared at Brunetti in astonishment, as though all the reservations he had harbored for almost two decades had suddenly been proved true. 'What do you think I am, a spy?'

'I'm sorry,' Brunetti said, offering the count his handkerchief to dry his lapel. 'It's the job. I forget.'

'Yes, I can see that,' the count agreed, though his tone was void of any assent. 'I'll go and see if I can find Paola and her mother.' He left, retaining the handkerchief, which Brunetti feared would be washed, starched, ironed, and sent back by special courier.

Brunetti pushed himself away from the bar and set out into the sea of people to begin his own search for Paola. He knew many of those in the room but, as it were, at second hand. Though he had never been introduced to most of them, he knew their scandals, their histories, their affairs, both legal and romantic. Part of this came from his being a policeman, but most of it came from living in what was really a provincial town where gossip was the real cult and where, had it not been at least a nominally Christian city, the reigning deity would surely have been Rumor.

During the more than five minutes it took him to find Paola, he exchanged greetings with a number of people and turned down repeated offers of a fresh drink. The countess was nowhere in sight; her husband had no doubt warned her of the risk of moral infection that stalked the room.

When Paola came up to him, she grabbed his arm and whispered into his ear. 'I've found just what you want.'

'A way to leave?' he said, but only to himself. With her, he practiced some restraint. 'What?'

'The voice of gossip, the real thing. We were at university together.'

'Who? Where?' he asked, interested in his surroundings for the first time that night.

'He's over there, at the door to the balcony.' She nudged him with her elbow and pointed with her chin to a man who stood across the room, at the central windows that overlooked the canal. The man looked to be about the same age as Paola, though he had clearly had a harder time getting there. From this distance, all Brunetti could distinguish was a short beard, mottled with gray, and a black jacket that seemed to be made of velvet.

'Come on; I'll introduce you,' urged Paola, tugging at his arm and leading him across the room toward the man, who smiled when he recognized Paola coming toward him. His nose was flat, as though it had once been broken, and his eyes were sad, as though his heart had been. He looked like a stevedore who wrote poetry.

'Ah, the lovely Paola,' he said as she reached him. He switched his drink into his left hand, took Paola's with his right, and bent to place a kiss in the air just above it. 'And this,' he said, turning to Brunetti, 'must be the famous Guido, about whom all of us grew so tired of hearing more years ago than it is discreet of me to remember.' He took Brunetti's hand and shook it firmly, making no attempt to disguise the interest with which he studied him.

'Stop it, Dami, and stop staring at Guido as if he were a painting.'

'Force of habit, my treasure, peering and prying at everything I observe. Next I'll no doubt peel back his jacket and try to see where he's signed.'

None of this made any sense to Brunetti, whose confusion must have been obvious to both of the others, for the man hastened to explain. 'As I can see, Paola will never introduce us, and she apparently has chosen to keep our past together a secret from you.' Before Brunetti could respond to the suggestion here, he continued: 'I am Demetriano Padovani, former classmate of your fair wife and currently a critic of things artistic.' He made a small bow.

Brunetti was, like most Italians, familiar with the name. This was the bright new art critic, the terror of both painters and museum directors. Paola and he had read his articles with shared delight, but he'd had no idea that they had gone to university together.

The other man grabbed a fresh drink from a passing waiter. 'I must apologize to you, Guido—if I may take the liberty of calling you Guido at our first meeting and of giving you the *tu*, an evidence of growing social and linguistic promiscuity—and confess to having spent years hating you.' Brunetti's confusion at this remark obviously delighted him. 'Back in those dark ages when we were students and all desperately in love with your Paola, we were convulsed by jealousy and, I admit, loathing for this Guido who seemed to have arrived from the stars to carry her heart away from us. First she wanted to know all about him, then it was "Will he take me for a coffee?" which as quickly developed into "Do you think he likes me?" until all of us, much as we loved the daffy girl, were quite ready to throttle her one dark night and toss her into a canal, just to have some freedom from the dark incubus that was Guido and so be left in peace to study for our exams.' Delighting in Paola's obvious discomfiture, he continued: 'And then she married him. You, that is. Much to our delight, as nothing is such an effective remedy for the mad excesses of love,' and here he paused to sip from his drink, before adding, 'as is marriage.' Content with having made Paola blush and Brunetti look around for another drink, he said, 'It's really a very good thing you did marry her, Guido, else not a one of us would have managed to pass our exams, so smitten were we with the girl.'

'It was my only purpose in marrying her,' Brunetti replied.

Padovani understood. 'And for that charity, let me offer you a drink. What would you like?'

'Scotch for us both,' Paola answered, then added, 'But come back quickly. I want to talk to you.'

Padovani bowed his head in false submission and headed off in pursuit of a waiter, moving like a very royal yacht of politeness as he made his way through the crowd. In a moment, he was back, holding three glasses in his hands.

'Are you still writing for *L'Unità*?' Paola asked as he handed her the drink.

At the sound of the name of the newspaper, Padovani pulled down his head in mock terror and shot conspiratorial glances around the room. He gave a very theatrical hiss and waved them close to him. In a whisper, he told them, 'Don't dare pronounce the name of that newspaper in this room, or your father will have the servants turn me out of the house.' Though Padovani's tone made it clear he was joking, Brunetti suspected that he was far closer to the truth than he realized.

The critic stood up to his full height, sipped at his drink, and changed to a voice that was almost declamatory. 'Paola, my dear, could it be that you have abandoned the ideals of our youth and no longer read the proletarian voice of the Communist Party? Excuse me,' he corrected himself, 'the Democratic Party of the Left?' Heads turned at the sound of the name, but he went on. 'God above, don't tell me you've accepted your age and begun to read *Corriere* or, even worse, *La Repubblica*, the voice of the grubbing middle class, disguised as the voice of the grubbing lower class?'

'No, we read *L'Osservatore Romano*,' Brunetti said, naming the official organ of the Vatican, which still fulminated against divorce, abortion, and the pernicious myth of female equality.

150

'How wise of you,' Padovani said, voice unctuous with praise. 'But since you read those glowing pages, you wouldn't know that I am, however humbly, the voice of artistic judgment for the struggling masses.' He dropped his voice and continued, aping perfectly the orotund voices of the RAI newscasters announcing the most recent fall of the government. 'I am the representative of the clear-eyed laborer. In me you see the rude voiced and grubby-fingered critic who seeks the values of true proletarian art in the midst of modern chaos.' He nodded in silent greeting to a passing figure and continued. 'It seems a great pity that you are not familiar with my work. Perhaps I can send you copies of my most recent articles. Pity I don't carry them about with me, but I suppose even genius must display some humility, however spurious.' They had all begun to enjoy this, so he continued. 'My most recent favorite was a wonderful piece I wrote last month about an exhibition of contemporary Cuban art—you know, tractors and grinning pineapples.' He made a moue of feigned distress until the exact words of his review came back to him. 'I praised its—how did I put it?—"its wonderful symmetry of refined form and purposeful integrity."' He leaned forward and whispered in Paola's ear, but so loud that Brunetti had no trouble hearing. 'I lifted that from one I wrote two years ago about Polish woodblocks, where

I praised, if memory serves, "refined symmetry of purposeful form."'

'And do you?' Paola asked, glancing at his velvet jacket, 'go to the office like that?'

'How deliciously bitchy you have remained, Paola.' He laughed, leaning forward to kiss her lightly on the cheek. 'But to answer your question, my angel, no, I do not think it seemly to take this opulence to the halls of the working class. I don more suitable attire, namely a dreadful pair of trousers my maid's husband would no longer wear and a jacket my nephew was going to give to the poor. Nor'—he held up a hand to prevent any interruption or question—'do I any longer drive there in the Maserati. I thought that would establish the wrong tone; besides, parking is such a problem in Rome. I solved the problem, for a while, by borrowing my maid's Fiat to drive to the office. But it would be covered with parking tickets, and then I lost hours taking the commissario of police to lunch to see that they were taken care of. So now I simply take a cab from my house and have myself left off just around the corner from the office, where I deliver my weekly article, speak angrily about social injustice, and then go down the street to a lovely little pasticceria, where I treat myself to a shockingly rich pastry. Then I go home and have a long soak in a hot tub and read Proust.

'"And so, on each side, is simple truth

152

suppressed,"' he said, quoting from a Shakespeare sonnet, one of the texts to which he had devoted the seven years he spent getting a degree in English literature at Oxford. 'But you must want something, some information, dearest Paola,' he said with a directness that was out of character or, at least, out of the character he was playing. 'First your father calls me personally with an invitation to this party, and then you attach yourself to me like a button, and I doubt that you'd do that unless you wanted something from me. And as the divine Guido is here with you, all you can legitimately want is information. And since I know just what it is Guido does for a living, I can but surmise it has to do with the scandal that has rocked our fair city, struck dumb the music world, and, in the doing, removed from the face of the planet a *nasty piece of work*.' The introduction of the British expression had the intended effect of surprising them both to gasps. He covered his mouth and gave a giggle of purest delight.

'Oh, Dami, you knew all along. Why didn't you just say so?'

Though Padovani's voice was steady when he answered, Brunetti could see that his eyes were bright, perhaps with alcohol, perhaps with something else. It mattered little to him what it was, so long as the man would explain his last remark.

'Come on,' Paola encouraged. 'You were the

only person I could think of who would be bound to know about him.'

Padovani fixed her with a level glance. 'And do you expect me to blacken the memory of a man who is not yet cold in his grave?'

From the sound of things, Brunetti thought that might well add to Padovani's fun.

'I'm surprised you waited that long,' said Paola.

Padovani gave her remark the attention it deserved. 'You're right, Paola. I will tell you all—that is, if the delicious Guido will go and get us all three enormous drinks. If he doesn't do it soon, I might begin to rail at the predictable tedium to which your parents have once again subjected me and, I note with wonder, half of what passes for the most famous people in the city.' Then, turning to Brunetti, 'Or better yet, Guido, if you could perhaps procure an entire bottle, we could, all three of us, steal away to one of the many ill-decorated rooms with which, alas, your parents' home is filled.' But he wasn't finished and turned back to Paola. 'And there, you using the blandishment of your beauty and your husband his unspeakable policeman's methods, you could together pry the nasty, niggling, dirty truth out of me. After which, if you were so minded, you, or perhaps'—he broke off and gave Brunetti a long look—'both of you, could have your way with me.' So that's the way things were, Brunetti suddenly realized, surprised that he had so successfully missed all the clues.

Paola shot Brunetti an entirely unnecessary warning glance. He liked the man's excess. He had no doubt that the invitation, wildly put as it had been, was entirely sincere, but that hardly seemed something to become angry about. He went off, as directed, to see about finding a bottle of Scotch.

It was a comment on either the count's hospitality or the laxity of the staff that he was given a bottle of Glenfiddich for the mere asking. When he got back to them, he found them arm in arm, whispering like conspirators. Padovani hushed Paola to silence and explained to Brunetti, 'I was just asking her whether, if I were to commit a really heinous crime, perhaps tell her mother what I think of the drapes, you'd take me down to your office to beat me until I confessed.'

'How do you think I got this?' Brunetti asked, and held up the bottle.

Padovani and Paola both laughed. 'Lead us, Paola,' the writer commanded, 'to a place where we can have our way with this, if not'— with a cow-eyed glance at Brunetti—'with one another.'

Ever practical, Paola said flatly, 'We can use the sewing room,' and led them out of the main salon and through a set of massive double doors. Then, like Ariadne, she led them unerringly down one corridor, turned to

155

the left, down another, through the library, and into a smaller room, in which a number of delicate brocade-covered chairs stood in a semicircle around an enormous television.

'Sewing room?' asked Padovani.

'Before "Dynasty",' explained Paola.

Padovani threw himself down into the most substantial chair in the room, swept his patent-leather shoes up onto the intaglio table, and said, 'Right, darlings, shoot,' no doubt lapsing into English by the mere force of the presence of the television. When neither of them asked a question, he prompted them. 'What is it you want to know about the late and not by anyone I can think of lamented Maestro?'

'Who would want to see him dead?' Brunetti asked.

'You are direct, aren't you? No wonder Paola capitulated with such alarming speed. But to answer your question, you'd need a phone book to hold the list of names.' He stopped speaking for a while and held out his glass for some whisky. Brunetti poured him a generous glassful, gave himself some as well, and poured a smaller amount into Paola's glass. 'Do you want me to give it to you chronologically, or perhaps by nationality, or a breakdown according to voice type or sexual preference?' He rested his glass on the arm of his chair and continued slowly. 'He goes back in time, Wellauer does, and the reasons people hated him go back along with him. You've probably heard the rumors about his having been a Nazi during the war. It was impossible for him to stop them, so like the good German he was, he simply ignored them. And no one seemed to mind at all. Not at all. No one does much anymore, do they? Look at Waldheim.'

'I've heard the rumors,' Brunetti said.

Padovani sipped at his glass, considering how to phrase it. 'All right, how about nationality? There are at least three Americans I could name, two Germans, and half a dozen Italians who would have been glad to see him dead.'

'But that hardly means they'd kill him,' Paola said.

Padovani nodded, granting this. He kicked off his shoes and pulled his feet up under him in the chair. He might be willing to vilify the countess's taste, but he would never stain her new brocade. 'He was a Nazi. Take that as given. His second wife was a suicide, which is something you might look into. The first left him after seven years, and even though her father was one of the richest men in Germany, Wellauer gave her a particularly generous settlement. There was talk at the time of nasty things, nasty sexual things, but that,' he added, sipping again, 'was when there still existed the idea that there were sexual things that could be nasty. But before you ask, no, I don't know what those sexual things were.'

'Would you tell us if you did?' Brunetti

157

asked.

Padovani shrugged.

'Now for things professional. He was a notorious sexual blackmailer. Any list of the sopranos and mezzo-sopranos who sang with him ought to give you an idea of that; bright, young, anonymous things who suddenly sang a Tosca or a Dorabella and then just as suddenly disappeared. He was so very good that he was permitted these lapses. Besides, most people can't tell the difference between great singing and competent singing anyway, so few people noticed, and no great harm was done. And I have to give him the credit that they were always at least competent singers. A few of them even went on to become great singers, but they probably would have done that without him.'

To Brunetti, this hardly sounded sufficient to provoke murder.

'Those were the careers he helped, but there are just as many he ruined, especially among men of my particular persuasion and,' he added, sipping at his drink, 'women of similar taste. The late Maestro was incapable of believing that he was unattractive to any woman. If I were you, I would look into the sexual stuff. The answer might not be there, but it might be a good place to begin. But that,' he said, pointing with his glass to the enormous television that loomed in front of them, 'might merely be a response to an

158

overexposure to that.'

He seemed to realize how unsatisfactory his information had been, so he added, 'In Italy, there are at least three people who had good reason to hate him. But none of them is in a position to have done him any harm. One is singing in the chorus of the Bari Opera Company. He might have become an important Verdi baritone had he not, in the dreadful sixties, made the mistake of not bothering to hide his sexual preference from the Maestro. I've even heard that he made the mistake of approaching the Maestro himself, but I can't believe that anyone could have been that stupid. Probably a myth. Whatever the cause, Wellauer is said to have dropped his name with a columnist who was a friend of his, and the articles started soon thereafter. That's why he's singing in Bari. In the chorus.

'The second is teaching music theory at the Palermo conservatory. I'm not sure what happened between them, but he was a conductor who had received a good deal of excellent publicity. This was about ten years ago, but then his career stopped after a few months of devastating reviews. Here, I admit, I have no direct information, but Wellauer's name was mentioned in relation to the reviews.

'The third is only a faint bell in my gossip's mind, but it involves someone who is said to be living here.' When he saw their surprise, he amended, 'No, not in the *palazzo*. In Venice. But she's hardly in a state to have done anything, since she must be close to eighty and is said to be a recluse. And I'm not sure that I've got the story straight or even remember it correctly.'

When he saw Paola's look, he held up his glass in excuse and explained, 'It's this stuff. Destroys brain cells. Or eats them.' He swirled the liquid around in the glass, watching the small waves he created, waiting for them to produce the tide of memory.

'I'll tell you what I remember or what I think I remember. Her name is Clemenza Santina.' When neither of them showed any sign of recognition, he explained: 'She was one of the most famous sopranos right before the war. Same thing happened to her that happened to Rosa Ponselle in America— discovered singing in a music hall with her two sisters, and within a few months she was singing at La Scala. One of those natural, perfect voices that come along only a few times a century. But she never recorded anything, so the only memory we have of her is what people heard, what they recall.' He saw their growing impatience, so he dragged himself back to the point. 'There was something between her and Wellauer, or between him and one of the sisters. I can't remember what it was or who told me, but she might have tried to kill him, or she threatened

160

to kill him.' He waved his glass in the air, and Brunetti saw how drunk the man was. 'Anyway, I think someone got killed or died, or maybe it was just a threat. Maybe I'll remember in the morning. Or maybe it's not important.'

'What made you think of her?' asked Brunetti.

'Because she sang Violetta with him. Before the war. Someone I was talking to, I can't remember who it was, told me that they'd tried to interview her recently. Let me think for a minute.' Again he consulted his drink, and again the memory came floating back. 'Narciso, that's who. He was doing an article on great singers of the past, and he went to see her, but she refused to speak to him, was very unpleasant about it. Didn't even open the door, I think he said. And then he told me the story he'd heard about her and Wellauer, before the war. In Rome, I think.'

'Did he say where she lives?'

'No, he didn't. But I can call him in the morning and ask.'

Either the alcohol or the waning conversation drained the sparkle from Padovani. As Brunetti watched, the foppishness subsided, and he became a middle-aged man with a thick beard and the beginnings of a substantial paunch, sitting with his feet tucked under him, exposing an inch of calf above black silk socks. Paola, he noticed, looked tired, or was she simply tired of having had to keep up the level of university banter with her former classmate? And Brunetti felt himself to be at that balance point that alcohol brought: if he continued drinking, he would soon be fuzzy and content; if he stopped, he would just as quickly be sober and somber. Choosing the second, he set his glass on the floor under his chair, sure a roving servant would find it before morning.

Paola set hers down as well and moved to the edge of her seat. She glanced over at Padovani, waiting for him to move, but he waved them off and picked up the bottle from the table. He poured himself a generous drink and said, 'I'll finish this before I return to the revels.' Brunetti wondered if he was as bored with the fiction of scintillating chatter as Paola seemed to be. The three of them exchanged bright nothings, and Padovani promised to call in the morning if he managed to get the address of the soprano.

Paola led Brunetti back through the labyrinth of the *palazzo*, toward the lights and the music. When they entered the main salon, they noticed that more people had arrived and the music had increased in volume, keeping pace with the sound of conversation.

Brunetti looked around, filled with anticipatory boredom at the sight and sound of these well-dressed, well-fed, well-versed people. He sensed that Paola had registered his feelings and was about to suggest they leave, when he saw someone he recognized. Standing at the bar, glass in one hand and cigarette in the other, was the doctor who had first examined Wellauer's body and declared him dead. At the time, Brunetti had wondered how someone who was wearing jeans had managed to be sitting in the orchestra. Tonight she was dressed much the same, a pair of gray slacks and a black jacket, with an obvious lack of concern for her own appearance that Brunetti would have thought impossible in an Italian woman.

He told Paola he had seen someone he wanted to talk to, and she replied that she would try to find her parents to thank them for the party. They separated, and he went across the room toward the doctor, whose name he had forgotten. She made no attempt to disguise the fact that she recognized and remembered him.

'Good evening, Commissario,' she said when he came up beside her.

'Good evening, Doctor,' he replied, and then added, as if they had managed sufficient homage to the rule of formality, 'My name is Guido.'

'And mine is Barbara.'

'How small the city is,' he observed, the banality of the remark allowing him, a formal man, to avoid having to commit himself to addressing her as either *lei* or *tu*.

'Sooner or later, everyone meets everyone,'

she concurred, avoiding with equal skill any direct address.

Deciding on the formal *lei*, he said, 'I'm sorry I never thanked you for your help the other night.'

She shrugged this away and asked, 'Was my diagnosis correct?'

'Yes,' he said, wondering how she could have avoided reading about it in every newspaper in the country. 'It was in the coffee, as you said.'

'I thought so. But I have to confess I recognized the smell only from reading Agatha Christie.'

'Me too. It's the only time I ever smelled it in real life.' Both of them ignored the awkwardness of that last word.

She stubbed out her cigarette in a potted palm the size of an orange tree. 'How would a person get it?' she asked.

'That's what I wanted to ask you, Doctor.'

She paused and considered for a few moments before she suggested, 'In a pharmacy, a laboratory, but I'm sure it would be a controlled substance.'

'It is and it isn't.'

She, being an Italian, understood immediately. 'So it could disappear and never be reported, or even missed?'

'Yes, I think so. One of my men is checking the pharmacies in the city, but we could never hope to check all the factories in Marghera or

Mestre.'

'It's used for developing film, isn't it?'

'Yes, and with certain petrochemicals.'

'There's enough of that in Marghera to keep your man busy.'

'For days, I'm afraid,' he admitted.

Noticing that her drink was gone, he asked, 'Would you like another?'

'No, thank you. I think I've had enough of the count's champagne for one evening.'

'Have you been here other evenings?' he asked, frankly curious.

'Yes, a few. He always invites me, and if I'm free, I try to come.'

'Why?' The question slipped out before he had a chance to think.

'He's my patient.'

'You're his doctor?' Brunetti was too astonished to disguise his response.

She laughed. What was more, her amusement was entirely natural and without resentment. 'If he's my patient, then I suppose I've got to be his doctor.' She relented. 'My office is just on the other side of the *campo*. I was the servants' doctor first, but then, about a year ago, I met the count when I was here to visit one of them, and we began to talk.'

'About what?' Brunetti was astonished at the possibility that the count was capable of an action so mundane as talking, especially with someone as unpretentious as this young woman.

'That first time, we talked about the servant, who had influenza, but when I came back, we somehow started to talk about Greek poetry. And that led to a discussion, if I remember correctly, of Greek and Roman historians. The count is particularly fond of Thucydides. Since I'd gone to the classical *liceo*, I could talk about them without making a fool of myself, so the count decided I must be a competent doctor. Now he comes to my office every so often, and we talk about Thucydides and Strabo.' She leaned back against the wall and crossed her ankles in front of her. 'He's very much like my other patients. Most of them come to talk about ailments they don't have and pain they don't feel. The count is more interesting to talk to, but I suppose there's really not much difference between them. He's lonely and old, just like them, and he needs someone to talk to.'

Brunetti was shocked to silence by this assessment of the count. Lonely? A man who could pick up the phone and triumph over a Swiss bank's code of secrecy? A man who could find out the contents of a man's will before the man was buried? So lonely that he would go and talk to his doctor about Greek historians?

'He talks about you sometimes as well,' she said. 'About all of you.'

'He does?'

'Yes. He carries your pictures in his wallet.

He's shown them to me a number of times. You, your wife, the children.'

'Why are you telling me this, Doctor?'

'As I told you, he's a lonely old man. And he's my patient, so I try to do whatever I can to help him.' When she saw that he was going to object, she added, 'Whatever I can, if I think it will help him.'

'Doctor, is it normal for you to accept private patients?'

If she saw where this was leading, she made no sign of it. 'Most of my patients are public health patients.'

'How many private patients do you have?'

'I don't think that's any of your business, Commissario.'

'No, I suppose it's not,' he admitted. 'Would you answer one about your politics?' It was a question that, in Italy, still had some meaning, the parties not yet all being carbon copies of one another.

'I'm Communist, of course, even with the new name.'

'Yet you accept as your patient one of the richest men in Venice? Probably one of the richest in Italy?'

'Of course. Why shouldn't I?'

'I just told you. Because he's a very rich man.'

'What's that got to do with my accepting him as a patient?'

'I thought that . . .'

'That I'd have to refuse him as a patient because he's rich and can afford better doctors? Is that what you meant, Commissario?' she asked, making no attempt to disguise her anger. 'Not only is that personally offensive, but it also shows a rather simplistic vision of the world. I suppose neither surprises me very much.' That last made him wonder what the count might have said about him during their talks.

He felt that the entire conversation had gotten out of hand. He had intended no offense, had not meant to suggest that the count could find better doctors. His surprise was entirely about this doctor's having accepted him. 'Doctor, please,' he said, and held out a hand between them. 'I'm sorry, but the world I work in *is* a simplistic one. There are good people.' She was listening, so he dared to add, with a smile, '. . . like us.' She had the grace to return his smile. 'And then there are people who break the law.'

'Oh, I see,' she said, her anger not diminished, after all. 'And does that give us all the right to divide up the world into two groups, the one we're in and all the others? And I get to treat those people who share my politics and let the rest die? You make it sound like a cowboy film—the good guys and the lawbreakers, and never the least bit of difficulty in telling the difference between the two.'

Struggling to defend himself, he said, 'I didn't say which law; I just said they broke the law.'

'Isn't there only one law in your vision of the world—the law of the state?' Her contempt was open, and he hoped it was for the law of the state and not for him.

'No, I don't think so,' he answered.

She threw up her hands. 'If this is when poor old God gets dragged down from heaven and put into the conversation, I'm going to get more champagne.'

'No, let me,' he said, and took her glass from her. He soon returned with a fresh glass of champagne and some mineral water for himself. She accepted the champagne and thanked him with an entirely friendly and normal smile.

She sipped, then asked him, 'And this law of yours?' She said it with such real interest and lack of rancor that the last exchange was entirely erased. On both sides, he realized.

'Clearly, the one we have isn't enough,' he began, surprised to hear himself saying this, for it was this law he had spent his career defending. 'We need a more human—or perhaps more humane—one.' He stopped, aware of how foolish it made him feel to say this. And, worse, to mean it.

'That would certainly be wonderful,' she said with a blandness that made him immediately suspicious. 'But wouldn't that interfere with your profession? After all, it's your job to enforce that other law, the law of the state.'

'They're really the same.' Realizing how lame and stupid this sounded, he added, 'Usually.'

'But not always?'

'No, not always.'

'And when they're not?'

'I try to see the point where they intersect, where they're the same.'

'And if they're not?'

'Then I do what I have to do.'

She burst into laughter so spontaneous that he joined her, aware of how much he had sounded like John Wayne just before he went out to that last gunfight.

'I apologize for baiting you, Guido; I really do. If it's any consolation to you, it's the same sort of decision we doctors have to make, though not too often, when what we think is right isn't the same as what the law says is right.'

He was, they both were, saved by Paola, who came up to him and asked if he was ready to go.

'Paola,' he said, turning to present her to the other woman. 'This is your father's doctor,' hoping to surprise her.

'Oh, Barbara,' Paola exclaimed. 'I'm so glad to meet you. My father talks about you all the time. I'm sorry it's taken us this long to meet.'

Brunetti watched and listened while they talked, amazed at the ease with which women made it obvious that they liked each other, at their enormous mutual trust, even at first meeting. United in a common concern for a man he had always found cool and distant, these two were talking as though they had known each other for years. There was none of the abrasive moral stocktaking that had transpired between him and the doctor. She and Paola had performed some sort of instant evaluation and been immediately pleased with what they found. He had often observed this phenomenon but feared he would never understand it. He had the same ability to become quickly friendly with another man, but somehow the intimacy stopped a few layers down. This immediate intimacy he was watching went deep, to some central place, before it stopped. And evidently it hadn't stopped; it had only paused until the next meeting.

They had arrived at the point of discussing Raffaele, the count's only grandson, before Paola and Barbara remembered that Brunetti was still there. Paola could tell from his restless foot-shifting that he was tired and wanted to leave, so she said, 'I'm sorry, Barbara, to tell you all this about Raffaele. Now you'll have two generations to worry about, instead of one.'

'No, it's good to get a different view about

the children. He's always so worried about them. But so proud of both of you.' It took Brunetti a moment before he realized she meant him and Paola. This was becoming, indeed, a night of many marvels.

He didn't notice how it was done, but the two women decided it was time for them all to leave. The doctor set her glass down on a table beside her, and Paola turned to take his arm at the same moment. They exchanged farewells, and he was again struck by how much warmer the doctor was with Paola than with him.

CHAPTER THIRTEEN

As fortune would have it, it was the next morning that his first report was due on Patta's desk 'before eight.' Since the clock, when he opened his eyes and saw it, read eight-fifteen, that was clearly going to be impossible.

A half hour later, feeling more recognizably human, he came into the kitchen and found Paola reading *L'Unità*, which reminded him it was Tuesday. For reasons he had never understood, she read a different newspaper each morning, spanning the political spectrum from right to left, and languages from French to English. Years ago, when he had first met her and understood her even less, he had asked about this. Her response, he came to

172

realize only years later, made perfect sense: 'I want to see how many different ways the same lies can be told.' Nothing he had read in the ensuing years had come close to suggesting that her approach was wrong. Today it was the Communist lie; tomorrow the Christian Democrats would get their chance.

He bent and kissed her on the back of the neck. She grunted but didn't bother to look up. Silently, she pointed to the left, where a plate of fresh brioches sat on the counter. As she turned a page, he poured himself a cup of coffee, spooned in three sugars, and took the seat opposite her. 'News?' he asked, biting into a brioche.

'Sort of. We don't have a government as of yesterday afternoon. The President's trying to form one, but it looks like he hasn't got a chance. And at the bakery this morning, all anyone talked about was how cold it's turned. No wonder we have the sort of government we do: we deserve it. Well,' she said, pausing over the photo of the most recent President-designate, 'perhaps we don't. No one could deserve that.'

'What else?' he asked, falling into the decade-old ritual. It allowed him to learn what was happening without having to read the papers, and it also usually gave him a very precise idea of her mood.

'Train strike next week, in protest to the firing of an engineer who got drunk and drove his train into another one. The men who worked with him had been complaining about him for months, but no one paid any attention. So three people are dead. And now, because he's been fired, the same people who complained about him are threatening to go on strike because he was fired.' She turned a page. He took another brioche. 'New threat of terrorist attacks. Maybe that will keep the tourists away.' She turned another page. 'Review of opening night at the Rome opera. A disaster. Lousy conductor. Dami told me last night that the orchestra had been complaining about him for weeks, all during rehearsals, but no one listened. Makes sense. No one listens to the men who run the trains, so why should anyone listen to musicians who get to hear him all during rehearsals?'

He set his coffee down so suddenly that some of it splashed onto the table. Paola's only response was to pull the paper closer to her.

'What did you say?'

'Hmm?' she asked, not really listening.

'What did you say about the conductor?'

She looked up because of the tone, not the words. 'What?'

'About the conductor, what did you just say?'

As happened with most of the dicta she delivered each morning, this one appeared to have been forgotten as soon as she was free of it. She flipped back to the page where the

174

article appeared and looked at it again. 'Oh, yes, the orchestra. If anyone had paid any attention to them, they would have known he was a lousy conductor. After all, they're the best sort of judge about how good a musician is, aren't they?'

'Paola,' he said, pushing the paper down from in front of her, 'if I weren't married to you, I'd leave my wife for you.'

He was glad to see he had surprised her; it was something he rarely achieved. He left her like that, peering over her reading glasses, not at all sure what she had done.

He ran down all the ninety-four steps, eager to get to work and start making phone calls.

When he arrived fifteen minutes later, there had still been no sign of Patta, so he dictated a short paragraph and sent it to be placed on his superior's desk. That done, he called the main office of the *Gazzettino* and asked to speak to Salvatore Rezzonico, the chief music critic. He was told he was not at the office but could be found either at home or at the music conservatory. When he finally located the man, at home, and explained what he wanted, Rezzonico agreed to speak to him later that morning at the conservatory, where he was teaching a class at eleven. Next Brunetti called his dentist; he had once mentioned a cousin who played first violin in the La Fenice orchestra. Traverso was his name, and Brunetti called and arranged to speak to him

175

before the performance that night.

He spent the next half hour talking with Miotti, who had come up with little more at the theater, save for another member of the chorus who was sure he had seen Flavia Petrelli go into the conductor's dressing room after the first act. Miotti had further learned the reason for the *portiere*'s obvious antipathy for the soprano: his belief that she was somehow involved with '*l'americana.*' Beyond this, Miotti had learned nothing. Brunetti sent him off to the archives of the *Gazzettino* to look for anything about a scandal involving the Maestro and an Italian singer, sometime 'before the war.' He avoided Miottits look at the vagueness of this and suggested that there might be a filing system that would facilitate things.

Brunetti now left his office and walked across the city to the music conservatory, fitted into a small *campo* near the Accademia Bridge. After much asking, he found the professor's classroom on the third floor and the professor waiting there, either for him or for his students.

As so often happened in Venice, Brunetti recognized the man from having walked past him many times in that part of the city. Though they had never spoken to one another, the warmth of the man's greeting made it obvious that he was familiar with Brunetti for the same reason. Rezzonico was a small man

176

with a pallid complexion and beautifully manicured nails. Clean-shaven, with hair cut very short, he wore a dark-gray suit and a somber tie, as if he were intentionally dressing for the role of professor.

'What is it I can do for you, Commissario?' he asked after Brunetti had introduced himself and taken a seat at one of the desks that filled the classroom.

'It's about Maestro Wellauer.'

'Ah, yes,' responded Rezzonico, his voice growing predictably somber. 'A sad loss to the world of music.' This was, after all, the man who had written his obituary.

Brunetti waited for the requisite time to pass, then continued. 'Were you going to review that performance of *Traviata* for the paper, Professor?'

'Yes, I was.'

'But the review never appeared?'

'No, we decided—that is, the editor decided—that out of respect for the Maestro and because the performance was not completed, we would wait for the new conductor and review one of his performances.'

'And have you written that review?'

'Yes. It appeared this morning.'

'I"m sorry, Professor, but I haven't had time to read it. Could you tell me if it was a favorable review?'

'On the whole, yes. The singers are good,

177

and Petrelli is superb. She's probably the only Verdi soprano singing today, the only real one, that is. The tenor is less good, but he's still very young, and I think the voice will mature.'

'And the conductor?'

'As I said in my review, anyone coming in new under these circumstances has an especially difficult task. It's not an easy thing to lead an orchestra that has been rehearsed by someone else.'

'Yes, I can understand that.'

'But considering all the difficulties he encountered,' continued the professor, 'he did remarkably well. He's a very talented young man, and he seems to have a special feeling for Verdi.'

'And what about Maestro Wellauer?'

'I beg your pardon?'

'If you had written a review of the opening night, the performance Wellauer began, what would you have said?'

'About the performance as a whole or about the Maestro?'

'Either. Both.'

It was clear that the question confused the professor. 'I'm not sure how to answer that. The Maestro's death made it all unnecessary.'

'But if you had written it, what would you have said about his conducting?'

The professor tilted his chair back and locked his hands behind his head, just the way Brunetti remembered his own professors doing. He sat like that for a while, pondering the question, then allowed his chair to slam back down onto the floor. 'I'm afraid the review would have been a different one.'

'In what way Professor?'

'For the singers, much the same. Signora Petrelli is always magnificent. The tenor sang well, as I said, and will certainly grow better with more experience on the stage. The night of the opening, they sang much the same way, but the result was different.' Seeing Brunetti's confusion, he attempted to explain. 'You see, I have so many years of his conducting to erase. It was difficult to listen to the music that night without having all those years of genius interfere with what I was actually hearing.

'Let me try to explain it this way. During a performance, it is the conductor who keeps things together, sees that the singers maintain the right tempi, that the orchestra supports them, that the entrances are on time, that neither is allowed to get away from the other. And he must also see that the orchestra's playing doesn't get too loud, that the crescendi build and are dramatic but, at the same time, don't drown out the singers. When a conductor hears this happening, he can quiet them with a flick of his hand or a finger to the mouth.' To illustrate, the musician demonstrated the gestures that Brunetti had seen performed during many concerts and operas.

'And he must, at every moment, be in charge of everything: chorus, singers, orchestra, keeping them in balance perfectly. If he doesn't do this, then the whole thing falls apart, and all anyone hears is the separate parts, not the whole opera as a unit.'

'And that night, the night the Maestro died?'

'The central control wasn't there. There were times when the orchestra grew so loud that I couldn't hear the singers, and I'm sure they must have had trouble hearing one another. There were other times when the orchestra played too fast and the singers had to struggle to keep up with them. Or the opposite.'

'Was anyone else in the theater aware of this, Professor?'

Rezzonico raised his eyebrows and snorted in disgust. 'Commissario, I don't know how familiar you are with the Venetian audience, but the most complimentary thing that can be said of them is that they are dogs. They don't go to the theater to listen to music or hear beautiful singing; they go to wear their new clothes and be seen in them by their friends, and those friends are there for the same reasons. You could bring the town band from the smallest town in Sicily and put them in the orchestra pit and have them play, and no one in the audience would notice the difference. If the costumes are lavish and the scenery is elaborate, then we have a success. If the opera is modern or the singers aren't Italian, then we are sure to have a failure.' The professor realized that this was turning into a speech, so he lowered his voice and added, 'But to answer your question: no, I doubt that very many people in the theater realized what was happening.'

'The other critics?'

The professor snorted again. 'Aside from Narciso at *La Repubblica*, there isn't a musician among them. Some simply go to the rehearsals and then write their reviews. Some can't even follow a score. No, there's no judgment there.'

'What do you think the cause of Maestro Wellauer's failure, if that's the proper term, might have been?'

'Anything. A bad night. He was an old man, after all. He could have been upset, perhaps by something that happened before the performance. Or, ridiculous as this sounds, it could have been nothing more than indigestion. But whatever it was, he was not in control of the music that night. It got away from him; the orchestra did what they wanted, and the singers tried to stay with them. But there was very little sense of command from him.'

'Anything else, Professor?'

'Do you mean about the music?'

'That, or anything else.'

Rezzonico considered for a moment, this

time lacing his fingers together on his lap, and finally said, 'This will perhaps sound strange. And it sounds strange to me because I don't know why I say it or believe it. But I think he knew.'

'I beg your pardon.'

'Wellauer. I think he knew.'

'About the music? About what was going on?'

'Yes.'

'Why do you say that, Professor?'

'It was after the scene in the second act where Germont pleads with Violetta.' He looked at Brunetti to see if he knew the plot of the opera. Brunetti nodded, and the professor continued. 'It's a scene that always gets a great deal of applause, especially if the singers are as good as Dardi and Petrelli. They were, and so there was long applause. During the applause, I watched the Maestro. He set his baton down on the podium, and I had the oddest sensation that he was getting ready to leave, simply step down from the podium and walk away. Either I saw it or I invented it, but he seemed just about to be making that step when the applause stopped and the first violins raised their bows. He saw them, nodded to them, and picked up the baton. And the opera continued, but I still have the peculiar feeling that if he hadn't seen their motion, he would simply have walked away from there.'

'Did anyone else notice this?'

'I don't know. No one I've spoken to has wanted to say much about the performance, and what little they've said has been very guarded. I was sitting in one of the front tier of boxes, off on the left, so I had a clear view of him. I suppose everyone else was watching the singers. Later, when I heard the announcement that he couldn't continue, I thought he'd had an attack of some sort. But not that he had been killed.'

'What have these other people said?'

'As I told you, they have been, well, almost cautious, not wanting to say anything against him, now that he's dead. But a few of the people here have said much the same thing, that the performance was disappointing. Nothing more than that.'

'I read your article about his career, Professor. You spoke very highly of him.'

'He was one of the great musicians of the century. A genius.'

'You make no mention of that last performance in your article, Professor.'

'You don't condemn a man for one bad night, Commissario, especially not when the total career has been so great.'

'Yes, I know; not for one bad night and not for one bad thing.'

'Precisely,' agreed the professor, and he turned his attention to two young women who came into the room, each carrying a thick musical score. 'But if you will excuse me,

Commissario, my students are beginning to arrive, and my class is about to begin.'

'Of course, Professor,' Brunetti said, getting to his feet and extending his hand. 'Thank you very much for both your time and your help.'

The other man muttered something in return, but Brunetti could tell that his attention had clearly shifted to his students. He left the room and went down the broad steps, out into Campo San Stefano.

It was a *campo* he walked through often, and he had come to know not only the people who worked there, in the bars and shops, but even the dogs that walked or played there. Lazing in the pale sunlight was a pink-and-white bulldog whose lack of muzzle always made Brunetti uneasy. Then there was that odd Chinese thing that had grown from what looked like a pile of furred tripe into a creature of surpassing ugliness. Last, lolling in front of the ceramics store, he saw the black mongrel that remained so motionless all day that many people had come to believe he was part of the merchandise.

He decided to have a coffee at Caffè Paolin. Tables were still set up outside, but the only people at them today were foreigners, desperately trying to convince themselves that it was warm enough to have a cappuccino at a table in the open air. Sensible people went inside.

He exchanged hellos with the barman, who

184

had tact enough not to ask him if there was any news in the case. In a city where there were no secrets of any sort, people had developed a capacity to avoid asking direct questions or remarking on anything other than the casual. He knew that no matter how long the case dragged on, none of the people with whom he interacted at this level—barman, newsdealer, bank teller—would ever say a word about it to him.

After downing an espresso, he felt restless, not at all hungry for the lunch that everyone around him seemed to be hurrying toward. He called his office, to be told that Signore Padovani had called and left a name and address for him. No message, just the name: Clemenza Santina; and the address: Corte Mosca, Giudecca.

CHAPTER FOURTEEN

The island of the Giudecca was a part of Venice Brunetti seldom visited. Visible from Piazza San Marco, visible, in fact, from the entire back flank of the island, in places no more than a hundred meters away, it nevertheless lived in strange isolation from the rest of the city. The grisly stories that appeared in the paper with embarrassing frequency, of children being bitten by rats or people found dead of overdoses, always seemed to take place on the Giudecca. Even the presence of a dethroned monarch and a fading movie star of the fifties couldn't redeem it in the popular consciousness as a sinister, backward place where nasty things happened.

Brunetti, along with a large part of the city, usually went there in July, during the Feast of the Redeemer, which celebrated the cessation of the plague of 1576. For two days, a pontoon bridge joined the Giudecca with the main island, allowing the faithful to walk across the water to the Church of the Redeemer, there to give thanks for yet another instance of the divine intervention that seemed so frequently to have saved or spared the city.

As the number 8 boat slapped its way across the choppy waters, he stood on the deck and looked off in the distance at the industrial inferno of Marghera, where smokestacks tossed up fluffy clouds of smoke that would gradually sneak across the *laguna* to dine on Venice's white Istrian marble. He wondered what divine intercession could save the city from the oil slick, this modern plague that covered the waters of the *laguna* and had already destroyed millions of the crabs that had crawled through the nightmares of his childhood. What Redeemer could come and save the city from the pall of greenish smoke that was slowly turning marble to meringue? A man of limited faith, he could imagine no salvation, either divine or human.

He got off at the Zittele stop, turned to the left, and walked along the water, searching for the entrance to Corte Mosca. Back across the water lay the city, glittering in the weak winter sunlight. He passed the church, closed now for God's afternoon siesta, and saw, just beyond it, the entrance to the courtyard. Narrow and low, the heavily shadowed passageway stank of cat.

At the end of the stone tunnel, he found himself at the edge of a rank garden that grew rampant at the center of the inner courtyard. To one side, something that might have been a cat was gnawing at a feathered thing. At the sound of his footsteps, the cat backed under a rosebush, pulling with it the thing it had been eating. On the opposite side of the courtyard stood a warped wooden door. He went across, occasionally freeing himself from a clinging thorn, to knock, then pound, on it.

After minutes, the door was pulled back a handsbreadth, and two eyes looked out at him. He explained that he was looking for Signora Santina. The eyes studied him, squinting in confusion, then retreated a bit into the complete darkness of the house. In deference to the infirmities of age, he repeated his question, this time almost shouting. At that, a small hole opened up under the two eyes, and a man's voice told him that the signora lived over there, at the opposite side of the courtyard.

Brunetti turned and looked back across the garden. Near the tunnel entrance, but almost hidden by a pile of decomposing grass and branches, was another low door. As he turned around to express his thanks, the door slammed shut in his face. Careful, he crossed the garden and knocked on the other door.

He had to wait even longer this time. When the door opened, he saw a pair of eyes at the same height as the others, and he wondered if this creature had somehow managed to run from one side of the building to the other. But closer examination showed him that these eyes were lighter and the surrounding face was clearly that of a woman, though it was as scored by wrinkles and pinched by cold as the first one had been.

'Yes?' she asked, looking up at him. She was a little pile of a woman, wrapped tight in layers of sweaters and scarves. From the bottom of the lowest skirt hung what appeared to be the hem of a flannel nightgown. She wore a pair of thick woolen slippers like those his grandmother had worn. Over everything, a man's overcoat, unbuttoned, hung open.

'Signora Santina?'

'What do you want?' The voice was high and sharp with age, making it difficult for him to believe that it belonged to one of the great singers of the prewar era. In that voice, too, he heard all the suspicion of authority that was instinctive to Italians, especially the old. That suspicion had taught him to delay as long as possible telling anyone who he was.

'Signora,' he said, leaning forward and speaking in a clear, loud voice, 'I'd like to speak to you about Maestro Helmut Wellauer.'

Her face registered nothing that indicated she had heard about his death. 'You don't have to shout. I'm not deaf. What are you, a journalist? Like that other one?'

'No, Signora. I'm not. But I would like to speak to you about the Maestro.' He spoke carefully now, intent upon his effect. 'I know that you sang with him. In the days of your glory.' At this word, her eyes shot up to his, and some trace of softness slipped into them.

She studied him, looking for the musician behind the conservative blue tie. 'Yes, I sang with him. But that was long ago.'

'Yes, Signora, I know that. But I would be honored if you would talk about your career.'

'So long as it's my career with him, you mean?' He saw the very instant when she realized who, or what, he was.

'You're police, aren't you?' she asked, as though the news had come to her as a smell, not an idea. She pulled the overcoat closed in front of her, crossing her arms over her chest.

'Yes, Signora, I am, but I've always been an admirer of yours.'

'Then why haven't I seen you here before? Liar.' She said it in description, not in anger.

189

'But I'll talk to you. If I don't, you'll come back with papers.' She turned abruptly and stepped back into darkness. 'Come in, come in. I can't afford to heat the whole courtyard.'

He went in behind her and was immediately assailed by cold and damp. He didn't know if it was the effect of being so suddenly cut off from the sun, but the apartment seemed far colder than the open courtyard had been. She brushed past him and pushed the door closed, cutting off entirely the light and the memory of warmth. With her foot, she pushed a thick roll of flannel into place against the narrow opening under the door. Then she locked the door, slipping its bolts home. With a policeman inside, she double-locked the door.

'This way,' she muttered, and set off down a long corridor. Brunetti was forced to wait until his eyes adjusted to the dimness before he followed her along the dank passageway and into a small, dark kitchen, in the middle of which was an antique kerosene heater. The lowest of flames flickered at its base; a heavy armchair, as layered with blankets as the old woman was with sweaters, was pulled up close to it.

'I suppose you want coffee,' she said as she closed the door to the kitchen, again kicking rolled rags against the crack beneath the door.

'That would be very kind of you, Signora,' he said.

She pointed to a straight-backed chair that

190

faced hers, and Brunetti moved to sit in it, though not before noticing that the woven wicker seat was worn, or chewed, through in a number of places. He sat down carefully and looked around the room. He saw the signs of desperate poverty: the cement sink with only one faucet, the lack of refrigerator or stove, the moldy patches on the walls. He smelled, more than he saw, the poverty, smelled it in the fetid air, the stink of sewer common on the ground floors of Venice, of the salami and cheese left open and unrefrigerated on the counter, and smelled it from the raw, unwashed odor that seeped across to him from the blankets and shawls heaped on the old woman's chair.

With motions grown circumscribed by age and lack of space, she poured coffee from an espresso pot into a low saucepan and walked haltingly toward the kerosene stove, on top of which she placed the pan. Slowly she made her way back to the cement counter beside the sink and returned to place two chipped cups on the table beside her chair. Then back again, this time to return with a small crystal sugar bowl that held a mound of grubby, solidified sugar in its center. Sticking her finger into the saucepan and judging the temperature correct, she poured its contents into the two cups, one of which she shoved roughly toward him. She licked her finger clean.

She stooped to pull back the covers on her

chair and then, like a person about to slip nto bed, lowered herself into the chair. Automatically, as if after long training, the covers slipped down from the back and arms of the chair to cover her.

She reached beside her to take her cup from the table, and he noticed that her hands were knobbed and deformed with arthritis, so much so that the left had become a sort of hook from which protruded a thumb. He realized that the same disease caused her slowness. And then, as the cold and damp continued to lay siege to his body, he considered what it must be like for her to live in this apartment.

Neither of them had said a thing during the preparation of the coffee. Now they sat in an almost congenial silence until she leaned forward and said, 'Have some sugar.'

She made no move to unwrap herself, so Brunetti picked up the single spoon and chipped away a piece of sugar. 'Allow me, Signora,' he said, and dropped it into her cup, using the spoon to move it around. He chopped off another piece of sugar and put it into his own cup, where it lay, solid and undissolvable. The liquid he sipped was thick, lukewarm, and lethal. A lump of sugar banged against his teeth, having done nothing to fight the acrid taste of the coffee. He took another sip, then set it down on the table. Signora Santina left her own untouched.

He sat back in his chair and, making no

attempt to disguise his curiosity, looked around the room. If he had expected to find any evidence of a career as meteoric as it was brief, he was mistaken. No poster of past opening nights hung upon these walls, no photos of the singer in costume. The only object that might have been a sign from her past was a large portrait photo in a silver frame that stood on top of a chipped wooden bureau. Arranged in a formal, artificial V, three young women, girls really, sat and smiled at the camera.

Still ignoring the cup at her side, she asked abruptly, 'What do you want to know?'

'Is it true that you sang with him, Signora?'

'Yes. The season of 1937. But not here.'

'Where?'

'Munich.'

'And what opera, Signora?'

'*Don Giovanni.* The Germans were always mad for their own. And the Austrians. So we gave them Mozart.' She added, with a small snort of contempt, 'And Wagner. Of course he gave them Wagner. He loved Wagner.'

'Who? Wellauer?'

'No. *L'imbianchino,*' she said, using the word for house-painter and, with it, conveying the sentiments that had cost countless people their lives.

'And the Maestro, did he like Wagner as well?'

'He liked anything the other one liked,' she

193

said with contempt she made no effort to disguise. 'But he liked him on his own, liked Wagner. They all do. It's the brooding and pain. It appeals to them. I think they like suffering. Their own or others'.'

Ignoring this, he asked, 'Did you know the Maestro well, Signora?'

She looked away from Brunetti, over toward the photo, then down at her hands, which she held carefully separated, as if even the most casual contact could cause them pain. 'Yes, I knew him well,' she finally said.

After what seemed a long time, he asked, 'What can you tell me about him, Signora?'

'He was vain,' she finally said. 'But with reason. He was the greatest conductor I ever worked with. I didn't sing with them all; my career was too short. But of those I sang with, he was the best. I don't know how he did it, but he could take any music, no matter how familiar it was, and he could make it seem new, as if it had never been played, or heard, before. Musicians didn't like him, usually, but they respected him. He could make them play like angels.'

'You said your career was too short. What caused it to end?'

She looked at him then, but she didn't ask how anyone who said he was a fan of hers could fail to know the story. After all, he was a policeman, and they always lied. About everything. 'I refused to sing for Il Duce. It was in Rome, at the opening night of the 1938 season. *Norma.* The general manager came backstage just before the curtain and told me that we had the honor of having Mussolini in the audience that night. And . . .' Her voice trailed off, seeking a way to explain this. 'And I was young and brave, and I said I wouldn't sing. I was young and I was famous, and I thought that I could do something like that, that my fame would protect me. I thought that Italians loved art and music enough to allow me to do that and be safe.' She shook her head at the thought.

'What happened, Signora?'

'I didn't sing. I didn't sing that night, and I didn't sing in public again. He couldn't kill me for that, for not singing, but he could arrest me. I stayed in my home in Rome until the end of the war, and when it was over, when it was over, I didn't sing anymore.' She shifted around in her chair. 'I don't want to talk about that.'

'About the Maestro, then. Is there anything else you can remember about him?' Though neither of them had mentioned his death, both of them spoke of him as among the dead.

'No, nothing.'

'Is it true, Signora, that you had personal difficulties with him?'

'I knew him fifty years ago.' She sighed. 'How can that be important?'

'Signora, I want only to get an idea of the man. All I know about him is his music, which is beautiful, and his body, which I saw and which was not. The more I know about him, the more I might be able to understand how he died.'

'It was poison, wasn't it?'

'Yes.'

'Good.' There was no malice, no venom in her voice. She could have been remarking on a passage of music or a meal, for all the enthusiasm she showed. He noticed that her hands were joined together now, fingers nervously weaving in and out. 'But I'm sorry someone killed him.' Which was it? he asked himself. 'Because I would have liked it to be suicide, so he would damn his soul as well as die.' Her tone remained level, dispassionate.

Brunetti shivered; his teeth started to chatter. Almost involuntarily, he got up from his seat and began to walk around in an effort to bring some warmth back into his limbs. At the bureau, he stopped in front of the photo and studied it. The three girls wore the exaggerated fashions of the thirties: long lace dresses trailing to the floor, open-toed shoes with immense heels. All three had the same dark, bow-shaped lips and razor-thin eyebrows. Under the makeup and marcelled hair, he could see that they were very young. They were arranged in descending order of age, the oldest to the left. She might have been in her early twenties, the middle one a few years younger. The last seemed little more than a child, perhaps in her early teens.

'Which one are you, Signora?'

'In the center. I was the middle one.'

'And the other two?'

'Clara. She was older. And Camilla. She was the baby. We were a good Italian family. My mother had six children in twelve years, three girls and three boys.'

'Did your sisters sing too?'

She sighed, then gave a small snort of disbelief. 'There was a time when everyone in Italy knew the three Santina sisters, the Three C's. But that was a long time ago, so there is no reason that you should know.' He saw the way she looked at the photo and wondered if they were still, to her, the way they were in that photo, young and beautiful.

'We began singing in the music halls, after the films. There was little money in our family, so we sang, the daughters, and we made some money. And then we began to be recognized, so there was more money. Somehow I discovered that I had a real voice, so I started singing in the theaters, but Camilla and Clara continued to sing in the music halls.' She stopped talking and picked up her coffee, drank it down in three quick swallows, then hid her hands under the warmth of the blankets.

'Did your trouble with him involve your sisters, Signora?'

Her voice was suddenly tired and old. 'That

197

was too long ago. Does it matter?'

'Did it involve your sisters, Signora?'

Her voice shot up into the soprano register. 'Why do you want to know? What does it matter? He's dead. They're dead. They're all dead.' She pulled the loose covers more tightly around her, protecting herself from the cold and from the cold sound of his voice. He waited for her to continue, but all he heard was the low puff and hiss of the kerosene heater giving voice to its futile attempt to keep the killing chill from the room.

Minutes passed. Brunetti could still taste the bitterness of the coffee in his mouth, and he could do nothing to lessen the cold that continued to seep into his bones.

Finally, she spoke, her voice absolute. 'If you've finished your coffee, you can go.'

He went back to the table and took the two cups over to the sink. When he turned, she had unburied herself and was already at the door to the room. She shuffled ahead of him down the long corridor, which, if possible, had grown even colder while they had been in the other room. Slowly, scrabbling at the locks with her twisted hands, she pulled back the bolts and held the door open enough for him to slip through. As he turned to thank her, he heard the bolts being driven home. Though it was early winter and cold, he sighed with relief and pleasure at the faint touch of the afternoon ⌐is back.

CHAPTER FIFTEEN

As the boat carried him back to the main island, he tried to think of who would be able to tell him what had happened between the singer and Wellauer. And between him and her sister. The only person he could think of was Michele Narasconi, a friend of his who lived in Rome and somehow managed to make a living as a travel and music writer. Michele's father, now retired, had done the same sort of thing, though with far greater success. He had been, for two decades, the leading reporter of the superfluous in Italy, a nation that demanded a steady stream of that sort of information. The older man had written, for years, weekly columns in both *Gente* and *Oggi*, and millions of readers had depended upon him for reports—accuracy being no requirement—about the various scandals of the Savoia family, stars of stage and screen, and the limitless flock of minor princelings who insisted upon migrating to Italy both before and after their abdications. Though Brunetti had no clear idea of what he was looking for, he knew that Michele's father would be the person to ask for it.

He waited until he was back at the office to place the call. It had been so long since he had spoken to Michele that he had to ask the interurban operator for the number. While the phone rang, he tried to think of a way to ask for what he wanted without insulting his friend.

'*Pronto*. Narasconi,' a woman's voice answered.

'*Ciao*, Roberta,' he said. 'It's Guido.'

'Oh, Guido, it's so nice to hear from you again. How are you? And Paola? And the children?'

'We're all fine, Roberta. Listen, is Michele there?'

'Yes; let me go and get him for you.' He heard the solid clunk of the phone's being set down, Roberta's voice calling to her husband. Various slammings and thumps ensued, and then Michele's voice said, '*Ciao*, Guido. How are you, and what do you want?' The laugh that followed the question removed any possibility of malice from it.

Brunetti decided not to waste time or energy in being coy. 'Michele, this time I need your father's memory. It's too far back for yours. How is he?'

'Still working. RAI wants him to write a program about the early days of television. If he does, I'll let you know so you can watch it. What is it you want to know?' A reporter by instinct as well as profession, Michele wasted no time.

'I want to know if he remembers an opera singer named Clemenza Santina. She sang right before the war.'

Michele made a faint noise. 'Sounds faintly familiar, though I can't remember why. If it was around the war, Papa will remember.'

'There were two other sisters. They all sang,' Brunetti explained.

'Yes, I remember now. The Singing C's, or the Beautiful C's; something like that. What do you want to know about them?'

'Anything at all, anything he can remember.'

'Is this related to Wellauer?' Michele asked out of an instinct that was seldom wrong.

'Yes.'

Michele gave a long, appreciative whistle. 'Is it yours?'

'Yes.'

Again, the whistle. 'I don't envy you that, Guido. The press will eat you alive if you don't find out who did it. Scandal to the Republic. Crime against Art. All that stuff.'

Brunetti, who had already had three days of this, said a simple 'I know.'

Michele's response was immediate. 'Sorry, Guido, sorry. What do you want me to ask Papa?'

'If there was ever any talk about Wellauer and the sisters.'

'The usual kind of talk?'

'Yes, or any other kind of talk. He was married at the time. I don't know if that's important.'

'Is that the one who committed suicide?' So

201

Michele had read the papers too.

'No; that was the second one. He was still married to number one. And I wouldn't mind if your father could remember anything about that, as well. But this was right before the war—'38, '39.'

'Wasn't there some sort of political trouble she got herself into? Insulted Hitler or something?'

'Mussolini. She spent the war under house arrest. If she had insulted Hitler, she would have been killed. I want to know what her connection to Wellauer was. And, if possible, the sister's.'

'How urgent is this, Guido?'

'Very.'

'All right. I saw Papa this morning, but I can go over this evening. He'll be delighted. It'll make him feel important, being asked to remember. You know how he likes to talk about the past.'

'Yes, I do. He was the only person I could think of, Michele.'

His friend laughed at this. Flattery was still flattery, no matter how true it happened to be. 'I'll tell him you said that, Guido.' Then, laughter gone, he asked, 'What about Wellauer?' This was as close as Michele would permit himself to come to asking a direct question, but that is what it was.

'Nothing yet. There were more than a thousand people in the theater the night it happened.'

'Is there a connection with the Santina woman?'

'I don't know, Michele. I can't know until I hear what your father remembers.'

'All right. I'll call you tonight after I talk to him. It'll probably be late. Should I still call?'

'Yes, I'll be there. Or Paola will. And thanks, Michele.'

'It's nothing, Guido. Besides, Papa will be proud you thought of him.'

'He's the only one.'

'I'll be sure to tell him.'

Neither of them bothered to say they had to get together soon; neither had the time to travel half the country to see an old friend. Instead they said goodbye and wished each other well.

When he had finished speaking to Michele, he realized it was time to go back to the Wellauer apartment for his second talk with the widow. He left a message for Miotti, saying he wouldn't be back in the office that afternoon, and scribbled a short note, asking one of the secretaries to place it on Patta's desk at eight the next morning.

He was a few minutes late getting to the Maestro's apartment. This time it was the maid who let him in, the woman who had been sitting in the second row of pews at the funeral mass. He introduced himself, gave her his coat, and asked if he might trouble her for a few words after he had spoken to the signora. She nodded and said no more than '*Sì*,' then led him to the room where he had spoken with the widow two days before.

She rose and came across the room to shake his hand. The intervening time had not been gentle to her, Brunetti thought, seeing the dark circles under her eyes, the skin that had become drier, rougher in texture. She went back to where she had been sitting, and Brunetti saw that there was nothing near her— no book, no magazine, no sewing. Apparently she had been sitting and waiting for him, or for the future. She sat down and lit a cigarette. She held the package toward him, offering him one. 'Sorry; I forgot you don't smoke,' she said in English.

He took the same seat as before, but this time he didn't bother with the business of the notebook. 'Signora, there are some questions I have to ask you,' he said. She made no acknowledgment of this, so he continued. 'They are delicate questions, and I would prefer not to have to ask them, especially at this time.'

'But you want the answers to them?'

'Yes.'

'Then I'm afraid you'll have to ask them, Dottor Brunetti.' She was, he realized, merely being literal, not severe, and so he said nothing. 'Why do you have to ask these questions?'

'Because they might help me find the person responsible for your husband's death.'

'Does it matter?' she asked.

'Does what matter, Signora?'

'Who killed him.'

'Doesn't it matter to you, Signora?'

'No, it doesn't matter. It never did. He's dead, and there's no bringing him back. What do I care who did it, or why?'

'Don't you have any desire for vengeance?' he asked before he remembered that she wasn't Italian.

She tilted her head back and peered at him through the smoke of her cigarette. 'Oh, yes, Commissario. I have a great desire for vengeance. I have always had that. I believe that people should be punished for the evil things they do.'

'Isn't that the same thing as vengeance?' he asked.

'You're in a better position to judge that than I am, Dottor Brunetti.' She turned away from him.

Before he realized it, he spoke out of his lack of patience. 'Signora, I'd like to ask you some questions, and I'd like to get honest answers for them.'

'Then ask your questions, by all means, and I shall give you answers to them.'

'I said I would like honest answers.'

'All right. Honest answers, then.'

'I'd like to know about your husband's

opinion of certain kinds of sexual behavior.'

The question obviously startled her. 'What do you mean?'

'I've been told that your husband particularly objected to homosexuality.'

He realized that this was not the question she had been expecting. 'Yes, he did.'

'Do you have any idea of the reason for that?'

She stabbed out her cigarette and leaned back in her chair, crossing her arms. 'What is this, psychology? Next are you going to suggest that Helmut was really a homosexual and, all these years, disguised his guilt in the classic way, by hating homosexuals?' Brunetti had seen this often enough in his career, but he didn't think it was the case here, so he said nothing. She forced herself to laugh in contempt of the idea. 'Believe me, Commissario, he was not what you think he was.'

Few people, Brunetti knew, ever were. He remained silent, curious to hear what she would say next. 'I don't deny that he disliked homosexuals. Anyone who worked with him would soon know that. But it was not because he feared that in himself. I was married to the man for two years, and there was nothing homosexual in him, I assure you of that. I think he objected because it offended some idea he had of order in the universe, some Platonic ideal of human behavior.' Brunetti

206

had certainly heard stranger reasons than this.

'Did his dislike extend to lesbians as well?'

'Yes, but he tended to be more offended by males, perhaps because their behavior is often so outrageous. I suppose, if anything, he took a prurient interest in lesbians. Most men do. But it's not a subject we ever discussed.'

During his career, Brunetti had spoken to many widows, interrogated many, but few of them managed to sound as objective about their husbands as this woman did. He wondered if the reason for that resided in the woman herself or in the man she seemed not to be mourning.

'Were there any men, any gay men, against whom he spoke with special dislike?'

'No,' she answered immediately. 'It seemed to depend on whom he was working with at the moment.'

'Did he have a professional prejudice against them?'

'That would be impossible in this milieu. There are too many. Helmut didn't like them, but he managed to work with them when he had to.'

'And when he worked with them, did he treat them any differently from the way he treated other people?'

'Commissario, I hope you aren't trying to construct a scenario here of a homosexual murder, someone who killed Helmut because of a cruel word or a canceled contract.'

'People have been murdered for far less.'

'That's not worth discussing,' she said sharply. 'Have you anything else to ask?'

He hesitated, himself offended by the next question he had to put to her. He told himself that he was like a priest, a doctor, and that what people told him went no further, but he knew that wasn't true, knew that he would respect no confidence if it would lead him to find the person he was looking for.

'My next question is not a general one, and it is not about his opinions.' He left it at that, hoping she would understand and volunteer some information. No help came. 'I refer specifically to your relations with your husband. Were there any peculiarities?'

He watched her fight down the impulse to leave her chair. Instead she ran the middle finger of her right hand over her lower lip a few times, elbow propped on the arm of her chair. 'I take it you are referring to my sexual relations with my husband.' He nodded. 'And I suppose I could become angry and demand what do you mean, in this day and age, by "peculiarities." But I will simply tell you that, no, there was nothing "peculiar" about our sexual relations, and that is all I choose to tell you.'

She had answered his questions. Whether he now had the truth was another issue entirely, one he chose not to deal with then. 'Did he seem to have any particular difficulty with any of the singers in this production? Or with anyone else involved in it?'

'No more than the usual. The director is a known homosexual, and the soprano is currently rumored to be so.'

'Do you know either one of them?'

'I've never spoken to Santore, other than to say hello to him at rehearsals. Flavia I do know, though not well, because we've met at parties and spoken to each other.'

'What do you think of her?'

'I think she's superb singer, and so did Helmut,' she answered, deliberately misunderstanding him.

'And personally?'

'Personally, I think she's delightful. Perhaps a bit short on sense of humor at times, but a pleasant person with whom to pass a few hours. And she's surprisingly intelligent. Most singers are not.' It was obvious that she was still choosing to misunderstand his questions and wouldn't give him what he wanted until he asked directly.

'And the rumors?'

'I've never considered them sufficiently important to give them any thought.'

'And your husband?'

'I think he believed them. No, that's a lie. I know he believed them. He said something to that effect one night. I can't remember now just what it was he said, but he made it clear that he believed the rumors.'

'But it wasn't enough to convince you?'

'Commissario,' she said with exaggerated patience, 'I'm not sure you've understood what I've been saying. It's not whether Helmut could or could not convince me of the truth of these rumors. It's that he couldn't convince me that they mattered. So I forgot about it until you mentioned it now.'

He gave no sign whatsoever of his approval and, instead, asked, 'And Santore? Did your husband say anything in particular about him?'

'Not that I can remember.' She lit another cigarette. 'This was a subject we did not agree on. I had no patience with his prejudice, and he knew that, so we avoided, by mutual consent, any discussion of the subject. Helmut was enough of a musician to keep his personal feelings to the side. It was one of the things I loved about him.'

'Were you faithful to him, Signora?'

It was a question she had clearly been anticipating. 'Yes, I think I was,' she said after a long silence.

'I'm afraid that's a remark I can't interpret,' Brunetti said.

'It depends, I think, on what you mean by "faithful."'

Yes, he supposed so, but he also supposed that the meaning of the word was relatively clear, even in Italy. He was suddenly very tired of this. 'Did you have sexual relations with anyone else while you were married to him?'

Her answer was immediate. 'No.'

He knew it was expected of him, so he asked, 'Then why did you say only that you thought you were?'

'Nothing. I was simply tired of predictable questions.'

'And I of unpredictable answers,' he snapped.

'Yes, I imagine you would be.' She smiled, offering a truce.

Since he hadn't bothered with the charade of the notebook, he couldn't signal the end of the interview by putting it in his pocket. So he got to his feet and said, 'There is one more thing.'

'Yes?'

'His papers were brought back to you yesterday morning. I would like your permission to take another look at them.'

'Isn't that what you were supposed to do while you had them?' she asked, making no attempt to hide her irritation.

'There was some confusion at the Questura. The translators saw them, then they were returned before I saw them. I apologize for the inconvenience, but I'd like to take a look at them now, if I might. I'd also like to speak to your maid. I spoke to her briefly when I came in, but there are some questions I'd like to ask her.'

'The papers are in Helmut's office. It's the second door on your left.' She chose to ignore his question about the maid and remained seated, not bothering to extend her hand to him. She watched as he left the room, then she went back to waiting for her future.

Brunetti walked down the corridor to the second door. The first thing he saw when he entered the room was the buff envelope of the Questura, sitting on the desk, unopened, still plump with documents. He sat at the desk and pulled the envelope toward him. Only then did he glance out the window and notice the rooftops that soared away from him across the city. In the distance, he could see the steeply pointed bell tower of San Marco and, to his left, the grim facade of the opera house. He pulled his attention away from the window and ripped open the envelope.

The papers, which he had already read in translation, he placed to one side. They concerned, he knew, contracts, engagements, recordings, and he had judged them to be of no importance.

He pulled three photographs from the envelope. Predictably, the report he had read made no mention of photos, probably because there were no words written on them. The first was of Wellauer and his widow, taken at a lake. They appeared tan and healthy, and Brunetti had to remind himself that the man must have been over seventy years old when the photo was taken, for he didn't look much older than Brunetti, he imagined. The second photo showed a young girl standing by a horse, a docile short thing, as round as it was high. The girl had one hand raised to the bridle of the horse and one foot halfway between the ground and the stirrup. Her head was swung around at an awkward angle, obviously caught off guard by the photographer, who must have called to her just as she was about to mount. She was tall and slender and had her mother's light hair, which swung out in two long braids under her riding helmet. Taken by surprise, she hadn't had time to smile and looked curiously somber.

The third photo was of the three of them together. The girl, almost as tall as her mother, but awkward even in repose, stood in the center, the adults a bit behind her, with their arms wrapped around each other. The child seemed a bit younger than in the other photo. All three launched prepared smiles into the camera.

The only other thing inside the envelope was a leather-bound datebook, the year embossed in gold on the cover. He opened it and glanced through the pages. The names of the days were given in German, and many days bore inscriptions in the slanting Gothic script he remembered from the *Traviata* score. Most of the notes were the names of places and operas or concert programs, abbreviations he could easily understand: 'Salz—D.G.'; 'Vienna—Ballo'; 'Bonn—Moz 40'; 'Ldn—

213

Così.' Others appeared to be personal or, at least, non-musical: 'Von S—5PM'; 'Erich & H—8'; 'D&G tea—Demel—4.'

Starting with the date of the conductor's death, he paged backward through the book for a total of three months. He found a schedule that would have exhausted a man half Wellauer's age, a list of engagements that grew heavier, the further back in time he went. Interested in this gradual increase, he opened the book to August and read forward in time; this way, he saw the pattern in reverse, a gradual decline in the number of dinners, teas, luncheons. He took a sheet of paper from one of the drawers in the desk and quickly sorted out the pattern: personal engagements to the right, music to the left. In August and September, except for a two-week period when almost nothing was noted, there had been some sort of engagement almost every day. In October, the number started to dwindle, and by the end of the month, there were almost no social engagements at all. Even the professional engagements had diminished, from at least two a week to only one or two every few weeks.

He flipped into the next year, which Wellauer would never see, and found, noted for late January, 'Ldn—Così.' What caught Brunetti's attention was the small mark he saw after the name of the opera. Was it a question mark or only a carelessly drawn accent?

He took another sheet of paper and made a second list, this one of the personal notes he found, beginning in October. For the sixth, he read: 'Erich & H—9PM.' Already familiar with those names, he could make sense of that On the seventh: 'Erich—8AM.' On the fifteenth: 'Petra & Nikolai—8PM,' and then nothing until the twenty-seventh, when he saw a note that read: 'Erich—8AM.' It seemed an odd time to meet a friend. The final entry of this sort was made two days before they left for Venice: 'Erich—9AM.'

And that was all, save for a note that Brunetti saw on the page for the thirteenth of November: 'Venice—Trav.'

He closed the book and slipped it back into the envelope, along with the photos and papers. He folded the papers on which he had taken his notes and went back to the room where he had left Signora Wellauer. She was just as she had been when he left, sitting in front of the open fire, smoking.

'Have you finished?' she said, when he came in.

'Yes, I have.' Still holding the papers, he said, 'I noticed from your husband's datebook that during the last few months, he was far less active than he had been in the past. Was there a particular reason for this?'

She paused a moment before answering. 'Helmut said he felt tired, didn't have the energy he once had. We saw a few friends, but

215

not as many, as you noted, as we had in the past. But not everything we did was noted in the datebook.'

'I didn't know that. But I'm interested in this change in him. You said nothing when I asked you about him.'

'As you might recall, Commissario, you asked about my sexual relations with my husband. Unfortunately, they are not noted in the datebook.'

'I notice that the name Erich appears frequently.'

'And why is that supposed to be important?'

'I didn't say it was important, Signora; I simply said that the name appears regularly during the last months of your husband's life. It appears often, joined with the initial "H," but it also appears alone.'

'I told you that not all of our engagements were listed in the datebook.'

'But these were important enough for your husband to note them down. May I ask who this Eric is?'

'It's Erich. Erich and Hedwig Steinbrunner. They are Helmut's oldest friends.'

'And not yours?'

'They became my friends, but Helmut had known them for more than forty years, and I had known them for only two, so it is logical that I think of them as Helmut's friends rather than my own.'

'I see. Could you give me their address?'

'Commissario, I fail to see why this is important.'

'I've explained to you why I think it's important. If you're unwilling to give me their address, I'm sure there are other friends of your husband's who could give it to me.'

She reeled off a street address and explained that it was in Berlin, then paused while he took out his pen and poised it above the paper he still held in his hand. When he was ready, she repeated it slowly, spelling every word, even *Strasse*, which he thought was an excessive comment on his stupidity.

'Will that be all?' she asked when he had finished writing.

'Yes, Signora. Thank you. Now might I speak to your maid?'

'I'm not sure I see why that's necessary.'

He ignored her and asked, 'Is she here in the apartment?'

Saying nothing, Signora Wellauer rose to her feet and went to the side of the room, where a cord hung down one wall. She pulled it, saying nothing, and went to stand in front of the window that looked out upon the rooftops of the city.

Soon after, the door opened and the maid entered the room. Brunetti waited for Signora Wellauer to say something, but she remained rigid in front of the window, ignoring them both. Brunetti, having no choice, spoke so that she could hear what he said to the maid.

'Signora Breddes, I'd like to have a few words with you, if I might.'

The maid nodded but said nothing.

'Perhaps if we might use the Maestro's study,' he said, but the widow was unrelenting and refused to turn back from the window. He went and stood at the door, gesturing for the maid to pass through before him. He followed her down the corridor to the now familiar study. Inside, he closed the door and motioned to a chair. She took her seat, and he went back to the chair he had sat in when he examined the papers.

She was in her mid-fifties, and she wore a dark dress that could be a sign of either her employment or her grief. The midcalf length was unfashionable, and the cut emphasized the angularity of her body, the narrowness of her shoulders, the flatness of her chest. Her face matched her body perfectly, the eyes a bit too narrow and the nose more than a little too long. She reminded him, as she sat upright on the edge of the chair, of one of the long-legged, long-necked sea birds that perched on the pilings of the canals.

'I'd like to ask you a few questions, Signora Breddes.'

'Signorina,' she corrected automatically.

'I hope there will be no trouble if we speak in Italian,' he said.

'Of course not. I've lived here for ten years.' She said it in a way to suggest she was offended by his remark.

'How long did you work for the Maestro, Signorina?'

'Twenty years. Ten in Germany, and now ten years here. When the Maestro bought the apartment here, he asked me to come and take care of it. I agreed. I would have gone anywhere for the Maestro.' From the way she spoke, Brunetti realized that she saw having to live in a ten-room apartment in Venice as a sort of suffering she would be willing to endure only because of her devotion to her employer.

'Do you have charge of the house?'

'Yes. I've been here since shortly after he bought it. He came down and gave instructions about the furniture and the painting. I was in charge of getting it organized and then of seeing that it was taken care of while he was away.'

'And while he was here?'

'Yes; that too.'

'How often did he come to Venice?'

'Two or three times a year. Seldom more than that.'

'Did he come to work? To conduct?'

'Sometimes. But he also came to visit friends, go to the Biennale.' She managed to make all this sound like so much earthly vanity.

'And while he was here, what were your responsibilities?'

'I did the cooking, though there was an

219

Italian cook who would come in for parties. I chose the flowers. I oversaw the work of the maids. They're Italian.' This, he assumed, explained the need for the overseeing.

'Who did the shopping for the house? Food? Wine?'

'While the Maestro was here, I planned the meals and sent the maids to Rialto every morning to get fresh vegetables.'

Brunetti thought she might be ready, now, to begin answering the real questions. 'So the Maestro got married while you were working for him?'

'Yes.'

'Did this cause any changes? When he came to Venice, that is.'

'I don't know what you mean,' she said, though it was clear she did.

'In the running of the house. Were your duties any different after the Maestro was married?'

'No. Sometimes the signora cooked, but not often.'

'Anything else?'

'No.'

'Did the presence of the signora's daughter cause you any problems?'

'No. She ate a lot of fruit. But she was no trouble.'

'I see, I see,' Brunetti said, taking a piece of paper from his pocket and idly sketching some words on it. 'Tell me, Signorina Breddes, during these last weeks that the Maestro was here, did you notice anything, well, anything different about his behavior, anything that struck you as peculiar?'

She remained silent, hands clasped on her lap. Finally, she said, 'I don't understand.'

'Did he seem strange to you in any way?' Silence. 'Well, if not strange in any way'—and he smiled, asking her to understand how difficult this was for him—'unusual in any way, out of the ordinary.' When she still said nothing, he added, 'I'm sure you would have noticed anything out of the ordinary, since you had known the Maestro so long and were certainly more familiar with him than anyone else in the house.' It was a blatant sop to her vanity, but that didn't mean it might not work.

'Do you mean with his work?'

'Well,' he began, and flashed her a smile of complicity, 'it could have been with his work, but it could have been with anything, perhaps something personal, something that had nothing to do with his career or with his music. As I said, I'm sure your long familiarity with the Maestro would have made you particularly sensitive to anything like this.'

Watching as the bait floated toward her, he flicked at the line to bring it even closer. 'Since you had known him for so long, you would have noticed things that others would have overlooked.'

'Yes, that's true,' she admitted. She licked

221

her lips nervously, drawing closer to the bait. He remained silent, motionless, unwilling to disturb the waters. She played idly with one of the buttons at the front of her dress, twisting it back and forth in a semicircle. Finally, she said, 'There was something, but I don't know if it's important.'

'Well, perhaps it will be. Remember, Signorina, anything you can tell me will help the Maestro.' Somehow he knew that she was blind to the colossal idiocy of this statement. He put his pen down and folded his hands, priestlike, and waited for her to speak.

'There were two things. Ever since he came down this time, he seemed to be more and more distracted, as if his thoughts were somewhere else. No, that's not it, not exactly. It's as if he didn't care any longer what happened around him.' She trailed off, not satisfied.

'Perhaps you could give me an example,' he prompted.

She shook her head, not liking this at all. 'No, I'm not saying this right. I don't know how to explain it. In the past, he would always ask me what had happened while he was away, ask about the house, about the maids, and what I had been doing.' Was she blushing? 'The Maestro knew that I loved music, that I went to concerts and operas while he was away, and he was always very careful to ask me about them. But this time when he came, there was none of that. He said hello when he arrived, and he asked me how I was, but he didn't seem to care at all about what I said to him. A few times—no, there was one time. I had to go into the study to ask him what time he wanted me to have dinner ready. He had a rehearsal that afternoon, and I didn't know what time it was supposed to end, so I went to the study to ask him. I knocked and went in, just the way I always did. But he ignored me, pretended I wasn't there, made me wait a few minutes while he finished writing something. I don't know why he did it, but he kept me waiting there, like a servant. Finally, I was so embarrassed that I started to leave. After twenty years, he wouldn't do that to me, keep me waiting like a criminal in front of a judge.' As she spoke, Brunetti saw her agony rekindled in her eyes.

'At last, when I turned around to leave, he looked up and pretended that he had just seen me there. He pretended I had appeared out of nowhere to ask him a question. I asked him when he planned to be back. I'm afraid I spoke angrily. I raised my voice to him, for the first time in twenty years. But he ignored that and just told me what time he would be back. And then I suppose he was sorry about how he had treated me, because he told me how beautiful the flowers were. He always liked to have flowers in the house when he was here.' She trailed away, adding irrelevantly, 'They're

223

delivered from Biancat. From all the way across the Grand Canal.'

Brunetti had no idea whether what he was hearing was outrage or pain, or both. To be a servant for twenty years is certainly to win the right not to be treated like a servant.

'There were other things too, but I didn't think anything of them at the time.'

'What things?'

'He seemed . . .' she said, thinking as she spoke of a way to say something and not to say it at the same time. 'He seemed older. I know, it had been a year since I last saw him, but the difference was greater than that. He had always been so young, so full of life. But this time he seemed like an old man.' To offer evidence of this, she added, 'He had begun to wear glasses. But not for reading.'

'Did that seem strange to you, Signorina?'

'Yes; people of my age,' she said frankly, 'we usually begin to need them for reading, for things that are close to us, but he didn't wear them for reading.'

'How do you know this?'

'Because sometimes I'd take him his afternoon tea and I'd find him reading, but he wouldn't be wearing them. When he saw me, he'd pick them up and put them on, or he'd just signal me to put the tray down, as if he didn't want to be bothered or interrupted.' She stopped.

'You said there were two things, Signorina.

May I ask what the other was?'

'I think I'd rather not say,' she replied nervously.

'If it's not important, then it won't matter. But if it is, it might help us find whoever did this.'

'I'm not sure; it's nothing I'm sure about,' she said, weakening. 'It's only something I sensed. Between them.' The way she said the last word made it clear who the other part of the 'them' was. Brunetti said nothing, determined to wait her out.

'This time they were different. In the past, they were always . . . I don't know how to describe it. They were close, always close, talking, sharing things, touching each other.' Her tone showed how much she disapproved of this as a way for married people to behave. 'But this time when they came, they were different with each other. It wasn't anything other people would have noticed. They were still very polite with each other, but they never touched anymore, the way they used to, when no one could see them.' But when she could. She looked at him. 'I'm not sure if this makes any sense.'

'Yes, I think it does, Signorina. Have you any idea of what might have caused this coolness between them?'

He saw the answer, or at least the suspicion of an answer, surface in her eyes, but then he watched it just as quickly disappear. Though

225

he had seen it there, he could not be sure if she was aware of what had just happened. 'Any idea at all?' he prodded. The instant he spoke, he realized he had gone too far.

'No. None.' She shook her head from side to side, freeing herself.

'Do you know if any of the other servants might have seen this?'

She sat up straighter in her chair. 'That is not something I would discuss with servants.'

'Of course, of course,' he muttered. 'I certainly didn't mean to suggest that.' He could see that she already regretted having told him what little she had. It would be best to minimize what she had told him so that she would not be reluctant to repeat it, should this ever become necessary, or to add to it, should this ever become possible. 'I appreciate what you've told me, Signorina. It confirms what we've heard from other sources. There is certainly no need to tell you that it will be held in strictest confidence. If you think of anything else, please call me at the Questura.'

'I don't want you to think . . .' she began, but couldn't bring herself to name what he might think of her.

'I assure you that I think of you only as someone who continues to be very loyal to the Maestro.' Since it was true, it was the least he could give her. The lines in her face softened minimally. He stood and extended his hand. Hers was small, birdlike, surprisingly fragile.

She led him down the corridor to the door of the apartment, disappeared for a moment, and returned with his coat. 'Tell me, Signorina,' he asked, 'what are your plans now? Will you remain in Venice?'

She looked at him as though he were a madman who had stopped her on the street. 'No; I plan to return to Ghent as soon as possible.'

'Have you any idea of when that will be?'

'The signora will have to decide what she wants to do with the apartment. I will stay until she does that, and then I will go home, where I belong.' Saying that, she opened the door for him and then closed it silently behind him. On his way down the steps, Brunetti stopped at the first landing and gazed out the window. Off in the distance, the angel on top of the bell tower spread his wings in benediction above the city and all those in it. Even if exile is spent in the most beautiful city in the world, Brunetti realized, it is still exile.

CHAPTER SIXTEEN

Since he was already so close to the theater, he went there directly, stopping only long enough to have a sandwich and a glass of beer, not really hungry but feeling the vague uneasiness that came upon him when he went for long periods of time without eating.

At the stage entrance, he showed his ID card and asked if Signore Traverso had come in yet. The *portiere* told him that Signore Traverso had arrived fifteen minutes before and was waiting for the commissario in the backstage bar. There, when Brunetti arrived, he found a tall, cadaverous man who had a familial resemblance to his cousin, Brunetti's dentist. The noise and confusion of many people passing by, both in and out of costume, made it difficult for them to talk, so Brunetti asked if they could go someplace quiet.

'I'm sorry,' said the musician. 'I should have thought of that. The only place to go is one of the dressing rooms that aren't being used. I suppose we could go up there.' The man placed some money on the bar and picked up his violin case. He led the way back through the theater and up the stairs Brunetti had used the first night he had come. At the top of the staircase, a stout woman in a blue smock came forward to ask them what they wanted.

Traverso had a few words with her, explaining who Brunetti was and what they needed. She nodded and led them along the narrow corridor. Taking an immense bunch of keys from her pocket, she opened a door and stepped back to let them enter. No theatrical glamour here, just a small room with two chairs on either side of a low table and a bench in front of a mirror. They seated themselves on the chairs, facing each other.

'During the rehearsals, did you notice anything unusual?' Brunetti asked. Because he didn't want to suggest what he was looking for, he kept his question general—so general, he realized, as to be virtually meaningless.

'Do you mean about the performance? Or about the Maestro?'

'Either. Both.'

'The performance? Same old stuff. The sets and staging were new, but we've used the costumes twice before. Singers are good, though, except for the tenor. Ought to be shot. Not his fault, though. Bad direction from the Maestro. None of us had much of an idea what we were supposed to be doing. Well, not at the beginning, but by the second week. I think we played from memory. I don't know if you understand.'

'Can you be more specific?'

'It was Wellauer; like his age caught up with him all of a sudden. I've played with him before. Twice. Best conductor I've ever worked with. No one like him today, though there are a lot who imitate him. Last time, we played *Così* with him. We never sounded so good. But not this time. He was suddenly an old man. It was like he wasn't paying any attention to what he did. Part of the time, when we reached a crescendo, he'd perk up and point that baton at anyone who was as little as an eighth of a beat late. It was

229

beautiful then. But the rest of the time, it just wasn't any good. But no one said anything. We just seemed to decide among ourselves to play the music the way it was written and take the lead from the concertmaster. I suppose it worked. The Maestro seemed content with it. But it wasn't like those other times.'

'Do you think the Maestro was aware of this?'

'Do you mean did he know how bad we sounded?'

'Yes.'

'He must have. You don't get to be the best conductor in the world and not hear what your orchestra is doing, do you? But it was more like he was thinking about something else most of the time. Like he wasn't there, just not paying any attention.'

'How about the night of the performance? Did you notice anything unusual?'

'No, I didn't. We were all too busy trying to keep together, so it wouldn't sound as bad as it might have.'

'Nothing at all? He didn't speak to anyone in a strange way?'

'He didn't speak to anyone that night. We didn't see him except when he came to the podium, down in the orchestra pit with us.' He paused, chasing at memory. 'There was one thing, hardly worth mentioning.'

'What?'

'It was at the end of the second act, right

after the big scene where Alfredo throws the money at Violetta. I don't know how the singers got through the ensemble. We were all over the place. Well, it ended, and the audience—they haven't got ears—they began to applaud, and the Maestro, he gave this funny little smile, like someone had just told him something funny. And then he set his baton down. Didn't toss it down on the podium, the way he usually did. Set it down very carefully, and then he smiled again. Then he stepped down from the podium and went backstage. And that's the last I saw of him. I thought he was smiling because the act was over and maybe the rest would be easy. And then they changed conductors for the third act.' He glanced at his watch. 'I'm not sure that's the sort of thing you were looking for.'

He reached down for his violin, and Brunetti said, 'One last thing. Did the rest of the orchestra notice this? Not the smile, but the difference in him?'

'A number of us did, those who had played with him before. For the rest, I can't say. We get so many lousy conductors here, I'm not sure if they can tell the difference between them. But maybe it's because of my father.' He saw Brunetti's confusion and explained. 'My father. He's eighty-seven. He does the same thing, looks over his glasses at us as if we've been keeping a secret from him and he wants to know what it is.' He looked at his watch again. 'I've got to go. It's only ten minutes until the curtain.'

'Thank you for your help,' Brunetti said, though he wasn't sure what to make of what the musician had just told him.

'Sounded like a lot of useless gossip to me. Nothing more. But I hope it can help.'

'Would there be any trouble if I stayed in the theater during the performance?' Brunetti asked.

'No, I don't think so. Just tell Lucia when you leave, so she can lock this room.' Then, hurriedly, 'I've got to go.'

'Thank you again.'

'It was nothing.' They shook hands, and the musician left.

Brunetti stayed in the room, already planning that he would take the opportunity to see how many people walked around backstage during a performance and during intermissions and how easy it would be to go into or out of the conductor's dressing room unnoticed.

He waited in the room for a quarter of an hour, grateful for the chance to be by himself in a quiet place. Gradually, all the noise that had filtered through the door stopped, and he realized that the singers would have gone downstairs to take their places onstage. Still he lingered in the room, comforted by the silence.

He heard the overture, filtering up the stairs and through the walls, and decided it was time to find the conductor's dressing room. He stepped out into the hall and looked around for the woman who had let them into the room, but she was nowhere to be seen. Because he had been charged with seeing that the room was locked, he walked along the hall and glanced down the stairway. 'Signora Lucia?' he called, but there was no reply. He went to the door of the first dressing room and knocked, but there was no reply. Nor at the second. At the third, someone called '*Avanti!*' and he pushed the door open, ready to explain that he had left and the dressing room could be locked.

'Signora Lucia,' he began as he entered the room. but he stopped when he saw Brett Lynch sprawled in an easy chair, book open in her lap, glass of red wine in one hand.

She was as startled as he but recovered more quickly. 'Good evening, Commissario. May I help you in any way?' She set her glass down on the table beside her chair, flipped her book closed, and smiled.

'I wanted to tell Signora Lucia she could lock that other dressing room,' he explained.

'She's probably downstairs, watching from the wings. She's a great fan of Flavia's. When she comes back up, I'll tell her to lock it. Don't worry, it'll be taken care of.'

'That's very kind of you. Aren't you watching the performance?'

'No,' she answered. Seeing his response, she

asked, 'Does that surprise you?'

'I don't know if it does or it doesn't. But if I asked you, then I suppose it does.'

Her answering grin pleased him, both because it was not the sort of thing he expected from her and because of the way it softened the angularity of her face.

'If you promise not to tell Flavia, I'll confess to you that I don't much like Verdi and I don't much like *Traviata*.'

'Why not?' he asked, curious that the secretary and friend—he left it at that—of the most famous Verdi soprano of the day would admit to not liking the music.

'Please have a seat, Commissario,' she said, pointing to the chair opposite her. 'Nothing much goes on for another'—she glanced at her watch—'twenty-four minutes.'

He took the seat she indicated, turned it to face her more directly, and asked, 'Why don't you like Verdi?'

'It's not exactly that. I do like some of the music. *Otello*, for example. But it's the wrong century for me.'

'Which do you prefer?' he asked, though he was sure of the answer he'd get. Wealthy, American, modern-minded: she would have to prefer the music of the century in which she lived, the century that had made her possible.

'Eighteenth,' she said, surprising him. 'Mozart and Handel, neither of which, for my sins, Flavia feels any great desire to sing.'

'Have you tried to convert her?'

She picked up her glass and sipped at it, set it back down on the table. 'I've converted her to some things, but I can't seem to tempt her away from Verdi.'

'I think that must be considered our great fortune,' he answered, slipping easily into her tone, which implied far more than it said. 'The other must be yours.'

She surprised him by giggling, and he surprised himself by laughing with her. 'Well, that's done. I've confessed. Now perhaps we can talk like human beings and not like characters in a cheap novel.'

'I'd very much like that, Signorina.'

'My name is Brett, and I know yours is Guido,' she said, using the informal second person and thus making the initial step toward familiarity. She got up from her chair and went over to a small sink in the corner. Beside it was a bottle of wine. She poured some into a second glass, brought it and the bottle back, and handed the glass to him.

'Are you back here to talk to Flavia?' she asked.

'No, that wasn't my intention. But I'll have to talk to her, sooner or later.'

'Why?'

'To ask what she was doing in Wellauer's dressing room after the first act.' If she found this at all surprising, she gave no sign of it. 'Do you have any idea?'

'Why do you say she was there?'

'Because at least two people saw her go in. After the first act.'

'But not after the second?'

'No, not after the second.'

'She was up here, with me, after the second act.'

'The last time we spoke, you said she was up here, with you, after the first act, as well. And she wasn't. Is there any reason I should believe you're telling me the truth now, when you lied then?' He took a drink of the wine. Barolo, and very good.'

'It's the truth.'

'Why should I believe that?'

'I suppose there's no real reason.' She sipped at her wine again, as though they had the entire evening before them for discussion. 'But she was.' She emptied her glass, poured a little more into it, and said, 'She did go to see him after the first act. She told me about it. He'd been playing with her for days, threatening to write to her husband. So, finally, she went back to talk to him.'

'It seems a strange time to do it, during a performance.'

'Flavia's like that. She doesn't think much about what she does. She simply acts, does what she wants. It's one of the reasons she's a great singer.'

'I would imagine it's difficult to live with.'

She grinned 'Yes, it is. But there are

compensations.'

'What did she tell you?' When she didn't understand, he added, 'About seeing him.'

'That they'd had an argument. He wouldn't give a clear answer about whether or not he had written to her husband. She didn't say much more than that, but she was still shaking with anger when she came back up here. I don't know how she managed to sing.'

'And did he write to her husband?'

'I don't know. She hasn't said anything else about it. Not since that night.' She saw his surprise. 'As I said, she's like that. When she's singing, she doesn't like to talk about anything that bothers her.' She added ruefully, 'She doesn't much like to do it when she's not singing, either, but she says it destroys her concentration if she has to think about anything except the music. And I suppose everyone has always let her get away with it. God knows, I do.'

'Was he capable of doing it, writing to her husband?'

'The man was capable of anything. Believe me. He saw himself as some sort of protector of human morals. He couldn't stand it if someone lived in violation of his definition of right and wrong. It maddened him that anyone would dare. He felt some sort of divine right to bring them to justice, his justice.'

'And what was she capable of doing?'

'Flavia?'

'Yes.'

The question didn't surprise her. 'I don't know. I don't think she could do it like that, not in cold blood. She'd do anything to keep the children, but I don't think . . . no, not like that. Besides, she'd hardly be walking around with poison, would she?' She seemed relieved to have thought of this. 'But it isn't finished. If there's a trial or some sort of hearing, then it'll come out, won't it, what they argued about?' Brunetti nodded. 'And that's all her husband will need.'

'I'm not so sure of that,' Brunetti said.

'Oh, come on,' she snapped. 'This is Italy, the land of the happy family, the sacred family She'd be allowed to have as many lovers as she wanted, so long as they were men. That would put the father, or a sort of father, back into the house. But the instant this became public, she'd never have a chance against him.'

'Don't you think you're exaggerating?'

'Exaggerating what?' she demanded. 'My life's never been a secret. I've always been too rich for it to matter what people thought of me or said about me. But that didn't stop them from saying it. So even if nothing could be proved about us, just think what a clever lawyer could do: "The soprano with the millionairess secretary." No, it would look like exactly what it is.'

'She could lie,' Brunetti said, suggesting perjury.

'With an Italian judge, I don't think that would make any difference. Besides, I don't think she'd lie. I really don't think she would. No, not about this. Flavia really does think she's above the law.' Instantly, she seemed to regret saying that. 'But she's all words, only talk, just like on the stage. She'll shout and rage at people, but it's all gestures. I've never known her to be violent, not to anyone. Just words.'

Brunetti was enough of an Italian to believe that words might easily change to something else when a woman's children were involved, but he kept that opinion to himself. 'Do you mind if I ask you some personal questions?'

She sighed wearily, anticipating what was coming, and shook her head.

'Has anyone ever tried to blackmail either one of you?'

This was clearly not the sort of question she had feared. 'No, never. Not me, and not Flavia, or at least she's never told me.'

'And the children? How do you get on with them?'

'Pretty well. Paolo is thirteen and Vittoria's eight, so at least he might have some idea of what's going on. But again, Flavia has never said anything, nothing has ever been said.' She shrugged, openhanded, and in that gesture ceased to be in any way Italian and became entirely American.

'And the future?'

'You mean old age? Sipping tea together in the afternoon at Florian's?'

It was rather a more sedate picture than he might have painted, but it would do. He nodded.

'I have no idea. While I'm with her, I can't work, so I have to decide about that, about what I want.'

'What is it you do?'

'I'm an archaeologist. Chinese. That's how I met Flavia. I helped arrange the China exhibit in the Doge's Palace three years ago. The bigwigs brought her along because she was singing *Lucia* at La Scala. And then they brought her to the party after the opening. Then I had to go back to Xian; that's where the dig is, the one I'm working on. There are only three of us there, three Westerners. And I've been away for three months now, and I have to go back or I'll be replaced.'

'The soldiers?' he asked, memory still bright with the image of the terracotta statues he had seen at that show, each one perfectly individualized and looking like the portrait of a man.

'That's just the beginning,' she said. 'There are thousands of them, more than we have any idea of. We haven't even begun to excavate the treasure in the central tomb. There's so much red tape with the government. But last fall we got permission to begin work on the treasure mound. From the little I've seen, it's going to be the most important archaeological find since King Tut. In fact, that will look like nothing once we start to take out what's buried there.'

He had always believed the passion of scholars to be an invention of people who wrote books, an attempt to render them more recognizably human. Seeing her, he realized how wrong he had been.

'Even their tools are beautiful, even the small bowls the workers used to eat from.'

'And if you don't go back?'

'If I don't go back, I lose it all. Not the fame. The Chinese deserve that. But the chance to see those things, to touch them, to have a real sense of what the people who made them were like. If I don't go back, I lose all that.'

'And is that more important to you than this?' he asked, gesturing around the dressing room.

'That's not a fair question.' She made her own broad gesture, one that took in the makeup on the table, the costumes hanging behind the door, the wigs propped up on pedestals. 'This sort of thing isn't my future. Mine is pots and shards and pieces of a civilization thousands of years old. And Flavia's is here, in the middle of this. In five years, she'll be the most famous Verdi singer in the world. I don't think there's a place for me in that. It's not anything she's realized yet, but I told you what she's like. She won't think of it until it happens.'

'But you have?'

'Of course.'

'What will you do?'

'See what happens here, with all this.' She gestured again, this time encompassing the death that had taken place in this theater four nights before. 'And then I'll go back to China. Or I think I will.'

'Just like that?'

'No, not "just like that," but I'll still go.'

'Is it worth it?' he asked.

'Is what worth it?'

'China.'

She shrugged again. 'It's my work. It's what I do. And, in the end, I suppose it's what I love as well. I can't spend my life sitting in dressing rooms, reading Chinese poetry, and waiting for the opera to end so that I can live my life.'

'Have you told her?'

'Has she told me what?' demanded Flavia Petrelli, making a thoroughly theatrical entrance and slamming the door behind her. She swept across the room, trailing behind her the train of a pale-blue gown. She was entirely transformed, radiant, as beautiful as Brunetti had ever seen a woman be. And it wasn't a costume or makeup that had made this change; she was dressed as what she was and what she did. That had transformed her. Her eyes swept around the room, taking in the two glasses, the amiability of their postures. 'Has

242

she told me what?' she demanded a second time.

'That she doesn't like *Traviata*,' Brunetti said. 'I remarked that it was strange to find her here, reading, while you were singing, and she explained that it wasn't one of her favorite operas.'

'It's also strange to find you here Commissario. And I know it's not one of her favorite operas.' If she didn't believe him, she gave no sign of it. He had stood when she came in. She walked in front of him, took one of the glasses that stood on the counter, filled it with mineral water, and drank it down in four long swallows. She filled it again and drank off half. 'It's like being in a sauna, with all those lights.' She finished the water and set the glass down. 'What are you two talking about?'

'He told you, Flavia. *Traviata*.'

'That's a lie,' the singer snapped. 'But I don't have time to talk about it.' Turning to Brunetti, she said, voice tight with anger and high in the manner of singers' voices after they have sung, 'If you'd be so kind as to get out of my dressing room, I'd like to change into my costume for the next act.'

'Certainly, Signora,' he said, all politeness and apology. Nodding to Brett, who gave him a brief smile in return but stayed in her chair, he left the room quickly. Outside, he paused and listened, ear close to the door, not at all

243

ashamed of what he was doing. But whatever they had to say to each other they said in low voices.

The woman in the blue smock appeared at the top of the steps. Brunetti pulled himself away from the door and walked toward her. Explaining that he had finished with the dressing room, he handed her the key, smiled, thanked her, and went back down the stairs to the stage area, where he found a chaos that amazed him. Gowned figures slumped against the walls, smoking and laughing. Men in tuxedos talked about soccer. And stagehands roamed back and forth, carrying paper ferns and trays with champagne glasses glued solidly to the bottom.

Down the short corridor to the right was the door to the conductor's dressing room, closed now behind the new conductor. Brunetti stood at the end of the corridor for at least ten minutes, and no one bothered to ask him who he was or what he was doing there. Finally, a bell sounded and a bearded man in a jacket and tie went from group to group backstage, pointing in various directions and sending them off to whatever it was they were supposed to do.

The conductor left the dressing room, closed the door behind him, and walked past Brunetti without paying any attention to him. As soon as he was gone, Brunetti went casually down the corridor and into the room. No one saw him go in or, if they saw him, bothered to ask him what he was doing there.

The room was much as it had been the other night, save that a small cup and saucer were sitting on the table, not lying on the floor. He stayed only a moment, then left. His departure was as little noticed as his entrance, and this only four days after a man had died in that room.

CHAPTER SEVENTEN

By the time he got home, it was too late to take Paola and the children to dinner, as he had promised he would do that evening; besides, he could smell the mingled odors of garlic and sage as he climbed the stairs.

As he walked into the apartment, he had a moment of total disorientation, for the voice of Flavia Petrelli, which voice he had last heard singing Violetta twenty minutes before, was performing the end of the second-act in his living room. He took two sudden and completely involuntary steps forward, until he remembered that the performance was being broadcast live that evening. Paola wasn't much of an opera fan and was probably watching to figure out which of the singers was a murderer. In which curiosity, he was sure, she was joined by millions of households all over Italy.

From the living room, he heard the voice of his daughter, Chiara, call out, 'Papà's home,' over which Violetta begged Alfredo to leave her forever.

He went into the living room just as the tenor threw a fistful of paper money into Flavia Petrelli's face. She sank to the floor, gracefully, in tears, Alfredo's father hurried across the stage to reprove him, and Chiara asked, 'Why did he do that, Papà? I thought he loved her.' She glanced up at him from what looked like math homework and, receiving no answer, repeated the question. 'Why'd he do that?'

'He thought she was going out with another man,' was the best Brunetti could come up with by way of explanation.

'What difference would that make? It's not like they're married or anything.'

'*Ciao*, Guido,' Paola called from the kitchen.

'Well,' Chiara persisted. 'Why is he so angry?'

Brunetti walked in front of her and lowered the volume on the television, wondering what it was that rendered all teenagers deaf. He could tell from the way she held her pencil in front of her and wiggled it in the air that she had no intention of letting this one go. He decided to compromise. 'They were living together, weren't they?'

'Yes; so what?'

246

'Well, when people live together, they usually don't go out with other people.'

'But she wasn't going out with anyone. She did all that just to make him think she was.'

'I guess he believed her, and he got jealous.'

'He doesn't have any reason to be jealous. She really loves him. Anyone can see that. He's a jerk. Besides, it's her money, isn't it?'

'Hmm,' he temporized, trying to remember the plot of *Traviata*.

'Why didn't he go out and get a job? As long as she's supporting him, then she's got the right to do whatever she wants.' The audience thundered its applause.

'It's not always like that, angel.'

'Well, sometimes it is, isn't it, Papà? Why not? Most of my friends, if their mothers don't work, like Mamma does, then their fathers always decide everything—where they'll go on vacation, everything. And some of them even have lovers.' This last was delivered weakly, more as a question than as a statement. 'And they get to do it because they earn the money, so they get to tell everyone what they have to do.' Not even Paola, he believed, could so accurately have summed up the capitalist system. It was, in fact, his wife's voice he heard in Chiara's speech.

'It's not as easy as that, sweetheart.' He pulled at his tie. 'Chiara, would you be an angel of grace and mercy and go into the kitchen and get your poor old father a glass of

247

wine?'

'Sure.' She tossed down her pencil, more than willing to abandon the issue. 'White or red?'

'See if there's some Prosecco. If not, bring me whatever you think I'd like.' In family jargon, this translated to whatever wine she wanted to have a taste of.

He lowered himself into the sofa and kicked off his shoes, propping his feet on the low table. He listened as an announcer filled the audience in, rather unnecessarily, on the events of the last few days. The man's eager, ghoulish tone made it sound like something from an opera, of the more bloody verismo repertory.

Chiara came back into the room. She was tall, utterly lacking in physical grace. From two rooms away, he could tell when it was Chiara's turn to do the dishes by the crashes and bangs that filled the house. But she was pretty, would perhaps become beautiful, with wide-spaced eyes and a soft down just beneath her ears that melted his heart with tenderness each time he saw it caught in a revealing light.

'Fragolino,' she said from behind him, and passed the glass to him, managing to spill only a drop, and that on the floor. 'Can I have a sip? Mamma didn't want to open it. She said there was just one more bottle after this, but I said you were very tired, so she said it was all right.' Even before he could consent, she took

248

the glass back and sipped from it. 'How can a wine smell like strawberries, Papà?' Why was it that, when children loved you, you knew everything, and when they were angry with you, you knew nothing?

'It's the grape. It smells like strawberries, so the wine does too.' He smelled, then tasted, the truth of this. 'You doing your homework?'

'Yes, mathematics,' she said, managing to put into the word an enthusiasm that confused him utterly. This, he remembered, was the child who explained his bank statements to him every three months and who was going to try to complete his tax form for him this May.

'What sort of mathematics?' he asked with feigned interest.

'Oh, you wouldn't understand, Papà.' Then, with lightning speed, 'When are you going to get me a computer?'

'When I win the lottery.' He had reason to believe that his father-in-law was going to give her a laptop computer for Christmas, and he disliked the fact that he disliked that fact.

'Oh, Papà, you always say that.' She sat down opposite him, plunked her feet onto the table between them, and placed them, sole to sole, against his. She gave a soft push with one foot. 'Maria Rinaldi has one, and so does Fabrizio, and I'll never be any good in school, not really good, until I have one.'

'It looks like you're doing fine with a pencil.'

'Sure I can do it, but it takes me forever.'

'Isn't it better for your brain if you exercise it, rather than letting the machine do it?'

'That's dumb, Papà. The brain's not a muscle. We learned that in biology. Besides, you don't walk across the city to get information if you can use the phone to get it for you.' He pushed back with his foot, but he didn't answer. 'Well, you don't, do you, Papà?'

'What would you do with all the time you saved if you got one?'

'I'd do more complicated problems. It doesn't do it *for* me, Papà, honest. It just does it faster. That's all it is, a machine that adds and subtracts a million times faster than we can.'

'Do you have any idea of how much those things cost?'

'Sure; the little Toshiba I want costs two million.'

Luckily, Paola came into the room then, or he would have had to tell Chiara just how much chance she had of getting a computer from him. Because that might lead her to mention her grandfather, he was doubly glad to see Paola. She carried the bottle of Fragolino and another glass. At the same time, the chattering voices on the television faded away and were replaced by the prelude to the third act.

Paola set down the bottle and sat on the arm of the sofa, next to him. On the screen, the curtain rose to display a barren room. It was difficult to recognize Flavia Petrelli, whom he had seen in the full power of her beauty little more than an hour before, in the frail woman slumped under the shawl who lay on the divan, one hand fallen weakly to the floor below her. She looked more like Signora Santina than she did a famous courtesan. The dark circles under her eyes, the misery of her drawn mouth, spoke convincingly of sickness and despair. Even her voice, when she asked Annina to give what little money she had to the poor, was weak, charged with pain and loss.

'She's very good,' Paola said. Brunetti shushed her. They watched.

'And he's dumb,' Chiara added as Alfredo swept into the room and grabbed her up in his arms.

'Shhh,' they both hissed at her. She returned to her figures, muttering,for her parents to hear.

He watched Petrelli's face transform itself with the ecstasy of reunion, watched it flush with real joy. Together, they planned a future they would never have, and her voice changed; he heard it returning to strength and clarity.

Her joy pulled her to her feet, raised her hands toward heaven. 'I feel myself reborn,' she cried, whereupon, this being opera, she promptly collapsed and died.

'I still think he's a jerk,' Chiara insisted over Alfredo's lamentation and the wild applause of the audience. 'Even if she lived, how would they support themselves? Is she supposed to go back to what she was doing before she met him?' Brunetti wanted to know nothing of how much his daughter might understand about that sort of thing. Having voiced her opinion, Chiara scribbled a long row of numbers at the bottom of her paper, slipped the paper into her math book, and flipped the book shut.

'I had no idea she was that good,' Paola said respectfully, completely ignoring her daughter's comments. 'What's she like?' The question was typical of her. The woman's involvement in a murder case had not been enough to interest Paola in her, not until she had seen the quality of her performance.

'She's just a singer,' he said dismissively.

'Yes, and Reagan was just an actor,' Paola said. 'What's she like?'

'She's arrogant, afraid of losing her children, and wears brown a lot.'

'Let's eat,' Chiara said. 'I'm starved.'

'Then go and set the table, and we'll be there in a minute.'

Chiara pushed herself up from her chair with every show of reluctance and went toward the kitchen, but not before saying, 'And now I suppose you'll make Papà tell you what she's really like, and I'll miss all the good parts, just like always.' One of the great crosses of Chiara's life was the fact that she could never get information from her father to transform into the coin of schoolyard popularity.

'I wonder,' Paola said, pouring wine into both their glasses, 'how she learned to act like that. I had an aunt who died of TB years ago, when I was a little girl, and I can still remember the way she looked, the way she was always moving her hands nervously, just the way *she* did onstage, always shifting them around in her lap and grabbing one with the other.' Then, with characteristic abruptness, 'Do you think she did it?'

He shrugged. 'She might have. Everyone's busy trying to give me the idea that she's the Latin fireball, all passion, knife in the ribs the instant the offending word is spoken. But you've just seen how well she can act, so there's nothing to say she isn't cold and calculating and entirely capable of having done it the way it was done. And she's intelligent, I think.'

'What about her friend?'

'The American?'

'Yes.'

'I don't know about her. She told me Petrelli went to see him after the first act, but only to argue with him.'

'What about?'

'He'd been threatening to tell her ex-husband about the affair with Brett.'

If Paola was surprised at his use of the first name, she gave no sign of it.

'Are there children?'

253

'Yes. Two.'

'Then it's a serious threat. But what about *her*, about Brett, as you call her. Could she have done it?'

'No, I don't think so. The affair isn't that fundamental to her life. Or she won't let it be. No, it's not likely.'

'You still didn't answer me about Petrelli.'

'Come on, Paola, you know I'm always wrong when I try to work by intuition, when I suspect too much or I suspect too soon. I don't know about her. The only thing I know is that this has got to have something to do with his past.'

'All right,' she said, agreeing to leave it. 'Let's eat. I have chicken, and artichokes, and a bottle of Soave.'

'God be praised,' he said, getting to his feet and pulling her up from the arm of the chair. Together, they went into the kitchen.

As usual, the minute before dinner was on the table and they were ready to eat, Raffaele, Brunetti's firstborn, son, and heir appeared from his room. He was fifteen, tall for his age, and took after Brunetti in appearance and gesture. In everything else, he took after no one in the family and would certainly have denied the possibility that his behavior resembled that of anyone, living or dead. He had discovered, by himself, that the world is corrupt and the system unjust, and that men in power were interested in that and that alone.

Because he was the first person ever to have made this discovery with such force and purity, he insisted upon showing his ample contempt for all those not yet graced with the clarity of his vision. This included, of course, his family, with the possible exception of Chiara, whom he excused from social guilt because of her youth and because she could be counted on to give him half of her allowance. His grandfather, it seemed, had also somehow managed to slip through the eye of the needle, no one understood how.

He attended the classical *liceo*, which was supposed to prepare him for the university, but he had done badly for the last year and had recently begun to talk of not going anymore, since 'education is just another part of the system by which the workers are oppressed.' Nor, should he quit school, had he any intention of finding a job, as that would make him subject to 'the system that oppresses the workers.' Hence, to avoid oppressing, he would refuse to get an education, and to avoid being oppressed, he would refuse to get a job. Brunetti found the simplicity of Raffaele's reasoning absolutely jesuitical.

Raffaele slumped at the table, propped on his elbows. Brunetti asked him how he was, this still being a topic safe to mention.

'OK.'

'Pass the bread, Raffi.' This from Chiara.

'Don't eat that clove of garlic, Chiara. You'll

stink for days.' This from Paola.

'Chicken's good.' This from Brunetti. 'Should I open the second bottle of wine?'

'Yes,' piped up Chiara, holding out her glass. 'I haven't had any yet.'

Brunetti took the second bottle from the refrigerator and opened it. He moved around the table, pouring wine into each of their glasses. Standing behind his son, he rested his hand on the boy's shoulder as he leaned over to pour the wine. Raffaele shrugged off his hand, then changed the gesture into an attempt to reach for the artichokes, which he never ate.

'What's for dessert?' asked Chiara.

'Fruit.'

'No cake?'

'Piggy,' said Raffaele, but in definition, not in criticism.

'Anyone want to play Monopoly after dinner?' Paola asked. Before the children could agree, she established conditions. 'Only if your homework's done.'

'Mine is,' Chiara said.

'So's mine,' Raffaele lied.

'I'm banker,' insisted Chiara.

'Bourgeois piggy,' Raffaele amended.

'You two do the dishes,' Paola ordered, 'and then we'll play.' At the first squeak of protest, she wheeled on them. 'No one's playing Monopoly on this table until the dishes are off it, washed, and in the cabinet.' As Raffaele opened his mouth to protest, she turned to him. 'And if that's a bourgeois way to look at it, that's too damn bad. Eating chicken's pretty bourgeois too, but I didn't hear any complaints about the chicken. So do the dishes and we'll play.'

It never failed to amaze Brunetti that she could use that tone with Raffaele and get away with it. Anytime he came close to reprimanding his son, the scene ended with slammed doors and sulks that lasted for days. Knowing he'd been outgunned, Raffaele showed his anger by snatching plates from the table and slapping them down on the counter next to the sink. Brunetti showed his by taking the bottle and his glass into the living room to wait out the inevitable thump and clatter of obedience.

'At least he's not building bombs in his bedroom,' Paola offered as consolation when she came in to join him. From the kitchen, they heard the muted sound that said Raffaele was washing the dishes and the sharp clanks that declared that Chiara was drying them and putting them away. Occasionally there was a sharp burst of laughter.

'Do you think he'll be all right?' he asked.

'As long as she can still make him laugh, I suppose we don't have to worry. He'd never do anything bad to Chiara, and I doubt he'd blow anyone up.' Brunetti wasn't sure just how this was supposed to serve as sufficient consolation for his concern about his son, but he was willing to accept it as such.

Chiara stuck her head into the room and cried, 'Raffi's got the board. Come on, let's go.'

When he and Paola got there, the Monopoly board was set up in the middle of the kitchen table and Chiara, as she had insisted, was banker, already passing out the small piles of money. By general consent, Paola was forbidden to be banker, as she had been caught too many times, over the course of the years, with her hand in the till. Raffaele, no doubt nervous that accepting the position would leave him open to the accusation of avarice, refused. And Brunetti had enough trouble concentrating on the game without adding the responsibilities of banker, so they always left it to Chiara, who delighted in the counting and collecting, paying and changing.

They rolled to see who went first. Raffaele lost and had to go last, which was enough to make the other three nervous from the beginning. The boy's need to win at the game frightened Brunetti, and he often played badly to give his son every advantage.

After half an hour, Chiara had all the green: Via Roma, Corso Impero, and Largo Augusto. Raffaele had two reds and needed only Via Marco Polo, which Brunetti owned, to make his set complete. After four more rounds, Brunetti allowed himself to be cajoled into selling the missing red property to Raffaele for Acquedotto and fifty thousand lire. Family rules forbade comment, but that didn't prevent Chiara from giving her brother a fierce kick under the table.

Raffaele, predictably, protested the injustice. 'Stop that, Chiara. If he wants to make a bad deal, let him.' This from the boy who wanted to bring down the entire capitalist system.

Brunetti handed over the deeds and watched as Raffaele immediately built hotels on all three properties. While Raffaele was busy with that, making sure Chiara gave him the proper change, Brunetti noticed Paola calmly sliding a small pile of ten-thousand-lire notes from the banker's pile to her own. She glanced up, noticed that her husband had seen her stealing from her own children, and gave him a dazzling smile. A policeman, married to a thief, with a computer monster and an anarchist for children.

The next time around, he landed on one of Raffaele's new hotels and had to hand over everything he owned. Paola suddenly discovered enough cash to build herself six hotels, but at least she had the grace to avoid his eyes as she handed the money to the banker.

He sat back in his chair and watched the game progress toward the ending that his loss to Raffaele had made inescapable. Paola's elbow began to inch toward the stack of ten-thousand-lire notes, but she was stopped by an icy glare from Chiara. Chiara, in her turn, failed to persuade Raffaele to sell her Parco della Vittoria, landed on the red hotels twice in a row, and went bankrupt. Paola held out for two more turns, until she landed on the hotel on Viale Costantino and couldn't pay.

The game ended. Raffaele was immediately transformed from a successful captain of empire to the disaffected foe of the ruling class; Chiara went to raid the refrigerator; and Paola yawned and said it was time to go to bed. Brunetti followed her down the hall, reflecting that the commissario of police of the Most Serene Republic had spent yet another evening in the unrelenting pursuit of the person responsible for the death of the most famous musician of the age.

CHAPTER EIGHTEEN

Michele's call came at one, pulling Brunetti out of a fuddled, restless sleep. He answered on the fourth ring and gave his name.

'Guido, it's Michele.'

'Michele,' he repeated stupidly, trying to remember if he knew anyone named Michele. He forced his eyes open and remembered. 'Michele. Michele—good. I'm glad you called.'

He switched the bedside lamp on and sat up against the headboard. Paola slept beside him, rocklike.

'I spoke to my father, and he remembered everything.'

'And?'

'It was just like you said: if there's anything to know, he'll know.'

'Stop gloating and tell me.'

'There were rumors about Wellauer and the sister who sang in opera, Clemenza. Papà couldn't remember where, but he knew it started in Germany, where she was singing with him. There was some sort of scene between the wife and La Santina, at a party, after a performance. They insulted each other, and Wellauer left.' Michele paused for effect. 'With La Santina. After the performances— my father thinks it was in '37 or '38—Santina came down here, to Rome, and Wellauer went home to face the music.' Bad as it was, Michele laughed at his own joke. Brunetti didn't.

'It seems he managed to patch things up with his wife. Papà suggested there was a lot of patching to do, then and later.'

'Is that the way it was?' Brunetti asked.

'Yes; Papà said he was one of the worst. Or best, depending on how you look at it. They got divorced after the war.'

'Because of that sort of thing?'

'Papà wasn't sure. Seems a safe bet. Or it

might have been because he backed the wrong side.'

'Then what happened, when Santina came back to Italy?'

'He came down to conduct a *Norma*, the one she refused to sing. Do you know about that?'

'Yes.' It had been in the file Miottis from the Rome and Venice newspapers of decades ago.

'They found another soprano, and Wellauer had a triumph.'

'What happened? Did she continue to see him?'

'This is where things get very cloudy, Papà says. Some people said they stayed together for a while after that. Others say that he broke it off as soon as she wasn't singing anymore.'

'What about the sisters?'

'Apparently, when Clemenza stopped singing, Wellauer picked up the slack with another one.' Michele had never been known for his delicacy of expression, especially when talking about women.

'And then what?'

'That went on for a while. And then there was what used to be called an "Illegal operation." Very easy to get, even then, my father tells me, if you knew the right people. And Wellauer did. No one knew much about it at the time, but she died. It might not even have been his child, but people seemed to

262

think so at the time.'

'And then what?'

'Well, she died, like I said. Nothing was ever printed, of course. You couldn't write about that sort of thing back then. And the cause of death was given in the papers as "after a sudden illness." Well, I suppose it was, in a sense.'

'And what about the other sister?'

'Papà thinks she went to live in Argentina, either right at the end of the war or soon after. He thinks she might have died there, but not until years later. Do you want to see if Papà can find out?'

'No, Michele. She's not important. What about Clemenza?'

'She tried to make a comeback after the war, but the voice wasn't the same. So she stopped singing. Papà said he thinks she lives here. Is that true?'

'Yes. I've spoken to her. Did your father remember anything else?'

'Only that he met Wellauer once, about fifteen years ago. Didn't like him, but he couldn't give any specific reason for it. Just didn't like him.'

Brunetti heard the change in Michele's voice that marked his passage from friend to journalist. 'Does any of this help, Guido?'

'I don't know, Michele. I just wanted to get some idea of the sort of man he was, and I wanted to find out about Santina.'

'Well, now you know.' Michele's voice was curt. He had sensed the policeman in the last answer.

'Michele, listen, it might be something, but I don't know yet.'

'Fine, fine. If it is, then it is.' He wouldn't bring himself to ask for the favor.

'If it does turn out to be anything, I'll call you, Michele.'

'Sure, sure; you do that, Guido. It's late, and I'm sure you want to get back to sleep. Call me if you need anything else, all right?'

'I promise. And thanks, Michele. Please thank your father for me.'

'He's the one who thanks you. This has made him feel important again. Good night, Guido.'

Before Brunetti could say anything, the line went dead. He switched off the light and slid down under the covers, aware now only of how cold it was in the room. In the dark, the only thing he could see was the photo in Clemenza Santina's room, the carefully arranged V in which the three sisters posed. One of them had died because of Wellauer, and another had perhaps lost her career as a result of knowing him. Only the little one had escaped him, and she had had to go to Argentina to do it.

CHAPTER NINETEEN

Early the next morning, Brunetti padded into the kitchen well before Paola was awake and, not fully conscious of his actions, started the coffee. He wandered back to the bathroom, splashed water on his face, and toweled it dry, avoiding the eyes of the man in the mirror. Before coffee, he didn't trust anyone.

He got back to the kitchen just as the coffeepot erupted. He didn't even bother to curse, just grabbed the pot from the flame and slapped off the gas. Pouring coffee into a cup, he spooned in three sugars and took the cup and himself out onto the terrace, which faced west. He hoped the morning chill would succeed in waking him if the coffee failed.

Scraggy-bearded, rumpled, he stood on the terrace and stared off at the point on the horizon where the Dolomites began. It must have rained heavily in the night, for the mountains had manifested themselves, sneaking close in the night and now magically visible in the crisp air. They would pack up and disappear before nightfall, he was sure, forced out of sight by waves of smoke that rose up ever fresh and new from the factories on the mainland or by the waves of humidity that crept in from the *laguna*.

From the left, the bells of San Polo rang out

265

for the six-thirty mass. Below him, in the house on the opposite side of the *calle*, the curtains snapped back and a naked man appeared at the window, utterly oblivious of Brunetti, who watched him from above. Suddenly the man sprouted another pair of hands, with red fingernails, which came reaching around him from behind. The man smiled, backed away from the window, and the curtains closed behind him.

The morning chill began to bite at Brunetti, driving him back into the kitchen, glad of its warmth and the presence of Paola, who now sat at the table and looked far more pleasant than anyone had a right to look before nine in the morning.

She gave him a cheery good morning; he returned a grunt. He set his empty coffee cup in the sink and picked up a second, this one topped with hot milk, which Paola had placed on the counter for him. The first had begun to prod him toward humanity; this one might finish the job.

'Was that Michele who called last night?'

'Um.' He rubbed at his face; he drank more coffee. She pulled a magazine from the end of the table and paged through it, sipping at her own mug. Not yet seven, and she's looking at Giorgio Armani jackets. She turned a page. He scratched his shoulder. Time passed.

'Was that Michele who called last night?'

'Yes.' She was pleased to have gotten a real

word from him and asked nothing more. 'He told me about Wellauer and Santina.'

'How long ago was all that?'

'About forty years, after the war. No, just before it, so it was more like fifty years.'

'What happened?'

'He got the sister pregnant, and she died after an abortion.'

'Did the old woman tell you any of this?'

'Not a word.'

'What are you going to do?'

'I'll have to talk to her again.'

'This morning?'

'No; I've got to go to the Questura. This afternoon. Tomorrow.' He realized how reluctant he was to return to that cold and misery.

'If you do go, wear your brown shoes.' They would help to protect him against the cold; nothing would protect him, or anyone, against the misery.

'Yes, thanks,' he said. 'Do you want to take a shower first?' he asked, remembering that she had an early class that morning.

'No, go ahead. I'll finish this and make some more coffee.'

As he walked by her, he bent to kiss her head, wondering how she managed to remain civil, even friendly, with the grumbling thing he was in the morning. He smelled the flowery scent of her shampoo and noticed that the hair just above her temple was faintly flecked with gray. He had never noticed it before, and he bent to kiss her there again, trembling at the fragility of this woman.

When he got to his office, he collected all the papers and reports that had accumulated concerning the conductor's death and began to read through them all again, some for the third or fourth time. The translations of the German reports were maddening. In their exhaustive attention to detail—as in the list of items taken from Wellauer's home during each of the two robberies—they were monuments to Germanic efficiency. In their almost total lack of information about the conductor's activities, personal or professional, during the war years, they gave evidence to an equally Germanic ability to remove a truth by simply ignoring it. Given the current president of Austria, Brunetti had to admit it was a tactic that met with remarkable success.

Wellauer had discovered his second wife's body. She had called a friend shortly before going down into the cellar to hang herself and had invited the woman to join her for a cup of coffee, a blending of the macabre and the mundane that upset Brunetti each time he read the report. Delayed, the woman had arrived only after Wellauer had found his wife's body and phoned the police. That meant he could just as easily have found anything she might have left—a note, a letter—and destroyed it.

Paola had given him Padovani's number that morning and told him that the journalist was planning to go back to Rome the following day. Knowing that the lunch could go on his expense account as 'interviewing a witness,' Brunetti called Padovani and invited him to lunch at Galleggiante, a restaurant Brunetti liked but could seldom afford. The other man agreed to meet him there at one.

He called down to the office where the translators worked and asked that the one who worked with German be sent up to him. When she arrived, a young woman he had often nodded to on the stairs or in the corridors of the building, he explained that he needed to put a call through to Berlin and might need her help if the person he spoke to didn't speak either English or Italian.

He dialed the number Signora Wellauer had given him. The phone was picked up on the fourth ring, and a woman's voice said crisply—Germans always sounded crisp to him—'Steinbrunner.' He passed the phone to the translator and could understand enough of what she said to glean that the doctor was in his office, not in his home, which was the number he had been given. He signaled the translator to make the next call, listened while she explained who she was and what the call was about. She held up her hand in a waiting gesture and nodded. Then she handed the phone to him, and he thought that some

269

miracle had occurred and Dr. Steinbrunner had answered his phone in Italian. Instead of a human voice, however, he heard mild-mannered, innocuous music coming across the Alps at the cost of the city of Venice. He handed the phone back to her and watched while she beat time in the air with her hand while they waited.

Suddenly she pulled the phone closer and said something in German. She spoke a few more sentences and then told Brunetti, 'His receptionist is transferring the call. She said he speaks English. Do you want to handle it, then?'

He nodded, took the phone from her, but waved for her to stay there. 'Wait and see if his English is as good as your German.'

Before he had finished this sentence, he heard a deep voice at the other end say, 'This is Dr. Erich Steinbrunner. May I know to whom I'm speaking?'

Brunetti introduced himself and signaled to the translator that she could leave. Before doing so, she leaned across his desk and pushed a pad and pencil toward him.

'Yes, Commissario, what can I do for you?'

'I'm investigating Maestro Wellauer's death, and I've learned from his widow that you were a close friend of his.'

'Yes, I was. My wife and I were friends of his for many years. His death has hurt us both.'

'I'm sure it has, Doctor.'

270

'I wanted to go there for the funeral, but my wife is in very poor health and cannot travel, and I didn't want to leave her.'

'I'm sure Signora Wellauer understands,' he said, surprised at the internationality of platitudes.

'I've spoken to Elizabeth,' said the doctor. 'She seems to be bearing it well.'

Cued by something in his tone, Brunetti said, 'She seemed somewhat . . . I'm not sure how to express this. She seemed somewhat reluctant that I call you, Doctor.' When that got no answer, he added, 'Perhaps it is too soon after his death for her to want to remember happier times.'

'Yes, that's possible,' the doctor responded dryly, making it clear that he thought it wasn't.

'Doctor, might I ask you a few questions?'

'Certainly.'

'I've examined the Maestro's datebook and saw that for the last few months of his life, he saw you and your wife frequently.'

'Yes, we had dinner three or four times.'

'But there were other times when your name alone was listed, Doctor, early in the morning. From the hour, I guessed that it might have been a professional visit—that is, that he was seeing you as a doctor and not as a friend.' Rather belatedly, he asked, 'Doctor, may I ask if you're a . . .' He stopped, not wanting to offend the man by asking if he was a general practitioner, and said, 'I'm sorry I've

271

forgotten the word in English. Could you tell me what your specialization is?'

'Nose, ear, and throat. But particularly throat. That's how I met Helmut, years ago. Years ago.' The man's voice grew warmer as he said this. 'I'm known here in Germany as "the singers' doctor."' Did he sound surprised at actually having to explain this to anyone?

'Is that why he was seeing you, because one of his singers was having trouble? Or was he having trouble with his voice?'

'No, there was nothing wrong with his throat or his voice. The first time, he asked me to meet for breakfast, and it was to speak about one of his singers.'

'And after that, Doctor, there were other morning dates listed in the book.'

'Yes, I saw him twice. The first time, he came to the office and asked me to give him an exam. And then, a week later, I gave him the results.'

'Would you tell me what those results were?'

'Before I do, can you tell me why you think this is important?'

'It seems that the Maestro was deeply preoccupied, worried about something. I've learned that from the people I've spoken to here. And so I am trying to find out what it might have been—anything that might have influenced his state of mind.'

'I'm afraid I don't see how this is pertinent,'

272

the doctor said.

'Doctor, I'm trying to learn as much as I can about the state of his health. Remember, anything I learn might help me find the person responsible for his death and see that he is punished.' Paola had often told him that the only way to appeal to a German was to invoke the law. The swiftness of the man's response seemed to prove her right.

'In that case, I'll willingly help you.'

'What kind of exam was it that you gave him?'

'As I said, his voice and throat were fine. Eyesight perfect. There was a slight hearing loss, however, and it was this that made him ask for the exam.'

'And what were the results, Doctor?'

'As I said, a slight hearing loss. Minimal. The sort of thing that is to be expected in a man of his age.' He immediately corrected himself: 'Of our age.'

'When did you give him the exam, Doctor? The dates I have are for October.'

'Yes, it was sometime then. I'd have to check my records to give you the exact dates, but it was about that time.'

'And do you remember the exact results?'

'No, no, I don't. But the loss was certainly less than ten percent, or I would have remembered.'

'Is this a significant loss, Doctor?'

'No, it's not.'

'Is it noticeable?'

'Noticeable?'

'Would it have interfered with his conducting?'

'That's exactly what Helmut wanted to know. I told him that it was nothing of that order, that the loss was barely measurable. He believed me. But that same morning, I had some other news to give him, and that news disturbed him.'

'What was that?'

'He had sent a young singer to me because she was having vocal problems. I discovered that she had nodes on her vocal cords that would have to be removed surgically. I told Helmut that it would be six months before she could sing again. He had been planning to have her sing with him in Munich this spring, but that was impossible.'

'Is there anything else you remember?'

'No, nothing in particular. He said he'd see me when they got back from Venice, but I took that to mean socially, the four of us together.'

Brunetti heard the slight hesitation in the man's voice and asked, 'Anything else, Doctor?'

'He asked me if I knew anyone in Venice I could recommend. As a doctor. I told him not to be silly, that he was as healthy as a horse. If he got sick, the opera would find him the best doctor they could. But he was insistent, wanted to know if there was someone I could recommend.'

'A specialist?'

'Yes. I finally gave him the name of a doctor I've consulted with a few times. He teaches at the University of Padova.'

'His name, Doctor?'

'Valerio Treponti. He also has a private practice in the city, but I don't have his number. Helmut didn't ask for it, seemed content merely to have the name.'

'Do you remember if he made a note of the name?'

'No, he didn't. In fact, at the time, I thought he was simply being obstinate. Besides, we were really there to talk about the singer.'

'One last question, Doctor.'

'Yes?'

'During the last few times you saw him, did you notice any change in him, any sign that he might have been preoccupied or concerned about something?'

The doctor's answer came after a long pause. 'There might have been something, but I don't know what it was.'

'Did you ask him about it?'

'One did not ask Helmut that sort of question.'

Brunetti restrained himself from saying that men who had been friends for more than forty years sometimes did. Instead he asked, 'Have you any idea what it might have been?'

This pause was just as long as the first. 'I

thought it might have something to do with Elizabeth. That's why I didn't mention it to Helmut. He was always very sensitive about her, about the difference in their ages. But perhaps you could ask her, Commissario.'

'Yes, Doctor. I plan to do that.'

'Good. Is there anything else? If not, I really must get back to my patients.'

'No, nothing else. It was very kind of you to talk to me. You've been very helpful.'

'I hope so. I hope you find whoever did this and punish him.'

'I'll certainly do whatever I can, Doctor,' Brunetti said politely, failing to add that his only interest was in the first and he didn't care at all about the second. But perhaps Germans thought about such things differently.

As soon as the line was clear, he dialed information and asked for the number of Dr. Valerio Treponti in Padova. When he reached the doctor's office, he was told that Treponti was busy with a patient and could not come to the phone. Brunetti explained who he was, said the call was urgent, and told the receptionist he would hold on.

While he waited, Brunetti leafed through the morning papers. Wellauer's death had disappeared from the major national newspapers; it was present in the *Gazzettino*, on the second page of the second section, because a music scholarship in his name was being established at the conservatory.

The line clicked, and a deep, resonant voice said, 'Treponti.'

'Doctor, this is Commissario Brunetti of the Venice police.'

'So I was told. What do you want?'

'I'd like to know if, during the last month, you've had as a patient a tall, elderly man who spoke Italian, very good Italian, but with a German accent.'

'How old?'

'About seventy.'

'You mean the Austrian. What was his name? Doerr? That's it, yes, Hilmar Doerr. But he wasn't German; he was Austrian. Same thing, really. What do you want to know about him?'

'Could you describe him to me, Doctor?'

'Are you sure this is important? I've got six patients in my waiting room, and I have to be at the hospital in an hour.'

'Could you describe him to me, Doctor?'

'Haven't I done that? Tall, blue eyes, middle sixties.'

'When did you see him?'

In the background at the other end of the line, Brunetti heard another voice say something. Then all sound disappeared as the doctor covered the mouthpiece of the phone. A minute passed, and then he was back, sounding even more hurried and impatient. 'Commissario, I can't speak to you now. I have important things to do.'

Brunetti let that pass and asked, 'Could you see me today, Doctor, if I came to your office?'

'At five this afternoon. I can give you twenty minutes. Here.' He hung up before Brunetti could ask him the address. Patiently, forcing himself to remain calm, he redialed the number and asked the woman who answered if she would give him the address of the doctor's office. When she did so, Brunetti thanked her with deliberate politeness and hung up.

He sat and thought about the easiest way to get to Padova. Patta, he knew, would order a car, a driver, and perhaps a pair of motorcycle escorts, should the traffic in terrorists be especially heavy on the autostrada that day. Brunetti's rank entitled him to a car, but his desire to save time led him to call the station and ask when the afternoon trains to Padova left. The express to Milan would get him there in plenty of time to reach the doctor's office by five. He would have to go to the train station directly after lunch with Padovani.

CHAPTER TWENTY

Padovani was waiting inside the restaurant when Brunetti got there. The journalist stood between the bar and the glass case filled with various antipasti: periwinkles, cuttlefish, shrimp. They shook hands briefly and were shown to their table by Signora Antonia, the Junoesque waitress who reigned supreme here. Once seated, they delayed the discussion of crime and gossip while they consulted with Signora Antonia about lunch. Though a written menu did exist, few regular clients ever bothered with it; most had never seen it. The day's selections and specialties were listed in Antonia's head. She quickly ran through the list, though Brunetti knew that this was the merest of formalities. She quickly decided that what they wanted to eat was the antipasto di mare, the risotto with shrimp, and the grilled branzino, which she assured them had come fresh that morning from the fish market. Padovani asked if he might possibly, if the signora advised it, have a green salad as well. She gave his request the attention it deserved, assented, and said they wanted a bottle of the house white wine, which she went to get.

When the wine was on the table and the first glass poured, Brunetti asked Padovani how much work he had to do before he left Venice. The critic explained that he had two gallery openings to review, one in Treviso and one in Milan, but he'd probably do them by phone.

'Call the reviews down to the newspaper in Rome?' Brunetti asked.

'Oh, no,' Padovani replied, snapping a bread stick in two and eating half. 'I do the reviews by phone.'

279

'Art reviews?' Brunetti asked. 'Of paintings?'

'Certainly,' Padovani answered. 'You don't expect me to waste my time going to see that crap, do you?' When he saw Brunetti's confusion, he explained. 'I know both of the painters' work, which is worthless. Both of them have hired the galleries, and both of them will send friends along to buy the paintings. One of them is the wife of a lawyer in Milan, and the other is the son of a neurosurgeon in Treviso, who runs the most expensive private clinic in the province. Both of them have too much time and nothing to do, so they have decided to become artists.' He said the last word with undisguised contempt.

Padovani interrupted himself long enough to sit back and smile broadly as Signora Antonia placed the oblong plates of antipasto in front of them.

'What sort of reviews do you write?'

'Oh, that depends,' Padovani said, spearing a chunk of octopus with his fork. 'For the doctor's son, I say he shows "complete ignorance of color and line." But the lawyer is a friend of one of the directors of the newspaper, so his wife "displays a mastery of composition and draftsmanship," when, in fact, she couldn't draw a square without making it look like a triangle.'

'Does it bother you?' Brunetti asked.

'Does what bother me—writing what I don't

believe?' Padovani asked, breaking another bread stick in half.

'Yes.'

'In the beginning. I suppose it did. But then I realized it was the only way I could be free to write the reviews I really care about.' He saw Brunetti's look and smiled. 'Come now, Guido, don't tell me you've never ignored a piece of evidence or written a report in a way to suggest something other than what that evidence suggested.'

Before he could answer this, Antonia was back. Padovani finished the last shrimp on his plate and smiled up at her. 'Delicious, Signora.' She took his plate, then Brunetti's.

Immediately she was back with the risotto, steaming and rich. When she saw Padovani reach out for the salt on the table, she said, 'There's enough salt already.' He pulled his hand back as though it had been burned and picked up his fork.

'But come, Guido, you didn't invite me here—at the city's expense, I hope—to chat about the progress of my career, nor to examine my conscience. You said that you wanted more information.'

'I'd like to know what else you learned about Signora Santina.'

Delicately, Padovani extracted a small piece of shrimp shell from his mouth, placed it on the side of his plate, and said, 'I'm afraid, then, that I'll have to pay for my own lunch.'

'Why?'

'Because I can't give you any more information about her. Narciso was just on his way out when I called him, and all he had time to do was give me the address. So all I know is what I told you that night. I'm sorry.'

Brunetti thought it artless of him to make the remark about paying for his lunch. 'Well, then, perhaps you could tell me about some of the other people instead.'

'I'll confess, Guido, that I've been busy. I've called a number of my friends here, and in Milan and Rome, and you have but to speak their names and I shall become a very fountain of information.'

'Flavia Petrelli?'

'Ah, the divine Flavia.' He placed a forkful of risotto in his mouth and pronounced it excellent. 'You would no doubt also like to know about the equally divine Miss Lynch, I suppose?'

'I'd like to know whatever you know about either one of them.'

Padovani ate some more of his risotto and pushed it aside. 'Do you want to ask me specific questions, or do you want me simply to chatter on?'

'The chatter would probably be best.'

'Yes. No doubt. So I've often been told.' He sipped at his wine and began. 'I forget where Flavia studied. Possibly Rome. In any case, the unexpected happened, as it always does, and

282

she was asked to step in at the last minute and replace the ever ailing Caballé. She did, the critics went wild, and she was famous overnight.' He leaned forward to touch the back of Brunetti's hand with one finger. 'I thought I might, for dramatic purposes, divide the story into two parts: professional and personal.' Brunetti nodded.

'That, pretty much, was the professional. She was famous, and she remained that way. Remains that way.' He sipped at his wine again, poured some more into his glass.

'So now for the personal. Enter the husband. She was singing in the Liceo in Barcelona, about two or three years after her success in Rome. He was something important in Spain. Plastics, factories, I think; in any case, something very dull but very profitable. In any case, lots of money, lots of friends with big houses and important names. Fairy-tale romance, garlands of flowers, truckloads of the things wherever she happened to be singing, jewels, all the usual temptations, and La Petrelli—who is, between parentheses, just a simple little country girl from some small town near Trento—went and fell in love and married him. And his factories, and his plastics, and his important friends.'

Antonia arrived and carried away their plates, clearly disapproving of the fact that Padovani's was still half full.

'She continued to sing; she continued to

283

grow more famous. And he seemed to like traveling with her, liked being the Latin husband of the famous diva, meeting more famous people, seeing his picture in the papers—all the sort of thing that people of his class need. Then came the children, but she continued to sing, and she continued to become more famous. But it soon became evident that things were no longer as honeymoonish as they had been. She canceled a performance, then another. Soon after that, she stopped singing for a year, went back to Spain with him. And didn't sing.'

Antonia approached the table with a long metal tray upon which lay their branzino. She placed it on a small serving table next to them and very efficiently cut two portions of tender white fish from it. She placed the portions in front of them. 'I hope you like this.' The men exchanged a glance in silent acceptance of the threat.

'Thank you, Signora,' Padovani said. 'Might I trouble you for the green salad.'

'When you finish the fish,' she said, and went back toward the kitchen. This, Brunetti reminded himself, is one of the best restaurants in the city.

Padovani took a few bites of the fish. 'And then she was back, as suddenly as she had disappeared, and the voice, during the year when she hadn't sung in public, had grown bigger, become more that immense, clear voice she has now. But now the husband was no longer in sight, and then there was a quiet separation, and an even more quiet divorce, which she got here, and then, when it became possible, in Spain.'

'What were the grounds for the divorce?' Brunetti asked.

Padovani held up an admonitory hand. 'All in good time. I want this to have the sound and pace of a nineteenth-century novel. So she began to sing again, our Flavia, and as I said, she was more magnificent than ever. But we never saw her. Not at dinners, not at parties, not at the performances of other singers. She had become something of a recluse, lived quietly with her children in Milan, where she was singing regularly.' He leaned across the table. 'Is the suspense growing?'

'Agonizingly so,' said Brunetti, and took another mouthful of fish. 'And the divorce?'

Padovani laughed. 'Paola warned me about this, said you were a ferret. All right, all right, you shall have the truth. But unfortunately, the truth, as it so often has a habit of being, is quite pedestrian. It turns out that he beat her, quite regularly and quite severely. I suppose it was his idea of how a real man treats his wife.' He shrugged. 'I wouldn't know.'

'But she left?' Brunetti asked.

'Not until he put her in the hospital. Even in Spain, some people are willing to draw the line at this. She went to the Italian embassy with

285

her children. With no money and no passports. Our ambassador at the time, like all of them, was a lick-spittle and tried to send her back to her husband. But his wife, a Sicilian—and let not a word be said against them—stormed down to the consular section and stood there while three passports were made out, and then she drove Flavia and her children to the airport, where she charged three first-class tickets to Milan to the embassy account and waited with them until the plane took off. It appears that she had seen Flavia sing Odabella three years before and felt she owed her at least that much.'

Brunetti found himself wondering just how much of this could be important to Wellauer's death and, made suspicious by Padovani's ironical manner, wondering how much of it was true.

As if reading his mind, Padovani leaned forward and said, 'It's true. Believe me.'

'How did you learn all this?'

'Guido, you've been a policeman long enough to have learned that as soon as a person reaches a certain level of notoriety, there are no more secrets.' Brunetti smiled in agreement, and Padovani continued. 'Now we have the interesting part, the return of our heroine to life. And the cause, as always in stories like this, is love. Well, at any rate,' he added after a reflective pause, 'lust.'

Brunetti, aware of the man's obvious

enjoyment of the story he was telling, was tempted to take his revenge by telling Antonia that Padovani hadn't eaten all his fish but had hidden it in his napkin.

'Her period of seclusion lasted almost three years. And then there was a series of, well, involvements. The first was a tenor she happened to be singing with. A very bad tenor but, luckily for her, a very nice man. Unluckily for her, he had an equally nice wife, to whom he very quickly returned. Then there were, in quick succession'—he began to tick them off on his fingers as he named them—'a baritone, another tenor, a dancer, or perhaps that was the director, a doctor who seems to have slipped in unnoticed, and finally, wonder of wonders, a countertenor. And then, as quickly as all this had begun, it stopped.' So did Padovani, while Antonia set his salad down in front of him. He prepared it, adding far too much vinegar for Brunetti's taste. 'She was seen with no one for about a year. And suddenly *l'americana* was on the scene and seemed to have conquered the divine Flavia.' Sensing Brunetti's interest, he asked, 'Do you know her?'

'Yes.'

'And what do you think of her?'

'I like her.'

'So do I,' agreed Padovani. 'This thing between her and Flavia makes no sense at all.'

Brunetti felt uncomfortable about showing

287

any interest in this, so he didn't ask Padovani to expand on the subject.

Asking him to do so was hardly necessary. 'They met about three years ago, during that China exhibition. They were seen a few times after that, having lunch together, going to the theater, but then *l'americana* had to go back to China.'

All the coy archness dropped out of Padovani's voice. 'I've read her books on Chinese art, the two that have been translated into Italian and the short one in English. If she's not the most important archaeologist working in the field today, she soon will be. I don't understand what she sees in Flavia, for Flavia, though she might be a genius, is really something of a bitch.'

'But what about love?' Brunetti asked, then amended the question as Padovani had. 'Or lust?'

'That's all right for the likes of Flavia; it doesn't take her away from her work. But the other one has in her hands one of the most important archaeological discoveries of our time, and I think she has the judgment and the skill to—' Padovani stopped suddenly, picked up his wine, and emptied his glass. 'Excuse me. I seldom get carried away like this. It must be the influence of the stately Antonia.'

Even though he knew it had nothing to do with the investigation, Brunetti couldn't stop himself from asking, 'Is she the first, ah, woman lover Petrelli had?'

'I don't think so, but the others have been passing affairs.'

'And this? Is it different?'

'For which one?'

'Both.'

'Since it's gone on for three years, I'd say yes, it's serious. For both of them.' Padovani picked the last green leaf from the bottom of his salad bowl and said, 'Perhaps I'm being unfair to Flavia. It costs her a lot, this affair.'

'In what way?'

'There are a great number of lesbian singers,' he explained. 'Strangely enough, most of them seem to be mezzo-sopranos. But that's neither here nor there. The difficulty is that they are far less tolerated than their male colleagues who also happen to be gay. So none of them dare to be open about their lives, and most of them are very discreet, choosing to disguise their lover as their secretary or their agent. But Flavia can hardly disguise Brett as anything. And so there is talk, and I'm sure there are looks and whispers when they come into a room together.'

Brunetti had only to remember the *portiere*'s tone to know how true this was. 'Have you been to their apartment here?'

'Those skylights,' Padovani said, and they both laughed.

'How did she manage that?' asked Brunetti, who had been refused a permit to install thermal windows.

'Her family is one of those old American ones, which stole its money more than a hundred years ago and is, therefore, respectable. An uncle of hers left her the apartment, which I think he won at cards about fifty years ago. As for the windows, the story goes that she tried to get someone to do them for her, but no one would lift a finger without a permit. So, finally, she simply went up on the roof, took off the tiles, cut holes in the roof, and built the frames.'

'Didn't anyone see her?' In Venice, all a person had to do was lift a hammer to the outside of a building and phones would be lifted in every house in the area. 'Didn't anyone call the police?'

'You've seen how high she is. No one who saw her up there could really tell what she was doing and would assume she was just checking the roof. Or fixing a tile.'

'And then what?'

'Once the windows were in, she called the office of the city planner and told them what she had done. She asked them to send someone around to figure out how much the fine would be.'

'And?' marveled Brunetti, amazed that a foreigner would come up with so perfectly Italianate a solution.

'A few months later, that's what they actually did. But when they got there and saw how well the work had been done, they wouldn't believe her when she told them she had done the job herself and insisted that she give them the names of her "accomplices." She repeated that she had done it herself, and they continued to refuse to believe her. Finally, she picked up the phone and dialed the mayor's office and asked to speak to "Lucio." This with two architects from the city planning office standing there with their rulers in their hands. She had a few words with "Lucio" handed the phone to one of them, and said that the mayor wanted to have a word with him.' Padovani mimicked the whole thing, ending by passing an invisible phone across the table.

'So the mayor had a few words with them, and they climbed out on the roof and measured the skylights, calculated the fine, and she sent them back to their office with a check in their hands.' Brunetti threw back his head and laughed so loud that people sitting at other tables looked their way.

'Wait, it gets better,' Padovani said. 'The check was made out to cash, and she never received an acknowledgment that the fine had been paid. And I'm told that the blueprints in the office of deeds at city hall have been changed, and the skylights are on them.' They laughed together at this victory of ingenuity over authority.

'Where does all this money come from?' Brunetti asked.

'Oh, God, who knows? Where does American money come from? Steel. Railways. You know how it is over there. It doesn't matter if you murder or rob to get it. The trick is in keeping it for a hundred years, and then you're aristocrats.'

'Is that so different from here?' Brunetti asked.

'Of course,' Padovani explained, smiling. 'Here we have to keep it five hundred years before we're aristocrats. And there's another difference. In Italy, you have to be well-dressed. In America, it's difficult to tell which are the millionaires and which are the servants.' Remembering Brett's boots, Brunetti wanted to demur. But there was no stopping Padovani, who was off again. 'They have a magazine there. I can't remember which one it is, but each year they publish a list of the richest people in America. Only the names and where the money comes from. I think they must be afraid to publish all their pictures. The ones they do, it's enough to make a person believe that money really is the root of all evil or, at the very least, bad taste. The women all look as though they'd been hung over open fires and dried. And the men, good God, the men. God, who dresses them? Do you think they *eat* plastic?'

Whatever answer Brunetti might have given was cut short by Antonia's return. She asked if they wanted fruit or cake for dessert.

Nervously, they both said they would forgo dessert and have coffee instead. She didn't like it, but she cleared the table.

'But to answer your question,' Padovani said when she was gone, 'I don't know where the money comes from, but there seems to be no end to it. Her uncle was very generous to various hospitals and charities in the city, and she seems to be doing the same, though most of what she gives is specifically for restoration.'

'Then that would explain the help from "Lucio."'

'Certainly.'

'What about her personal life?'

Padovani gave him a strange glance, having long since realized how little any of this had to do with the investigation of Wellauer's death. But that could hardly be enough to stop him from telling what he knew. After all, gossip's greatest charms was its utter superfluity. 'Very little. I mean, there's not much that anyone knows for sure. She seems always to have been of this persuasion, but almost nothing is known about her personal life before she came here.'

'Which was when?'

'About seven years ago. That is, that it became her permanent address. She spent years here, with her uncle, when she was a child.'

'That explains the Veneziano, then.'

Padovani laughed. 'It is strange to hear someone who isn't one of us speak it, isn't it?'

'Yes.'

At this point, Antonia returned with the coffees, bringing with her two small glasses of grappa, which she told them were offered with the compliments of the restaurant. Though neither of them wanted the fiery liquid, they made a show of sipping at it and praising its quality. She moved off, suspicious, and Brunetti caught her looking back at them from the door of the kitchen, as if she expected them to pour the grappa into their shoes.

'What else about her personal life?' Brunetti asked, frankly curious.

'She keeps it very personal, I think. I have a friend in New York who went to school with her. Harvard, of course. Then Yale. After which she went to Taiwan and then to the mainland. She was one of the first Western archaeologists to go there. In '83 or '84, I think. She'd written her first book by then, while she was in Taiwan.'

'Isn't she young to have done all this?'

'Yes, I suppose she is. But she's very, very good.'

Antonia sailed past them, carrying coffees to the next table, and Brunetti signaled to her, mimed writing the check. She nodded.

'I hope some of this will be of help to you,' said Padovani, meaning it.

'So do I,' replied Brunetti, unwilling to admit that it wouldn't, equally unwilling to admit that he was simply interested in the two women.

'If there's any other way I can help you, please call,' Padovani said, then added, 'We could come here again. But if we do, I insist that you bring along two of your biggest policemen to protect me against . . . Ah, Signora Antonia,' he said effortlessly as she came up to the table and placed the bill in front of Brunetti. 'We have eaten superbly well and hope to return as soon as possible.' The results of this flattery astonished Brunetti. For the first time that afternoon, Antonia smiled at them, a radiant blossoming of pure pleasure that revealed deep dimples at either side of her mouth and perfect, brilliant teeth. Brunetti envied Padovani his technique; it would prove invaluable in questioning suspects.

CHAPTER TWENTY-ONE

The intercity train made its way slowly across the causeway that joined Venice to the mainland and was soon passing to the right of the industrial horror of Marghera. Like a person who cannot keep from prodding an aching tooth with his tongue, Brunetti failed to look away from the forest of cranes and smokestacks and the miasma of filthy air that drifted back across the waters of the *laguna* toward the city from which he had come.

Soon after Mestre, barren winter fields replaced the industrial blight, but the general prospect was not much improved. After the devastating drought of the summer, most of the fields were covered with unharvested corn that had proved too expensive to irrigate and too parched to pick.

The train was only ten minutes late, so he was on time for his appointment with the doctor, whose office was in a modern building not far from the university. Because he was Venetian, Brunetti didn't think to use the elevator and climbed the stairs to the third floor. When he opened the door to the office, he found the waiting room empty save for a white-uniformed woman who sat behind a desk. 'The doctor will see you now,' she said when he entered, not bothering to ask who he was. Did it show? Brunetti wondered yet again.

Dr. Treponti was a small, neat man with a short dark beard and brown eyes that were slightly magnified by the thick glasses he wore. His cheeks were as round and tight as a chipmunk's, and he carried a small marsupial paunch in front of him. He didn't smile when Brunetti came in, but he did offer his hand. Gesturing to a chair in front of his desk, he waited for Brunetti to sit down before resuming his own chair, and then he asked, 'What is it you'd like to know?'

Brunetti took a small publicity still of the

conductor from his inside pocket and held it out to the doctor. 'Is this the man who came to you? The man you said was Austrian?'

The doctor took the photo, studied it briefly, and handed it back to Brunetti. 'Yes, that's the man.'

'Why did he come to see you, Doctor?'

'Aren't you going to tell me who he is? If the police are involved in this and his name isn't Hilmar Doerr?'

Brunetti was amazed that anyone could live in Italy and not know about the death of the conductor, but he simply said, 'I'll tell you that after you tell me what you can about him, Doctor.' Before the other man could object, he added, 'I don't want anything you might tell me to be colored by that information.'

'This isn't political, is it?' the doctor asked, with the deep distrust that only Italians can put into the question.

'No, it has nothing to do with politics. I give you my word.'

However dubious the value of that commodity might have seemed to the doctor, he agreed. 'Very well.' He opened the manila folder on his desk and said, 'I'll have my nurse give you a copy of this later.'

'Thank you, Doctor.'

'As I said, he told me that his name was Hilmar Doerr, and he said he was an Austrian who lived in Venice. Because he was not part of the Italian health plan, he came to me as a private patient. I saw no reason not to believe him.' As he spoke, the doctor studied the notes on the lined paper in front of him. Brunetti could see how neat they were, even upside down.

'He said that he had suffered some loss of hearing during the last months and asked me to check it. This was,' the doctor said, flipping the chart back to the front and checking the date there, 'on the third of November.

'I performed the usual tests and found that there had been, as he said, a significant hearing loss.' He anticipated Brunetti's question and answered it. 'I estimated that he still had sixty to seventy percent of normal hearing.

'What confused me was his saying that he had not had any hearing problems before; they had suddenly appeared in the last month or so.'

'Would this sort of thing be common in a man of his age?'

'He told me he was sixty-two. I assume that, too, is a lie? If you could give me his proper age, I might be better able to answer the question.'

'He was seventy-four.'

Hearing this, Dr. Treponti turned the file back to the cover, crossed out something, and wrote a correction above it. 'I don't think that would change things,' he said, 'at least not substantially. The damage was sudden, and because it was to nerve tissue, it was irreversible.'

'Are you sure about that, Doctor?'

He didn't even bother to answer. 'Because of the nature of the loss, I suggested he return in two weeks, when I repeated the tests and found that there had been even more loss, and more damage. Also irreversible.'

'How much more?'

'I would estimate,' he said, glancing down again at the figures on the chart, 'another ten percent. Perhaps a bit more.'

'Was there anything you could do to help him?'

'I suggested one of the new hearing aids. I hoped—I didn't really believe—that it would help him.'

'And did it?'

'I don't know.'

'I beg your pardon?'

'He never returned to my office.'

Brunetti calculated for a moment. The second visit had taken place well into rehearsals for the opera. 'Can you tell me more about this hearing aid?'

'It's very small, mounted on a pair of normal-looking glasses, with clear or prescription lenses. It works on the principle of—' He broke off. 'I'm not sure why this is important here.'

Instead of explaining, Brunetti asked, 'Is it something that might have helped?'

'That's difficult to say. So much of what we hear, we don't hear with our ears.' Seeing Brunetti's confusion, he explained. 'We do a good deal of lipreading, we fill in missing words from the context of the others we do hear. When people wear these hearing aids, they've finally accepted the idea that something is wrong with their hearing. So all of their other senses begin to work overtime, trying to fill in the missing signals and messages, and because the only thing that's been added is the hearing aid, they believe it's the hearing aid that's helping them, when the only thing that's happened, really, is that their other senses are working to their maximum to make up for the ears that can no longer hear as well.'

'Was that the case here?'

'As I told you, I can't be sure. When I fitted him with the hearing aid, during the second appointment, he insisted that he could hear better. He responded more accurately to my questions, but they all do, no matter whether there's any real physical improvement. I'm in front of them, asking questions directly to them, looking at them, seen by them. With the tests, where the voices come to them through earphones and there are no visual signals, there's seldom any improvement, not in cases like his.'

Brunetti considered all this, then asked, 'Doctor, you said that when he returned for the second examination, there had been even more loss of hearing. Have you any idea what could cause a loss like that, so sudden?'

It was clear from his smile that the doctor had been anticipating this question. He folded his hands in front of him, much in the fashion of a television doctor on a soap opera. 'It could be age, but that really wouldn't explain a loss as sudden as his. It could be a sudden infection of the ear, but then there would very likely be pain, and he complained of none, or loss of balance, and he said he had not experienced that. It could have been continued use of diuretics, but he said he was taking none.'

'You discussed all this with him, Doctor?'

'Of course I did. He was more concerned about it than I've ever seen a patient be, and as my patient, he had a right to know.'

'Certainly.'

Placated, the doctor continued. 'Another possibility I mentioned to him was antibiotics. He seemed interested in this possibility, so I explained that the dosage would have to have been very heavy.'

'Antibiotics?' Brunetti asked.

'Yes. One of the side effects, not at all common but possible, is damage to the auditory nerve. But as I said, the dose would have to be massive. I asked him if he was taking any, but he said no. So with all the possibilities excluded, the only reasonable explanation would be his advanced age. As a doctor, I wasn't satisfied with that, and I still am not.' He glanced down at his calendar. 'If I could see him now, enough time has passed so I could at least check the deterioration. If it continued at the same rate as I observed in the second examination, he would be almost entirely deaf by now. Unless, of course, I was mistaken and it was an infection I didn't notice or that didn't show up on the tests I conducted.' He closed the file and asked, 'Is there any chance that he will return for another examination?'

'The man is dead,' Brunetti said flatly.

Nothing registered in the doctor's eyes. 'May I ask the cause of death?' he asked, then hastened to explain: 'I'd like to know in case there was some sort of infection I overlooked.'

'He was poisoned.'

'Poisoned,' the doctor repeated, then he added, 'I see, I see.' He considered that and then asked, strangely diffident, acknowledging that the advantage had passed to Brunetti, 'And what poison, may I ask?'

'Cyanide.'

'Oh.' He sound disappointed.

'Is it important, Doctor?'

'If it had been arsenic, there would have been some hearing loss, of the sort he appeared to have. That is, if it was given over a long period of time. But cyanide. No, I don't think so.' He considered this for a moment, opened the file, made a brief note, then drew a heavy horizontal line under what he had just added. 'Was an autopsy performed? I believe they are obligatory in cases like this.'

'Yes.'

'And was any note made of his hearing?'

'I don't believe any special search was made.'

'That's unfortunate,' the doctor said, then corrected himself: 'But it probably wouldn't have shown anything.' He closed his eyes, and Brunetti could see him leafing through textbooks in his mind, pausing here and there to read a passage with particular attention. Finally, he opened his eyes and looked across at Brunetti. 'No, it wouldn't have been evident.'

Brunetti stood. 'If you could have your nurse make me a copy of your file, Doctor, I won't take any more of your time.'

'Yes, certainly,' said the doctor, getting to his feet and following Brunetti to the door. In the outer office, he handed the file to his nurse and asked her to make a copy for the commissario, then he turned to one of the patients who had appeared while he was speaking to Brunetti and said, 'Signora Mosca, you may come in now.' He nodded to Brunetti and followed the woman into his office, closing the door behind them.

The nurse returned and handed him a copy of the file, still warm from the copying machine. He thanked her and left. In the elevator, which he remembered to take, he opened it and read the final note: 'Patient dead of cyanide poisoning. Results of suggested treatment unknown.'

CHAPTER TWENTY-TWO

He was home before eight, only to discover that Paola had taken the children to see a film. She had left a note saying that a woman had called twice during the afternoon but had not left her name. He rooted around in the refrigerator, finding only salami and cheese and a plastic bag of black olives. He pulled them all out and set them on the table, then went back to the counter and got himself a bottle of red wine and a glass. He popped an olive into his mouth, poured a glass of wine, then spat the pit into his cupped hand. He looked around for a place to put it while he ate another. And another. Finally, he tossed them into the garbage bag under the sink.

He cut two slices of bread, put some salami between them, and poured a glass of wine. On the table was that week's issue of *Epoca*, which Paola must have been reading at the table. He sat down, flipped open the magazine, and took a bite of his sandwich. And the phone rang.

Chewing, he walked slowly into the living

room, hoping that the ringing would stop before he got there. On the seventh ring, he picked it up and said his name.

'Hello. This is Brett,' she said quickly. 'I'm sorry to call you at home, but I'd like to talk to you. If that's possible.'

'Is it something important?' he asked, knowing it had to be for her to call but hoping, nevertheless, that it was not.

'Yes. It's Flavia.' He knew that too. 'She's had a letter from his lawyer.' There was no need to ask her whose lawyer. 'And we talked about the argument she had with him.' This would have to be Wellauer. Brunetti knew he should volunteer to meet her, but he lacked the will to do it.

'Guido, are you there?' He heard the tension in her voice, even as he heard her struggle to keep it calm.

'Yes. Where are you?'

'I'm at home. But I can't see you here.' Her voice caught at that, and he suddenly wanted to talk to her.

'Brett, listen to me. Do you know the Giro bar, the one just near Santa Marina?'

'Yes.'

'I'll meet you there in fifteen minutes.'

'Thank you, Guido.'

'Fifteen minutes,' he repeated, and hung up. He scribbled a note for Paola, saying he had to go out, and ate the rest of his sandwich as he went down the steps.

305

Giro's was a smoky, dismal place, one of the few bars in the city that stayed open after ten at night. The management had changed hands a few months before, and the new owners had done their best to tart the place up, adding white curtains and slick music. But it had failed to become a hip pub, while ceasing to be a local bar where friends met for a coffee or a drink. It had neither class nor charm, only overpriced wine and too much smoke.

He saw her when he walked in, sitting at a table in the rear, looking at the door and being looked at in her turn by the three or four young men who stood at the bar, drinking small glasses of red wine and talking in voices that were meant to float back and impress her. He felt their eyes on him as he made his way to her table. The warmth of her smile made him glad he had come.

'Thank you,' she said simply.

'Tell me about the letter.'

She looked at the table, where her hands lay, palms down, and she kept them there while she spoke to him. 'It's from a lawyer in Milan, the same one who fought the divorce. He says that he has received information that Flavia is leading "an immoral and unnatural life"—those were the words. She showed me the letter. "An immoral and unnatural life."' She looked up at him and tried to smile. 'I guess that's me, eh?' She brought one hand up, embracing emptiness. 'I don't believe it,' she said, shaking her head from side to side. 'He said that they were going to file a suit against her and ask . . . they would demand that the children be returned to the custody of their father. This was an official notice of their intention.' She stopped and covered her eyes with one hand. 'They're officially giving us notice.' She moved her hand to her mouth and covered it, as though keeping the words inside. 'No, not us, just Flavia. Only her—that they're going to reinstitute proceedings.'

Brunetti sensed the arrival of a waiter and waved him back with an angry hand. When the man had retreated out of hearing, he asked, 'What else?' She tried; he could see that she tried to push the words out, but she couldn't do it. She looked up and gave him a nervous grin, just the sort Chiara produced when she had done something wrong and had to tell him about it.

She muttered something, lowered her head.

'What, Brett? I didn't hear.'

She looked at the top of the table. 'Had to tell someone. No one else.'

'No one else?' She had spent much of her life in this city, and there was no one she could tell this to, only the policeman whose job it was to find out if she loved a murderess?

'No one?'

'I've told no one about Flavia,' she said, meeting his glance this time. 'She said she wanted no gossip, that it could damage her

307

career. I've never told anyone about her. About us.' He remembered, in that instant, Padovani's telling the tale of Paola's first blush of love for him, of the way she carried on, telling all her friends, talking of nothing else. The world had permitted her not only joy but public joy. And this woman had been in love, there was no question of that, for three years and had told no one. Except him. The policeman.

'Was your name mentioned in the letter?'

She shook her head.

'What about Flavia? What did she say?'

Biting her lips, she lifted one hand and pointed it at her heart.

'She blames you?'

Just like Chiara, she nodded and then dragged the back of her hand under her nose. It came away wet and gleaming. He pulled out his handkerchief and handed it to her. She took it, but seeming not to have any idea what she was supposed to do with it, she sat with it in her hand, tears running down her face, nose dripping. Feeling not a little foolish but remembering that, after all, he was someone's father, he took the handkerchief and patted at her face with it. She started back in her seat and took the handkerchief from him. She wiped her face, blew her nose, and put it in her pocket, the second he had lost in a week.

'She said it was my fault, that none of this would have happened if it weren't for me.' Her voice was tight and raspy. She grimaced. 'The awful thing is it's true. I know it's not really true, but I can't make it not be true, the way she says it is.'

'Did the letter say where the information came from?'

'No. But it had to be Wellauer.'

'Good.'

She looked at him in surprise. 'How can that be good? The lawyer said they were going to bring charges. That would make everything public.'

'Brett,' he said, voice level and calm. 'Think about it. If his witness was Wellauer, he'd have to testify. And even if he were still alive, he'd never get himself caught in something like this. It's just a threat.'

'But still, if they bring charges . . .'

'All he's trying to do is scare you. And look how he's succeeded. No court, even an Italian court, would admit anything on hearsay, and that's all the letter is, without the person who wrote it to give evidence.' He watched her as she considered this. 'There isn't any evidence, is there?'

'What do you mean by evidence?'

'Letters. I don't know. Conversations.'

'No, nothing like that. I've never written anything, not even from China. And Flavia's always too busy to write.'

'What about her friends? Do they know?'

'I don't know. It's not something that people

309

like to talk about.'

'Then I don't think you have anything to worry about.'

She tried to smile, tried to convince herself that he had somehow managed to bring her back from grief to safety. 'Really?'

'Really,' he said, and smiled. 'I spend a lot of time with lawyers, and all this one is trying to do is scare you and threaten you.'

'Well,' she began, with a laugh that turned into a hiccup, 'he certainly managed to do that.' Then, under her breath, 'The bastard.'

With that, Brunetti thought it was safe to order two brandies, which the waiter was very quick to bring. When the drinks arrived, she said, 'She was awful.'

He took a sip and waited for her to say more.

'She said terrible things.'

'We all do sometimes.'

'I don't,' she retorted immediately, and he suspected that she didn't, that she would use language as a tool and not a weapon.

'She'll forget it, Brett. People who say such things always do.'

She shrugged, dismissing that as irrelevant. She, clearly, wouldn't forget.

'What are you going to do?' he asked, really interested in her answer.

'Go home. See if she's there. See what happens.'

He realized that he had never so much as

bothered to learn if Petrelli had her own home in the city, had never initiated an investigation of her behavior, either before or after Wellauer's death. Was it that easy for him to be misled? Was he so different from the rest of men—show him a pretty face, cry a little, appear to be intelligent and honest, and he'd just cancel out the possibility that you could have killed a man or could love someone who did?

He was frightened by how easily this woman had disarmed him. He pulled some loose bills from his pocket and dropped them on the table. 'Yes, that's a good idea,' he finally said, pushing back his chair and getting to his feet.

He caught her sudden insecurity at seeing him so suddenly change from friend to stranger. He couldn't even do this well. 'Come on, I'll go as far as San Giovanni e Paolo with you.' Outside, because it was night and because it was habit, he linked his arm with hers as they walked. Neither one of them spoke. He was aware of how much she felt like a woman, of the wider arc of her hips, of how pleasant it was to have her move close against him when they passed people on the narrow streets. All this he realized as he walked her home to her lover.

They said goodbye under the statue of Colleoni, no more than that, just a simple goodbye.

CHAPTER TWENTY-THREE

Brunetti walked back through the quiet city, troubled by what he had just heard. He thought he knew something of love, having learned about it with Paola. Was he so conventional, then, that this woman's love— for there was no question that it was love—had to remain alien to him because it didn't conform to his ideas? He dismissed that all as sentimentality at its worst and concentrated, instead, on the question he had asked himself in the bar: whether his affection for this woman, his attraction toward something in her, had blinded him to what he was supposed to be doing. Flavia Petrelli just didn't seem to be someone who would kill in cold blood. He had no doubt that, in a moment of heat or passion, she would be capable of killing someone; most people are. For her, it would have been a knife in the ribs or a shove down the steps, not poison, administered coolly, almost dispassionately.

Who, then? The sister in Argentina? Had she come back and exacted vengeance for her older sister's death? After waiting almost half a century? The idea was ludicrous.

Who, then? Not the director, Santore. Not for a friend's canceled contract. Santore certainly had enough connections, after a lifetime in the theater, to find his friend a place to sing, even if he had the most modest of talents. Even if he didn't have any talent at all.

That left the widow, but Brunetti's instincts told him that her grief was real and that her lack of interest in finding the person responsible had nothing to do with protecting herself. If anything, she seemed to want to protect the dead man, and that led Brunetti back where he had begun, needing and wanting to know more about the man's past, about his character, about the crack in his careful pose of moral rectitude that would have led someone to put poison in his coffee.

Brunetti was uncomfortable with the fact that he didn't like Wellauer, had none of the compassion and outrage he usually felt for those whose lives had been stolen from them. He couldn't shake himself of the belief that— he couldn't express it any more clearly— Wellauer had somehow been involved in his own death. He snorted; everyone is involved in his own death. But no matter how he tried, the idea would neither disappear nor clarify, and so he kept searching for the detail that might have provoked the death, and he kept failing to find it.

The next morning was as dismal as his mood. A thick fog had appeared during the night, seeping up from the waters on which the city was built, not drifting in from the sea.

313

When he stepped out of his front door, cold, misty tendrils wrapped themselves around his face, slipped beneath his collar. He could see clearly for only a few meters, and then vision grew cloudy; buildings slipped into and out of sight, as though they, and not the fog, shifted and moved. Phantoms, clothed in a nimbus of shimmering gray, passed him on the street, floating by as though disembodied. If he turned to follow them with his eyes, he saw them disappear, swallowed up by the dense film that filled the narrow streets and lay upon the waters like a curse. Instinct and long experience told him there would be no boat service on the Grand Canal; the fog was far too thick for that. He walked blindly, telling his feet to lead, allowing decades of familiarity with bridges, streets, and turns to take him over to the Zattere and the landing where both the number 8 and the number 5 stopped on their way to the Giudecca.

Service was limited, and the boats, divorced from any idea of a schedule, appeared randomly out of clouds of fog, radar screens spinning. He waited fifteen minutes before a number 5 loomed up, then slammed heavily into the dock, rocking it and causing a few of the people waiting there to lose their balance and fall into one another. Only the radar saw the crossing; the humans huddled down in the cabin, blind as moles in sand.

When he got off the boat, Brunetti had no

choice but to walk forward until he could almost touch the front of the buildings along the waterfront. Keeping them an arm's length away, he walked toward where he remembered the archway to be. When he got to an opening in the line of facades, he turned into it, not really certain that this was Corte Mosca. He could not read the name, though it was painted on the wall only a foot above his head.

The humidity had worsened the smell of cat; the cold sharpened it. The dead plants in the courtyard now lay under a blanket of fog. He knocked at the door, knocked again more loudly, and heard her call out from the other side. 'Who is it?'

'Commissario Brunetti.'

Again he listened to the slow, angry rasp of metal on metal as she pulled back the heavy bolts that secured the door. She pulled it toward her. The sharp increase in humidity forced her to give it an upward tug in the middle of its arc to lift it from the uneven floor. Still wearing the overcoat, though it was now buttoned tight, she didn't bother to ask him what he wanted. She stepped back enough to allow him to enter, then slammed the door behind him. Again she bolted it securely before turning to lead him down the narrow passageway. In the kitchen, he went and sat near the stove, and she stopped to kick the rags back into place beneath the door.

She shuffled to her chair and collapsed into

315

it, to be immediately enveloped in the waiting scarves and shawls.

'You're back.'

'Yes.'

'What do you want?'

'What I came for last time.'

'And what's that? I'm an old woman, and I don't remember things.' The intelligence in her eyes belied that.

'I'd like some information about your sister.'

Without bothering to ask which one he meant, she said, 'What do you want to know?'

'I don't want to make you remember your grief, Signora, but I need to know more about Wellauer so that I can understand why he died.'

'And if he deserved to die?'

'Signora, we all deserve to die, but no one should get to decide for us when that will be.'

'Oh, my.' She chuckled dryly. 'You're a real Jesuit, aren't you? And who decided when my sister would die? And who decided how?' As suddenly as her anger had flared up, it died, and she asked, 'What do you want to know?'

'I know of your relation with him. I know that he was said to be the father of your sister's child. And I know that she died in Rome in 1939.'

'She didn't just die. She bled to death,' she said in a voice as bleak as blood and death. 'She bled to death in a hotel room, the room

316

he put her in after the abortion and where he didn't go to visit her.' The pain of age struggled in her voice with the pain of memory. 'When they found her, she had been dead for a day. Perhaps two. And it was another day before I learned about it. I was under house arrest, but friends came to tell me about her. I left the house. I had to strike a policeman to do it, knock him to the ground and kick him in the face to do it, to get away. But I left. And none of them, none of the people who saw me kick him, none of them stopped to help him.

'I went with my friends. To where she was. Everything that was necessary had already been done, and we buried her the same day. No priest came, because of the way she died, so we just buried her. The grave was very small.' Her voice trailed away, borne off by the power of memory.

He had seen this happen many times in the past, and he therefore had the sense to remain quiet. The words had started now, and she wouldn't be able to stop until she had said them all and gotten free of them. He waited, patient, living now in the past with her.

'We dressed her all in white. And then we buried her, in that tiny grave. That tiny hole. I went back to my home after the funeral, and they arrested me. But since I was already arrested, it didn't make any difference. I asked them about the policeman, and they said he was all right. I apologized to him when I saw him later. After the war, when the Allies were in the city, he hid in my cellar for a month, until his mother came and took him away. I had no reason to dislike him or want to hurt him.'

'How did it happen?'

She glanced up at him in confusion, honestly not understanding.

'Your sister and Wellauer?'

She licked her lips and studied her gnarled hands, just visible among the shawls. 'I introduced them. He had heard about the way my singing career started, so when they came to Germany to see me sing, he asked me to introduce him to them, to Clara and to little Camilla.'

'Were you involved with him then?'

'Do you mean, was he my lover?'

'Yes.'

'Yes, he was. It started almost immediately, when I went up there to sing.'

'And his affair with your sister?' he asked.

Her head snapped back as though he had hit her. She leaned forward, and Brunetti thought she was going to strike out at him. Instead she spat. A thin, watery gobbet landed on his thigh and slowly sank into the fabric of his trousers. He was too stunned to wipe it away.

'Damn you. You're all the same. Still all the same,' she shouted in a wild, cracked voice.

318

'You look at something, and you see the filth you want to see.' Her voice grew louder, and she repeated what he had said, mockingly. 'His affair with my sister. His affair.' She leaned closer to him, eyes narrowed with hatred, and whispered, 'My sister was twelve years old. Twelve years old. We buried her in her First Communion dress; she was still that small. She was a little girl.

'He raped her, Mr. Policeman. He didn't have an affair with my little sister. He raped her. The first time, and then the other times, when he threatened her, threatened to tell me about her, about what a bad girl she was. And then, when she was pregnant, he sent us both back to Rome. And I didn't know anything about it. For he was still my lover. Making love to me and then raping my little baby sister. Do you see, Mr. Policeman, why I'm glad he's dead and why I say he deserved to die?' Her face was transformed by the rage she had carried for half a century.

'Do you want to know it all, Mr. Policeman?'

Brunetti nodded, seeing it, understanding.

'He came back to Rome, to conduct that *Norma* there with me. And she told him she was pregnant. She was too frightened to tell us, too afraid that we would tell her what a bad girl she was. So he arranged the abortion, and he took her there, and then he took her to that hotel. And he left her there, and she bled to

319

death. And when she died, she was still only twelve years old.'

He saw her hand move out of its wrapping of shawls and scarves, saw it swing up toward him. He did little more than move his head back, and the blow missed him. This maddened her, and she slammed her gnarled hand against the wooden arm of the chair and shrieked with the pain of it.

She lunged out of her chair, sending shawls and blankets slithering to the floor. 'Get out of my house, you pig. You pig.'

Brunetti leapt away from her, tripping over the leg of his chair, and stumbled down the corridor before her. Her hand remained raised in front of her, and he fled from screaming rage. She stopped, panting, while he fumbled with the bolts, pulling them back. In the courtyard, he could still hear her voice as she screamed at him, at Wellauer, at the world. She slammed and bolted the door, but still she raged on. He stood shivering in the fog, shaken by the anger he had raised in her. He forced himself to take deep breaths, to forget that first instant when he had felt real fear of the woman, fear of the tremendous impulse of memory that had pulled her up from her chair and toward him.

CHAPTER TWENTY-FOUR

He had to wait almost half an hour at the boat stop, and by the time the number 5 came, he was thoroughly chilled. There had been no change in the atmosphere, so during the trip back across the *laguna* to San Zaccaria, he huddled in the barely heated inner cabin and looked out on damp whiteness that clawed at the misty windows. Arrived at the Questura, he walked up to his office, ignoring the few people who greeted him. Inside, he closed the door but kept his coat on, waiting for the chill to pass from his body. Images crowded into his mind. He saw the old woman, a fury, screaming her way down the damp corridor; he saw the three sisters in the artful V of their pose; and he saw the little girl lying dead in her First Communion dress. And he saw it all, saw the pattern, saw the plan.

He finally took off his coat and tossed it on the back of a chair. He went to his desk and started to search through the papers littered across its top. He set files and folders aside, hunting until he found the green-covered autopsy report.

On the second page, he found what he remembered would be there: Rizzardi had made note of the small bruises on arm and buttock, listing them only as 'traces of subcutaneous bleeding, cause unknown.'

Neither of the two doctors he had spoken to had mentioned giving Wellauer any sort of injection. But a man who was married to a doctor would hardly have had to make an appointment to receive an injection. Nor did Brunetti believe he had to have an appointment to speak to that doctor.

He returned to the pile of papers and found the report from the German police and read through it until he found something that had tugged at his memory. Elizabeth Wellauer's first husband, Alexandra's father, not only taught at the University of Heidelberg but was chairman of the Department of Pharmacology. She had stopped to see him on her way to Venice.

* * *

'Yes?' Elizabeth Wellauer said as she opened the door for him.

'Again I apologize for disturbing you, Signora, but there is new information, and I'd like to ask you some more questions.'

'About what?' she asked, making no move to open the door any further.

'The results of the autopsy on your husband,' he explained, certain that this would be enough to give him entry. With a sharp, graceless motion, she pulled the door back and stood aside. Silently, she led him to the room

322

where they had had their two previous interviews and pointed to what he was beginning to think of as his chair. He waited while she lit a cigarette, a gesture so habitual with her that he now paid almost no attention to it.

'At the time of the autopsy'—he began with no preliminaries—'the pathologist said that he found signs of bruising on your husband's body that might have been caused by injections of some sort. The same thing is mentioned in his report.' He paused, giving her the opportunity to volunteer an explanation. When none came, he continued. 'Dr. Rizzardi said that they might have come from anything: drugs, vitamins, antibiotics. He said that the pattern of the bruises was inconsistent with your husband's having given them to himself—he was right-handed, wasn't he?'

'Yes.'

'The bruises on the arm were on the right side as well, so he couldn't have given himself those injections.' He allowed himself a minimal pause. 'If they were injections, that is.' He paused again. 'Signora, did you give your husband these injections?'

She ignored him, so he repeated the question. 'Signora, did you give your husband these injections?' No response. 'Signora, do you understand my question? Did you give your husband these injections?'

'They were vitamins,' she finally answered.

'What kind?'

'B-twelve.'

'Where did you get them? From your former husband?'

The question clearly surprised her. She shook her head in strong denial. 'No; he had nothing to do with it. I wrote a prescription for them while we were still in Berlin. Helmut had complained of feeling tired, so I suggested that he try a series of B-twelve injections. He had done so in the past, and they had helped him then.'

'How long ago did you begin with the injections, Signora?'

'I don't remember exactly. About six weeks ago.'

'Did he seem to improve?'

'What?'

'Your husband. Did he improve as a result of these injections. Did they have the effect you intended?'

She glanced up at him sharply when he asked this second question, but answered calmly. 'No, they didn't seem to help. So after six or seven, I decided to discontinue them.'

'Did you decide that, or did your husband, Signora?'

'What difference does it make? They didn't work, so he stopped taking them.'

'I think it makes a great deal of difference, Signora, who decided to stop them. And I think you know that.'

324

'Then I suppose he decided.'

'Where did you get the prescription filled? Here in Italy?'

'No; I'm not licensed to practice here. It was in Berlin, before we came down here.'

'I see. Then the pharmacist would surely have a record of it.'

'Yes, I suppose he would. But I don't remember where I had it filled.'

'You mean you just wrote a prescription and chose a pharmacy at random?'

'Yes.'

'How long have you lived in Berlin, Signora?'

'Ten years. I don't see why that's important.'

'Because it seems strange to me that a doctor would live in a city for ten years and not have a permanent pharmacy. Or that the Maestro wouldn't have a pharmacy where he usually went.'

Her response was just a second too long in coming. 'He did. We both do. But that day, I wasn't at home when I wrote the prescription, so I just took it to the first pharmacy I saw and asked them to fill it.'

'But surely you remember where it was. It wasn't so long ago.'

She looked out the window, concentrating, trying to remember. She turned to him and said, 'I'm sorry, but I can't remember where it was.'

'That's no matter, Signora,' he said

dismissively. it for us.' She glanced up at this, surprised, or something more. 'And I'm sure they'll be able to find out what the prescription was, what sort of'—he paused for just a second before saying the last word—'vitamin.'

Though her cigarette was still burning in the ashtray, she reached for the package, then changed the motion and simply pushed the pack around with one finger, giving it a precise quarter turn each time. 'Shall we stop this now?' she asked, voice neutral. 'I've never liked games, and you aren't very good at them, either.'

Through the years, he had seen this happen more times than he could count, seen people reach the point they couldn't go beyond, the point where they would, however reluctantly, tell the truth. Like a city under siege: their outer defenses gave in first, then came the first retreat, the first concession to the approaching enemy. Depending upon the defender, the struggle would be fast or slow, bogged down at this rampart or that; there could be a counterattack, or there could be none. But the first motion was always the same, the almost relieved shrugging off of the lie, which led, in the end, to the final opening of the gates to truth.

'It wasn't a vitamin. You know that, don't you?' she asked.

He nodded.

'And do you know what it was?'

'No, I don't know what it was, not exactly. But I believe it was an antibiotic. I don't know which one, but I don't think that's important.'

'No, it's not important.' She looked up at him with a small smile, its sadness centered in her eyes. 'Netilmicina. I believe that's the name it's sold under here in Italy. The prescription was filled at the Ritter Pharmacy, about three blocks from the entrance to the zoo. You shouldn't have any trouble finding it.'

'What did you tell your husband it was?'

'Just as I told you, B-twelve.'

'How many injections did you give him?'

'Six, at six-day intervals.'

'How soon was it before he began to notice the effect?'

'A few weeks. We weren't speaking much to each other then, but he still saw me as his doctor, so first he asked me about his fatigue. And then he asked me about his hearing.'

'And what did you tell him?'

'I reminded him of his age, and then I told him it might be a temporary side effect of the vitamin. That was stupid of me. I have medical books in the house, and he could easily have gone and checked what I told him.'

'Did he?'

'No, no, he didn't. He trusted me. I was his doctor, you see.'

'Then how did he learn? Or how did he begin to suspect?'

'He went to see Erich about it. You know

327

that, or you wouldn't be here now, asking these questions. And after we were here, he began to wear the glasses with the hearing aid, so I knew he must have gone to see another doctor. When I suggested another injection, he refused. He knew by then, of course, but I don't know how he found out. From the other doctor?' she asked.

Again he nodded.

She gave him the same sad smile.

'And then what happened, Signora?'

'We had come down here in the middle of the treatment. In fact, I gave him the last injection in this room. Even then he might have known but refused to believe what he knew.' She closed her eyes and rubbed at them with her hands. 'It becomes very complicated, this idea of when he knew everything.'

'When did you finally realize that he knew?'

'It must have been about two weeks ago. In a way, I'm surprised it took him so long, but that was because we were so much in love.' She looked across at him when she said this. 'He knew how much I loved him. So he couldn't believe that I'd do this to him.' She smiled bitterly. 'There were times, after I started, when I couldn't believe it, either, when I remembered how much I loved him.'

'When did you realize that he knew what the injections were?'

'I was in here one night, reading. I hadn't gone to the rehearsal that day, the way I usually did. It was too painful, listening to the music, to the bad chords, the entrances that came too soon or too late, and knowing that I'd done that, done it as surely as if I'd taken the baton from his hands and waved it crazily around in the air.' She stopped speaking, as though listening to the discordant music of those rehearsals.

'I was in here, reading, or trying to read, and I heard—' She looked up at the sound of the word and said, like an actor delivering an aside in a crowded theater, 'My God, it's hard to avoid that word, isn't it?' and slipped back into her role. 'He was early, had come back early from the theater. I heard him come down the hall and then open the door. He was still wearing his coat, and he was carrying the score of *Traviata*. It was one of his favorite operas. He loved to conduct it. He came in and stood there, just over there,' she said, pointing to a space where no one stood now. 'He looked at me, and he asked me, "You did this, didn't you?"' She continued looking at the door, waiting for the words to be said again.

'Did you answer him?'

'I owed him that much, didn't I?' she asked, voice calm and reasonable. 'Yes, I told him I'd done it.'

'What did he do?'

'He left. Not the house, just the room. And then we managed not to see each other again, not until the *prima*.'

329

'Did he threaten you in any way? Say that he was going to go to the police? Punish you?'

She seemed to be honestly puzzled by his question. 'What good would that have done? If you've spoken to the doctor, you know that the damage is permanent. There was nothing that the police could do, there was nothing that anyone could do, to get his hearing back. And there was no way he could punish me.' She paused long enough to light another cigarette. 'Except by doing what he did,' she said.

'And what is that?' Brunetti asked.

She chided him openly. 'If you know as much as you seem to know, then you must know that as well.'

He met her glance, keeping his face expressionless, 'I still have two questions, Signora. The first is an honest question that I ask out of ignorance. And the second is simpler, and I think I know the answer already.'

'Then start with the second one,' she said.

'It concerns your husband. Why would he try to punish you in this way?'

'By "in this way," do you mean by making it look as if I had murdered him?'

'Yes.'

He watched as she tried to speak, saw the words begin to form themselves and then drop, forgotten. At last she said, voice low, 'He saw himself as above the law, above the law the rest of us had to follow. I think he believed that it was his genius that gave him this power, this right. And God knows we all encouraged him in that. We made him a god of music, and we fell down and worshiped him.' She stopped and looked across at him. 'I'm sorry; I'm not answering your question. You wanted to know if he was capable of trying to make it look as if I was responsible. But you see,' she said, raising her hands to him, as if she wanted to pull understanding from him, 'I was responsible. So he did have a right to do this to me. It would have been less horrible if I had killed the man; that would have left the god untouched.' She broke off, but Brunetti said nothing.

'I'm trying to tell you how he would have seen it. I knew him so well, knew how he felt, what he thought.' Again she paused, then she continued with her attempt to make him understand. 'Something strange occurred to me after he died and I began to realize how careful he had been, inviting me back, letting me into the dressing room. It seemed to me then, and it still does now, that he had a right to do what he did, to punish me. In a way, he was his music. And I killed that instead of killing him. He was dead. Before he died, he was already dead. I'd killed his spirit. I saw it during the rehearsals, when he peered over those glasses and tried to hear through his useless hearing aid what was happening to the music. And he couldn't hear. He couldn't hear.' She shook her head at something she didn't understand. 'He didn't have to punish me, Mr. Brunetti. That's been done. I've spent my time in hell.'

She folded her hands in her lap and continued. 'Then, the night of the *prima*, he told me what he was going to do.' When she saw Brunetti's surprise, she explained: 'No, he didn't tell me, not like that, not clearly. I didn't realize it at the time.'

'Was this when you went backstage?' Brunetti asked.

'Yes.'

'What happened?'

'At first, he didn't say anything when he saw me at the door. Just looked up at me. But then he must have seen someone in the corridor behind me. Perhaps he thought they were coming toward the dressing room.' She bowed her head wearily. 'I don't know. All he said was something that sounded rehearsed: what Tosca says when she sees Cavaradossi's body—"*Finire così, finire così*." I didn't understand then—"to finish like this, like this"—but I should have. She says it just before she kills herself, but I didn't understand. Not then.' Brunetti was surprised to see a grin of near amusement flash across her face. 'That was very like him, to be dramatic at the last minute. Melodramatic, really. Later, I was surprised that he would take his last words from an opera by Puccini.' She looked up, serious. 'I hope that doesn't sound strange. But I thought he would want to be remembered quoting something by Mozart. Or Wagner.' He watched her struggle with mounting hysteria. He stood and went over to a cabinet that stood between the two windows and poured her a small glass of brandy. He stood for a moment, glass in hand, and looked out at the bell tower of San Marco. Then he went back to her and handed her the glass.

Not really conscious of what it was, she took it and sipped at it. He returned to the window and continued his observation of the bell tower. When he was sure it was the way it had always been, he resumed his seat opposite her.

'Will you tell me why you did it, Signora?'

Her surprise was genuine. 'If you were clever enough to find out how I did it, then surely you must know why.'

He shook his head. 'I won't say what I think, because if I'm wrong, I'll dishonor the man.' Even as he spoke the words, he knew how much he was himself sounding like a Puccini libretto.

'That means you do understand, doesn't it?' she asked, and leaned forward to place the still-full glass next to the package of cigarettes.

'Your daughter, Signora?'

She bit at her upper lip and gave a nod so small as to be imperceptible. When she released her lip, he saw the white marks where she had bitten into it. She extended her hand

333

toward the cigarettes, pulled it back, caught it in the other, and said in a voice so low he had to lean forward to hear her, 'I had no idea,' and shook her head at the ugliness of it. 'Alex is not a musical child. She didn't even know who he was when I started seeing him. When I told her that I wanted to marry him, she seemed interested. Then, when I told her that he had a farm and that he had horses, she was very interested. That's all she ever cared about, horses, like the heroine in an English book for children. Horses and books about horses.

'She was eleven when we were married. They got on well. After she learned who he was—I think her classmates must have told her—she seemed a little frightened of him, but that passed. Helmut was very good with children.' She stopped and grimaced at the grotesque irony of what she had just said.

'And then. And then. And then,' she repeated, unable to free herself from the grooves of memory. 'This summer, I had to go back to Budapest. To see my mother, who isn't well. Helmut said that everything would be all right while I was gone. I took a cab, and I went to the airport. But the airport was closed. I don't remember why. A strike. Or trouble with the customs officers.' She looked up then. 'It really doesn't matter why it was closed, does it?'

'No, Signora.'

'There was a long delay, more than an hour, and then we were told that there would be no flights until the following morning. So I took another cab and went home. It wasn't very late, not even midnight, so I didn't bother to call and tell him I was coming back. I went home and let myself into the house. There were no lights on, so I went upstairs. Alex has always been a restless sleeper, so I went to her room to check on her. To check on her.' She looked up at him, expressionless.

'When I got to the top of the stairs, I could hear her. I thought she was having a nightmare. It wasn't a scream, just a noise. Like an animal. Just a noise. Only that. And I went to her room. He was there. With her.

'This is the strange part,' she said quite calmly, as though she were sharing a puzzle with him, asking him what he thought of it. 'I don't remember what happened. No, I know that he left, but I don't remember what I said to him or he said to me. I stayed with Alex that night.

'Later, days later, he told me that Alex had had a nightmare.' She laughed in disgust and disbelief. 'That's all he said. We never talked about it. I sent Alex to her grandparents. To school there. And we never talked about it. Oh, how modern we were, how civilized. Of course, we stopped sleeping together, and stopped being with each other. And Alex was gone.'

'Do her grandparents know what happened?'

A quick shake of her head. 'No; I told them what I told everyone, that I didn't want her schooling interrupted when we came to Venice.'

'When did you decide? To do what you did?' Brunetti asked.

She shrugged. 'I don't know. One day, the idea was simply there. The only thing that was really important to him, the only thing he really loved, was his music, so I decided that was the thing I'd take away from him. At the time, it seemed fair.'

'And does it now?'

She considered this for a long time before she answered. 'Yes, it still does seem fair. Everything that's happened seems fair. But that's not the point, is it?'

To him, there was no point in any of it. No point, and no message, and no lesson. It was no more than human evil and the terrible waste that comes from it.

Her voice was suddenly tired. 'What happens now?'

'I don't know,' he answered honestly. 'Do you have any idea where he got the cyanide?'

She shrugged her shoulders, as though she thought the question irrelevant. 'It could have been anywhere,' she said. 'He has a friend who is a chemist, or it could have been one of his friends from the old days.' When she saw

336

Brunetti's puzzled glance, she explained. 'The war. He made a lot of powerful friends then, and many of them are important men now.'

'Then the rumors about him are true?'

'I don't know. Before we were married, he said they were all lies, and I believed him. I don't believe it anymore.' She said this bitterly, then forced herself back to her original explanation. 'I don't know where he got it, but I know it would have been no problem for him.' Her sad smile returned. 'I had access to it, of course. He knew that.'

'Access? How?'

'We didn't come down here together. We didn't want to travel together. I stopped in Heidelberg for two days on the way down, to see my former husband.' Who, Brunetti recalled, taught pharmacology.

'Did the Maestro know that you were there?'

She nodded. 'My first husband and I remained friends, and we hold property together.'

'Did you tell him what happened?'

'Of course not,' she said, raising her voice for the first time.

'Where did you see him?'

'At the university. I met him at his laboratory. He's working on a new drug to minimize the effects of Parkinson's. He showed me through the laboratory, and then we went to lunch together.'

337

'Did the Maestro know this?'

She shrugged. 'I don't know. I suppose I might have told him. I probably did. It was very difficult for us to find anything to talk about. This was a neutral topic, so we were glad to have it to talk about.'

'Did you and the Maestro ever talk about what happened?'

She couldn't bring herself to ask what he meant; she knew. 'No.'

'Did you ever talk about the future? What you were going to do?'

'No, not directly.'

'What does that mean?'

'One day, when I was coming in and he was going to rehearsal, he said, "Just wait until after *Traviata*." I thought he meant that we would be able to decide what to do then. But I had already decided to leave him. I'd written to two hospitals, one in Budapest and one in Augsburg, and I'd talked to my former husband about his help in finding me a position in a hospital.'

Either way, Brunetti realized, she was trapped. There was evidence that she had been planning a separate future, even before he died. And now she was a widow, and enormously rich. And even if the information about her daughter was made public, there was evidence that she had stopped on the way to Venice to talk to the girl's father, a man who surely had access to the poison that had killed

338

the Maestro.

No Italian judge would convict a woman for what she had done, not if she explained about her daughter. Given the evidence Brunetti had—Signora Santina's testimony about her sister, the interviews with the doctors, even the suicide of his second wife at a time when their daughter was twelve years old—there was no court in Italy that would bring a charge of murder against her. But all of this would hang upon the testimony of the girl, upon the tall girl Alex, in love with horses and still a child.

Brunetti knew that this woman would never let that testimony take place, regardless of the consequences if she did not. Further, he knew that he would never allow it to happen, either.

And without the testimony of the daughter? There was the obvious coolness between them, her easy access to the poison, her presence in the dressing room that night, wildly out of keeping with what they had always done. All that had the appearance of truth. If she was charged only with having given him injections that she knew would destroy his hearing, she would be freed of the accusation of murder, but this scenario would work only if her daughter's name was mentioned. He knew that was impossible.

'Before he died, before any of this ever happened,' he began, leaving it to her to interpret what he meant by 'this,' 'did your husband ever speak about his age; was he afraid of a physical decline?'

She paused for a while before she answered him, puzzled by the irrelevance of his question. 'Yes, we talked about it. Not often, but once or twice. Once, when we'd all had more than enough to drink, we talked about it with Erich and Hedwig.'

'And what did he say?'

'It was Erich, if I remember correctly. He said that in the future, if anything should ever stop him from working—not just stop him from doing surgery but make him be, well, not himself anymore, not able to be a doctor in any way—he said he was a doctor and knew how to take care of that himself.

'It was very late, and we were all very tired, so perhaps that made the conversation more serious than it might have been. He said that, and then Helmut said that he understood him perfectly and would do the same thing.'

'Would Dr. Steinbrunner remember this conversation?'

'I think so. It was only this summer. The night of our anniversary.'

'Did your husband ever say anything more specific than that?' Before she could answer, he completed the question: 'When there were other people present?'

'Do you mean, when there were witnesses?'

He nodded.

'No, not that I can remember But that night, the conversation was so serious that it was clear to us all just what they meant.'

'Will your friends remember it as meaning what you say it did?'

'Yes, I think so. I don't think they approve of me, not as a wife for Helmut.' After she said that, she looked up at him suddenly, eyes wide with horror. 'Do you think they knew?'

Brunetti shook his head, hoping to assure her that, no, they didn't know, couldn't have known something like that about him and remained silent. But he had no reason to believe that. He veered away and asked, 'Can you remember any other time your husband might have made reference to that subject?'

'There were the letters he sent me before we were married.'

'What did he say?'

'He was joking, trying to dismiss the difference in our ages. He said that I'd never be burdened with a feeble, helpless old husband, that he'd see that this never happened.'

'Do you still have those letters?'

She bowed her head and said softly, 'Yes. I still have everything he ever gave me, all the letters he sent me.'

'I still don't understand how you could do it,' he said, not shocked or outraged; simply puzzled.

'I don't know anymore, either. I've thought about it so much that I've probably invented new reasons for it, new justifications. To

341

punish him? Or maybe I wanted to weaken him so much that he'd be absolutely, completely dependent on me. Or maybe I knew that it would force him to do what he did. I simply don't know anymore, and I don't think I'll ever understand why.' He thought she had finished, but she added, voice icy, 'But I'm glad I did it, and I'd do it again.'

He looked away from her then. Because Brunetti was not a lawyer, he had no idea of the nature of the crime. Assault? Theft? If you steal a man's hearing, what do you steal from him? And is the crime worse if the victim's hearing is more important to him than other people's hearing is to them?

'Signora, do you believe he invited you backstage to make it look as if you had killed him?'

'I don't know, but he might have. He believed in justice. But if he wanted that, he could have arranged things to look far worse for me. I've thought about this, since that night. Maybe he left it like this so that I wouldn't ever be sure what he intended. And this way, he wouldn't be responsible for whatever happened to me because of it.' She gave a small smile. 'He was a very complex man.'

Brunetti leaned toward her and placed his hand on her arm. 'Signora, listen very carefully to what happened during this interview,' he said, deciding, thinking of Chiara and

342

deciding. 'We talked about the way your husband had confided in you his fears about his growing deafness.'

Startled, she began to protest. 'But—'

He cut her off before she could say anything else. 'How he told you of his deafness, how he feared it. That he had gone to his friend Erich in Germany and then to another doctor, in Padova, and that both of them had told him that he was growing deaf. That this explains his behavior here, his obvious depression. And that you told me you were afraid that he had killed himself when he realized that his career was over, that he had no future as a musician.' His voice sounded as tired as he felt.

When she started to protest, he said only, 'Signora, the only person who would suffer because of the truth is the only innocent one.'

She was silenced by the truth of this. 'How do I do all this?'

He had no idea how to advise her, never before having helped a criminal invent an alibi or deny the evidence of a crime. 'The important thing is that you told me about his deafness. From that, everything will follow.' She looked at him, still puzzled, and he spoke to her as he would to a dull child who refused to understand a lesson. 'You told me this the second time I spoke to you, the morning I came to visit you here. You told me that he had been having serious trouble with his hearing and had spoken to his friend Erich.'

343

She began to protest, and he could have shaken her for her dullness. 'He also told you he had been to another doctor. All of this will be in the report of our meeting.'

'Why are you doing this?' she finally asked.

He dismissed the question with a gesture.

'Why are you doing this?' she repeated.

'Because you didn't kill him.'

'And the rest? What I did do to him?'

'There's no way you can be made to suffer for that without making your daughter suffer even more.'

She winced away from this truth. 'What else do I have to do?' she asked, obedient now.

'I'm not sure yet. Just remember that we talked about this the first morning I came here to see you.'

She started to speak and then stopped.

'What?' he asked.

'Nothing, nothing.'

He got suddenly to his feet. It made him uncomfortable, sitting here and plotting. 'That's all, then. I imagine you'll have to testify at the inquest, when it happens.'

'Will you be there?'

'Yes. I'll have filed my report by then and given my opinion.'

'And what will that be?'

'It will be the truth, Signora.'

Her voice was level. 'I don't know what the truth is anymore.'

'I will tell the *procuratore* that my

investigation revealed that your husband committed suicide when he realized that he was going deaf. Just as it was.'

'Yes,' she echoed. 'Just as it was.'

He left her sitting in the room where she had given her husband the last injection.

CHAPTER TWENTY-FIVE

At eight the next morning, just as ordered, Brunetti placed his report on Vice-Questore Patta's desk, where it sat until his superior officer arrived at his office, just past eleven. When, after returning three personal phone calls and reading through the financial newspaper, the vice-questore brought himself to read the report, he found it both interesting and illuminating:

The results of my investigation lead me to conclude that Maestro Helmut Wellauer took his own life as a result of his growing deafness.

1. During the last months, his hearing had deteriorated to the point where he had less than 40 percent of normal hearing. (See attached interviews with Drs. Steinmbrunner and Treport; and attached medical records.)

2. This loss of hearing resulted in increasing inability to function as a conductor. (See attached interviews with Prof. Rezzonico and

Signore Traverso.)

3. The Maestro was in a depressed state of mind. (See attached interviews with Signora Wellauer and Signorina Breddes.)

4. He had access to the poison used. (See attached interviews with Signora Wellauer and Dr. Steinbrunner.)

5. He was known to favor the idea of suicide, should he arrive at a point in which he could no longer function as a musician (See attached telephone interview with Dr. Steinbrunner. Personal correspondence to follow from Germany.)

Given the overwhelming weight of this information, plus the logical exclusion of suspects who might have had either motive or opportunity to commit a crime, I can conclude only that the Maestro accepted suicide as an alternative to deafness.

Respectfully submitted,
Guido Brunetti
Commissario of Police

'I suspected this from the beginning, of course,' Patta said to Brunetti, who had answered his superior's request that he come to his office to discuss the case. 'But I didn't want to say anything at the beginning and thus prejudice your investigation.'

'That was very generous of you, sir,' Brunetti said. 'And very intelligent.' He studied the facade of the church of San Lorenzo, part of which was visible beyond his superior's shoulder.

'It was unthinkable that anyone who loved music could have done such a thing.' It was evident that Patta included himself among that number. 'His wife says here . . .,' he began, looking down at the report. Brunetti studied, this time, the small diamond tie tack in the form of a rose that Patta wore in his red tie. '. . . that he was "visibly disturbed."' This reference convinced Brunetti that Patta had indeed read the report, an event of surpassing rarity. 'Revolting as the behavior of those two women is,' Patta continued, making a small moue of disgust at something that did not appear in the report, 'it is unlikely that either of them would have the psychological profile of a murderer.' Whatever that meant.

'And the widow—impossible, even if she is a foreigner.' Then, even though Brunetti had not asked for clarification of the remark, Patta gave it. 'No woman who is a mother could have done something as cold-blooded as this. There's an instinct in them that prevents such things.' He smiled at the brilliance of his perception, and Brunetti, too, smiled, delighted to hear it.

'I'm having lunch with the mayor today,' Patta said, with a studied casualness which relegated that fact to the events of daily life, 'and I'll explain the results of our investigation to him.' Hearing that plural, Brunetti was in no doubt that by lunchtime, the investigation would have slipped back into the singular, but it would not be in the third person.

'Will that be all, sir?' he asked politely.

Patta glanced up from the report, which he appeared to be committing to memory. 'Yes, yes. That will be all.'

'And the *procuratore*? Will you inform him too?' Brunetti asked, hoping that Patta would insist upon this as well, adding the weight of his office to any recommendation for nonprosecution that would be passed to the chief magistrate.

'Yes, I'll see to that.' Brunetti watched as Patta considered the possibility of inviting the chief magistrate to lunch with the mayor, saw him reject it. 'I'll take care of that when I get back from lunch with His Honor.' That, Brunetti reflected, would give him two scenes to play.

Brunetti got to his feet. 'I'll get back to my office, then, sir.'

'Yes, yes,' Patta muttered absently, still reading the page in front of him.

'And, Commissario,' Patta said from behind him.

'Yes, sir,' Brunetti said, turning and smiling as he set up the conditions of today's bet.

'Thanks for your help.'

'It was nothing, sir,' he said, thinking that a dozen red roses would do.

Seven months later, a letter arrived, addressed to Brunetti at the Questura. His attention was caught by the stamps, two lilac rectangles with a delicate tracery of calligraphy flowing down their sides. Below each was printed, 'People's Republic of China.' He knew no one there.

There was no return address on the envelope. He tore it open and from it slid a Polaroid photo of a jeweled crown. A sense of scale was missing, but if it had been designed for a human to wear, then the stones that encircled the central jewel must have been the size of pigeons' eggs. Rubies? No other stone he could think of so resembled blood. The central stone, massive and square-cut, could only have been a diamond.

He flipped the photo over to the back and read: 'Here is a part of the beauty I have returned to.' It was signed, 'B. Lynch.' There was no other message. Nothing else was in the envelope.